the LONELINESS of DISTANT BEINGS

the LONELINESS of DISTANT BEINGS

KATE LING

LITTLE, BROWN BOOKS FOR YOUNG READERS
www.lbkids.co.uk

LITTLE, BROWN BOOKS FOR YOUNG READERS

First published in Great Britain in 2016 by Hodder and Stoughton

1 3 5 7 9 10 8 6 4 2

A CIP catalogue record for this book
is available from the British Library.

ISBN 978-1-51020-016-6

Typeset by M Rules
Printed and bound in Great Britain by
Clays Ltd, St Ives plc

The paper and board used in this book are made
from wood from responsible sources.

MIX
Paper from
responsible sources
FSC® C104740

Little, Brown Books for Young Readers
An imprint of
Hachette Children's Group
Part of Hodder and Stoughton
Carmelite House
50 Victoria Embankment
London EC4Y 0DZ

An Hachette UK Company
www.hachette.co.uk

www.hachettechildrens.co.uk

Chapter One

I know that they're birds, but only because I've been told. So many of them, sitting in a long line and waiting, and I don't know what it is that eventually makes them lift but they do, all of them, all at once, flickering into the sky on a thousand tiny wings. And the sky I've only ever lived outside of is blue, so blue, swept across with clouds like brushstrokes.

They always show this, this same bit of movie, on the big screen at funerals. I guess we all get the metaphor or whatever. Then they show some pictures of the dead person, just a few, normally their crew shots at passing out or Christmas balls or them in their dress uniform or what have you. But this time is different; right at the beginning there is an image of my great-grandmother on the planet she left behind, peach-cheeked, tanned, squinting in the sun, sand clinging to her legs. There's this kind of gasping sound from everyone when they show it.

Great Granny Bea had a lot of photographs, some printed on to card so you could hold them in your hand. Hold them and peer into them like windows. And when you looked into them, there she was looking out. Younger. Now she looks out of them alive, when in reality she is dead.

The funeral is the same as the others. Once we've laid the flowers Production have sent we stand and look, look at a box, and then Grandpa makes a speech. He doesn't even mention the fact that Bea was the last one in this place who ever lived on Earth, but I know we are all thinking it. I know the reason so many people have come today is because this is it – somehow now we really are all alone.

And then we leave the airlock, leave her there and walk away. Grandpa is the last to leave and it seems he only remembers to go at all because I take his arm just then. I guess that this part never gets any easier, no matter how many times you do it.

The lock doors slide over and we watch through the thick circular windows as the outer door opens, both sides simultaneously like giant jaws, and then she is gone. Out there, flying through space to who knows where. Just like she was before, really, but now she's doing it all alone.

I barely hear the first-session circuit announcement. I left the wake early only to fall into a horrible, deep zombie sleep. And this is why I am dreaming still while I pull on my trainers and tracksuit and head to Main gangway where I stand there yawning so much that I am trembling and wet-eyed by the time the runners streak past me and I join them, like jumping into moving water. I have music on my pod but I guess I'm not even listening to it, or even really thinking as we head down Main, irresistibly falling into step with each other until we're banging along like a beating drum. People on their way home from their third-session shifts walk one side, single file, eyes on the floor. Some of the noisy pumped-up guys at the front reach up and touch the trunking that's low overhead as we pass, just like they always do, and I could scream for the gaping chasm of boredom that this has become.

This is prescribed by Dr Maddox. That's the only reason I do it, have to do it, to keep myself out of Correctional. Dr Mad isn't a believer in long-term medication for 'children', preferring natural remedies, such as telling him all the horrible things that are going on in your head and running around in pointless circles, which he claims will produce endorphins, but I'm pretty much still on the fence about it. I spend quite a lot of time thinking the medication would be the better option, even if it does make you feel like someone pulled your brain out and replaced it with a damp sponge.

But anyway, this is why I find myself running

circuits with all the flyboys from Engineering and the people who have somehow managed to get fat on the miserable rations we get dished out at the cantinas. I have been doing this every day now for more than a year, since I managed to get myself sprung out of Dr Mad's clutches in Correctional, where I was held for five weeks because I kind of decided to stop speaking for a while and then (one particularly bad night) tried to dig my way out of this place through the metal walls with my bare hands, tearing all my nails off in the process, and everyone decided it was because I was crazy. But look, it's something that I don't particularly like to talk about because, you know, it's pretty embarrassing, and the whole thing created a load of miserable memories I'd rather not take ownership of, whatever Dr Mad says.

So I do my circuits and I get to be normal again. I get to not be nuts. Except I reckon if you've lost your mind once you never really feel like it won't happen again. You're always looking over your shoulder. Running from it.

The best part of the circuit for most people is when we hit View. View on West Main deck is about a hundred strides long. It has a bank of staggered seating up one side and some space in front for walking (or in our case running), and on our right as we pass through is floor-to-ceiling quadruple-pane vacuum-sealed glass

4

and an infinity of galaxy punching you right in the face. I guess you can't help but look at it but it doesn't do anything for me the way it does for other people. Well, it hasn't until recently, anyway.

These last few weeks we have been nearing star system Huxley, and seeing an actual sun has made me like this view more. There hasn't been sun for so long and in some way it brings you back to life, regardless of the fact that, being a middle-aged K-dwarf, Huxley is pretty small and dim. Whatever, it wakes you up, wakes you up on a cellular level that I guess we don't even understand, and don't have to. Huxley is the first possible life-supporting system that we have passed in eighty-four years. And, OK, the relevance is only limited since we are a First Contact vessel rather than a Pioneer, but we are the first ones here, we are the first to pass through this place, and we have no idea what we could find here; and this is the only thing that makes me want to be alive right now; this is the only thing that makes me want to live in my own skin.

After running I don't really feel like going back to quarters, so instead I go to see Emme. She and I haven't been on super good terms lately, and I am pretty aware that it's the whole me-being-crazy thing. That's the problem with going nuts: once you've done it, nobody ever looks at you the same way again.

But when I buzz at her door she lets me straight

in and we stand there in the tight grey space of her family's galley, which is a mess, but thankfully empty of people.

'Where are your folks?' I ask her, before accidentally zoning out and missing her answer. Then I follow her to her room where we sit on her bunk and I bend forward over my knees, looking at the floor.

'Wanna play chess?' she says.

I nod and slide further back on the bed, leaning against the wall where it is cold on my back. Neither of us speaks while we are loading the game on to our pods. I sneak my eyes to her though and she is watching me.

'I'm sorry about your Great Granny Bea,' she says.

'You know, it's OK, she was old.' I shrug, shutting her down.

'Hmm,' she says. 'But still ... with graduation and everything.'

'Yeah, I don't care about that though, not really.'

'Yeah, me neither,' she says.

The pods beep and we play a couple of moves. Then she pauses it.

'OK, I do care,' she says. 'I lied about that.'

I wait, looking at her.

'I'm not ready,' she says, leaving a silence that I don't fill. 'What, you are?'

'I just ... I guess I don't see the point in thinking about it when there's nothing I can do to change it.'

'So going into Service? Your Union? You're not worried about any of it?'

'Why bother worrying when it's all going to happen whether I want it to or not?'

She looks at me, up from under her eyebrows, lips stiff, then she unpauses the game for a bit, makes another move, pauses it again. 'So who do you think you'll get? For your Union?'

I shrug. 'The whole thing's a joke so what difference does it make?'

She watches me with the same expression in her pretty, wide-spaced eyes.

'When did you get like this?' she asks me.

'Like what?'

'Like nothing matters.'

And this is the point at which I realise why Emme and I haven't been getting on lately: she still thinks you can make sense of this pointless existence of ours and I already know that you can't.

Chapter Two

My sister, Pandora, married Cain almost a year ago and now, at nineteen, she is seven months pregnant. And man is she a pig in muck. All she does is laugh, and make little clothes, and invite all the young mums round so they can give her stuff and rub her belly. Cain thinks it's all so great too. And to think that I once thought he was cool. To see him now, dumb as anything and cooing over her and her belly, I hardly even know this guy. I used to be so jealous of my sister that her life partner was actually someone OK, and now he is just such a loser I can hardly even look at him. I'm not so disappointed in Pandora because I always knew she was lame. But sometimes I'm amazed how little we actually have in common. All those years in the same quarters and now all she does is knit booties.

Normal people would have moved into their own family quarters by now but my sister isn't normal and only just applied for hers. This is because she is under the misconception that my dad and I actually like having her around. I know this because Cain told me she was so worried about how we would cope without her that she was planning for them to stay even after the baby was born, to which I answered that I had far graver concerns about how we would cope WITH her than without. I mean, the whole thing is dysfunctional beyond words. My dad doesn't even seem to know how to sit between us any more at leisure time. He's been sitting there silent while we argued over his head for a long time now, and he wouldn't say anything, maybe just laugh sometimes at things we said and sometimes say, 'Girls, come on,' but we always knew he was kind of enjoying it, especially as we would both kiss him on the head before we went to bed. But now, I don't know, it's like Cain and Pandora are being dumb and only talking to each other and Dad and I are just watching the screens, but mostly I'm just thinking about what an idiot Pan is for being so happy at the prospect of the miserable existence that lies ahead of her.

So maybe, the day I wake up and it's my last day in Education, I'm just hoping I never turn into her; maybe I'm just hoping I get to the end of this day without my brain trickling out of my ear.

We have Father Seth first who has basically spent the last decade telling us Bible stories and has stopped by on our final day in this pokey little grey room to explain to us the meaning of life, or the meaning of life the way he sees it in any case. Naturally Jonah's the only person really paying attention; he's the only one who cares about this stuff. I mean, Emme's taking all the notes in the world because she always does but you can tell she's on autopilot.

'Now, Generation 84, this is your time.' This is just the kind of cheese Father Seth comes out with on a regular basis. There are thirty-five of us in this class, ranging from fifteen to seventeen; just the latest batch of workers churned out by what is, essentially, a production line. Education only have three classrooms so you spend three years in Education A, three in Education B, three in C, and then you're out, and they start making life miserable for a new consignment of six to eight year olds who are just about to begin wishing they'd never been born.

By the time I tune back in, Father Seth is warming to his theme, beaming through the beard that seems to be obligatory for guys who are into God. 'This is your moment, Generation 84. Your life path is just about to unfold before you; the life that God has chosen for you.'

Which, you know, is just more of him laying on the crap, because God has exactly ZERO to do with the stuff that goes down here, and he knows it.

'And tomorrow you will discover who among your classmates will be the one to accompany you into adulthood and parenthood, to fulfil your life's great purpose, here on Ventura.'

To which Ezra Lomax says, 'Try not to fight over me, girls. Sadly only one of you can be the lucky lady,' which is typical, and most people laugh, though you can even tell from the way some of the girls (including Emme) giggle that they're praying it's them. Idiots. I mean, he's the captain's son and he's so convinced he's hot he kind of manages to make other people believe it too, but that is the sum total of what he's got going for him.

After Father Seth, we have Lieutenant Maria Fernanda for the last time ever, and while all we're thinking about is going into Service on Monday and what our commissions will be she decides to show us a video about how life evolved on Earth. It's a pretty old show; you can tell it's from way back in a time when they hadn't even thought about all this, hadn't even considered that one day they would pack eight hundred and eighty-eight people into a big tin can and fire them off into the universe never to be seen again. And she then uses all this as her launch pad for going on about how lucky we are that we don't live like animals any more, how great it is that families are designed and regulated without the complications of erratic emotional and sexual attachments causing chaos, how blessed we are that Science come along and hoover up our eggs so they can make our babies for us on a Petri dish, a strictly controlled number in each five-year cycle, half males and half females, like some kind of interstellar cattle ranch. And as an added bonus, we don't have to be bothered with all the unsavoury unpredictability, illness and imperfection that used to plague us back when we were real human beings. Lucky us, because now we only have the diseases that we have created for ourselves.

Then we have the last of our unholy trinity, Dr Pen, who shows us the Ventura Communications Incorporated publicity video we have (by now) seen a million times, in which they play us the pulsey, surgey sound of the Signal, the one a whole team of people have already spent more than a hundred years trying to decode (to no avail) and which we are following all the way to Epsilon Eridani, even though it is taking us three hundred and fifty years each way, just to see what they have to say for themselves, if it even is a 'them' and not some fart of cosmic feedback. And I mean, in an odd way, even though I guess I should hate that signal, the stupid signal that is actually the only reason that any of this, including me, exists at all, I've always kind of liked it. It's so stubborn. It just keeps going. And for more than a hundred years, no one has been able to crack its code (if it has one), and it's just this mess, this absolute mess of sound, and yet enough people believed in it, believed it was calling to us, that it made all of this happen. I guess all that really proves is just how desperately we don't want to be alone.

This is all as a precursor to this incredibly lame party they throw between two and three – a bit of karaoke (that's what we do for fun round here) and all of us standing around super awkward while the teachers pretend to get teary and make dumb speeches about each of us and about how happy we're going to be.

I guess I don't talk to anyone much at this point since it is all way beyond weird. There's a few of the guys that I've been friends with over the last however long, mostly because I like video games and Emme doesn't that much, but I swear I can't even face them with it hanging over us that we might find out tomorrow that we're about to be husband and wife. Instead I keep my head down and stay tucked into the corner with Emme.

'So come on, really, who do you think you'll get?' she asks me.

I rest my chin on my palm as I look at her, amazed at how heavy my head feels. 'I told you, I—'

She raises her hands. 'OK, I know, you don't care. Then who do you think *I'll* get?'

'I know you're hoping to get Ezra.'

She grins. 'Who wouldn't though, right? Captain's son. Insanely hot.'

I make a face. 'Emme, haven't you ever noticed how much he loves himself?'

She shrugs. 'I know, but I think I could live with it.'

This is when Brandon finishes up on the karaoke and calls Emme for her turn, and while he's standing there waiting to hand her the microphone she is holding her hand out to me.

'Come on, Seren, duet with me, for old times' sake,' she says, and I swear I actually shudder.

'I think I'll sit this one out,' I say.

'Come on!' she says, jumping up and down a little and grabbing my hand, which I reclaim while glaring at her.

'No, Em. I mean it.' This is when she shrugs, only letting her smile slip a little before heading to the stage, and she literally gets there just in time to cue in.

Emme's not the best singer in the world but she can hit notes pretty proficiently and she has so much confidence that she makes it look good. I've always wished I could do it the way she does but even on the rare occasion I get talked into it I always decide the only way I can style it out is by playing some kind of even darker, broodier version of myself. It's not that I don't want to enjoy things – it just doesn't seem like something I can do. Like something I was born with. Or without.

I find myself looking round the room at all the people I have spent every miserable day with for way too long, sitting on desks and looking pale under the harsh lights, and my eyes come to rest on Jonah sitting reading in the corner diagonally opposite, probably the Bible knowing him, like none of it is even happening at all. Weird that, as identical twins, Ezra and he look so similar and yet couldn't be more different. Then we all write stupid messages on each other's T-shirts as if all the time we wasted in this little room actually meant anything of any real relevance, and then the beeps go for second session and thankfully we're done.

Chapter Three

Graduation day. We have to wear full-dress for it, and this is the first time I've ever had to do that so mine is brand-new, packet-fresh, shirt and tie and grey blazer that buttons all the way up and this weird round hat thing that has the same little Ventura emblem on the front of it that our usual clothes do, but this time it is silvery and metal and cold rather than just stitched in. I look at myself in the mirror for a while, thinking about it all, trying to get it to sink in. By the end of this day I will not be in Education any more. By the end of this day I will be in Service, two years, mandatory, before I specialise. Working eight-hour shifts five days a week. By the end of this day I will know who I will have to spend my life with, have genetically engineered children with, pretend to love.

Captain Katerina Lomax, aka Captain Kat, aka the master of all she surveys and the one who runs the show now that the old captain, Captain Lee, has been dead some four years, takes the stage in her navy-blue full-dress Command uniform. Despite being only in her mid-thirties and having two weird kids and a dead husband she has spent her life climbing up every level until she seems to have found herself exactly where she wants to be, that is to say, the top. She's this tall, insanely hot blonde, so you don't have to spend too long wondering how it is that all these doors have opened to her but, whatever, she has definitely made it her mission to maximise on the opportunities there were. My sister, for one, thinks she's pretty much the Lord God Almighty, but has never really been able to justify this opinion or shake me from mine that she's actually just kind of scary and possibly not all that sane. Anyway, here Dad is next to me, Pan on his far side with Cain, and Dad's taking my hand as we sit in the absolute ice-chill of the drill hall and watch the captain approach the podium.

'As you know, this year marks eighty-four years since the Ventura left Earth, and a projected two hundred and sixty-two remain until we reach our destination. We were the sacrifice the people of Earth were prepared to make to find out what may or may not exist in Epsilon Eridani. Yes, you heard me, I said *sacrifice*. I'm not denying, and I never will, that we have had to make huge sacrifices in the name of this mission.

'When Ventura Communications Incorporated first

became sponsors of NASA and the European Space Agency's joint SETI programme they could have no idea where it would take them. The coded message they discovered, originating in the region of the star system Epsilon Eridani, was just the beginning. When our mission was first conceived, there was a series of problems that needed to be solved. First were the ships: powerful, nuclear-fusion-fuelled, self-sufficient. The ability to generate artificial gravity. The capacity to synthesise virtually any food from a basis of fish and egg proteins and to filter water and air ad infinitum meant that the only weak link left in the chain was us, was our mortality. Once it became clear that the journey could never be covered within a lifetime, the concept of the multi-generational crew was born.

'We are one of the interstellar generations. We've never seen Earth; we'll never see where we're going. This ship, eighty-four years into a seven-hundred-year journey, will be all we ever know. All our children ever know. It was all our parents ever knew. Our descendants will be the ones to reach the destination, and their ancestors will one day return to Earth, carrying the most exciting news humanity has ever received. But in the meantime it is important that we remember who we are, that we carry with us the culture, the morals, the ideals of home. That we are of Earth, even if we've never seen it.

'For this reason the Education you are now finishing is absolutely vital to this mission, and I know that each and every one of you has done your best and appreciated every moment. Now it is your turn to take your place among your crew, to give back, to contribute to your society and become as productive a member of it as you can be, and step one of this is your Service. Two years in which you will serve in Maintenance, Production, Domestic and other divisions and during which time you will prove reliable, adaptable and hardworking, and hopefully discover your calling.

'No less important is your Union. Today you will find out who among your classmates will be your life partner. Our breeding programme is one of the cornerstones of our mission and we know you will play your role with pride and joy, just as your parents did and their parents before them.

'So, without further ado, it is with great honour that I announce the graduating class of Mission Date 84.'

Everyone claps and all I want to do is puke. Pan is reaching across Dad and squeezing my hand while he crunches my shoulder bones and smiles – SMILES for God's sake – as if there's any way this could turn out except horrible. I mean, really, he has no idea.

By the time I tune back in to Captain Kat it turns out she actually has something relatively interesting to say for once. 'Before we reveal the new Unions, we have a special announcement to make. One of this year's alumni has been chosen for a very special life path, and I am overjoyed to tell you that it is none other than my own son, Jonah Lomax, who has been called to a life in the priesthood, and we are, of course, so, so happy for him.' She has these glittering tears perfectly positioned in her eyes as she claps and he gets up to head to the stage and we all watch him, pretty much slack-jawed and what the heck. I mean, there is just no limit to the crap this woman can pull. It's not like it's totally out of the blue or anything because he has always been pretty heavily into that stuff, but it's way too convenient a way to deal with the unexpected splitting of an egg seventeen years ago. And I don't even know whether I feel sorry for Jonah as I watch him walk up there and stand looking dazed while Father Seth lays the purple sash around his neck or whether I'm actually incredibly jealous of him, because he just got himself a one-way ticket out of this mess.

Anyway there's no time to think about it; Captain Kat is in her element as the lights go down and the Union announcements begin, pictures popping up on the big screen to much hooting and applause. OK, so the good news is at least I don't get lumbered with Arthur (Phoebe does), and Erica gets Nico (oh man, that's the worst). Emme knows she's next, and so do I, and we catch each other's eye though she's all the way across the room with her mum and dad and grandma who are just about going mental with suspense and then there her picture is, really pretty actually though she knew what the picture was for so there's also this barely concealed look of terror on her face. And I can hardly look at the photo that appears next to her ... and it's Leon Witney, which, you know, could be worse actually. I mean, he's kind of weird and quiet and stuttery and boring, but I'm looking over and giving Emme the thumbs up because, jeez, it could have been Ezra, which is in fact the Worst Case Scenario no matter what she might have thought she wanted.

So, yeah, I bet you're way ahead of me now, and can already guess whose picture comes up next to mine. There are a few more people before me but ... yep. You got it. There's me, with a totally hacked-off expression and white as fish flesh, and there next to me is Ezra. Ezra Lomax. My life partner. The father of my unborn children. And announcing it, his mother, who has the cheek to raise an eyebrow a little as she takes it in. And then she's looking at him, her spawn, over to one side of the front row, his light hair falling all over his face as he slides a look at me over his shoulder in super slow motion, our eyes meeting once, and then we have to walk up there. We actually have to get up and make our legs work and go up there to get our certificates and it all happens to me but more like to someone else and then I'm there, standing there with him, HIM, the heat of his arm intercepting with the heat of my arm until I move it a little away and even over the sound of the crowd (who by the way I can't even see I am SO freaked) I can hear him and he is – WHAT? – humming. Humming. Not a tune or anything, just a sound, one long, flat sound, like an angry bee.

Here is Ezra Lomax in a few words: arrogant, bully, completely in love with himself. And, you know what, I'm standing there and it's slowly dawning on me that I always knew. Not in a good way, more in the way that I knew life would never actually go well for me.

And afterwards we stand there and it goes like this:

Him: Well …

Me: Well …

Him: That's um …

Me: Yeah.

Him: I guess, er …

Me: What?

Him (stuffing his hands in his pockets because he doesn't seem to know what else to do with them): I don't know, I guess …

Me: What?

Him (laughing): Man, like, I don't even know.

And all this time everyone is kind of shuffling around. I mean, they've had their big clapathon and there are lots of people dabbing their eyes and I suppose I should be feeling some big kind of watershed moment is happening but actually all I feel is dry-mouthed, sick, sweaty, a bit like my eyes aren't working. Maybe how it would feel to have a brain tumour or something like that. And since all the families are now gathering to do awkward hugs, mine appear and stand there looking at me like they're so terrified of what I might do that in the end I actually feel bad for them, so I force my face into something approximating a smile. Almost like it was a signal they were waiting for, they all come to life, Dad pulling me into this kind of headlock and kissing me on the eye, Cain circling me with one arm and reaching to shake Ezra's hand with the other, Pan crushing my hands and squealing in my face about how excited she is. Grandpa catches my eye from the back where he is in full-dress black Security uniform, tall and impenetrable and overseeing it all, and gives me one of his hardly visible winks.

I watch Dad take Ezra's hand and simultaneously slap him on the back so hard he staggers forward. 'Good man,' he says, probably trying to convince himself more than anything. I know for a fact that he isn't crazy about him or his family, but I can already guess that everyone thinks it's kind of a big deal that he's the captain's son and that, you know, there may be perks to this, but God knows what they are. I'm really not sure I want to find out.

Yeah, so at this point Captain Kat has been over with Jonah, doing her whole delighted mother bit (everyone knows he's her favourite though of course she isn't exactly spoilt for choice because they both have their issues), but then she's on her way over to us and then she's standing there, breathing out musically, looking at me first with these little diamond-like tears in her blue eyes.

'What a joy! What a precious moment this is, to stand here and look at each other and anticipate a lifetime of happiness,' she says, and I'm thinking how right my dad is when he says she's full of it. She's the kind of person who should only be seen on the screens; seriously, she is just too much for real life – too tall, too blonde, too much of everything.

She doesn't hug Ezra or me; instead she puts a hand on the side of each of our faces and looks from one to the other while acting like she's about to shed a tear. Then next thing you know she is holding Dad's hand between hers, then Pan's, then Cain's, though they barely seem to register with her because she is mostly just on her way to Grandpa.

'Oh Joshua,' she says, once she gets to him, resting her hand on his arm where it grips his hat into his side. 'How perfect this is! We couldn't even have hoped for this. Our families have been so fractured, so tested, and now we can be whole again and move forward together. I am, truly, overwhelmed by God's grace.'

I watch Grandpa then, the way he looks at Ezra, who's standing there doing this permanent scowl that he always does and messing around with his hair which is ridiculous by anyone's standards but definitely by Grandpa's, and you can tell he's wondering how it all came to this. This is mostly because he was so tight with the old captain, Captain Lee, as they were in Education together, and Captain Lee did things a certain way and since Captain Kat's been around there's been a sense of something new, but not in a good way, if you see what I mean.

Anyway, so all this goes on and then we're meant to drink fizzy wine (our first official alcohol) and eat these vile cakes the colour of raw meat that have been laid out on a table and, I don't know, mingle or something, but we don't. Or rather I don't. I just stand there with people talking around me and every time someone speaks to me the only thing I say is 'What?' because I swear to you I cannot even hear anyone or anything. And at one awful moment this guy from Cultural is going round taking pictures of everyone and he arrives and I realise, even though I still can't make out a word anyone says, that he wants one of us together, as the future Mr and Mrs Lomax. So we stand there and the way Ezra has his arm round me I smell him, the awful deodorant he uses that is sweet with this undertone that is almost urine-like, and all I can think about is that time, down in Engineering on a school trip, when we made a point of 'getting lost' all because he swore blind he had his own shuttle and he knew how to drive it and in the end all it was was him putting on his pretty lame moves. And now here we are and he has his hand spread across the small of my back and he is tapping me: *tap tap tap*. Morse code for something, probably, but nothing I would ever want to know.

Chapter Four

I don't think it's fair that Pan and Dad, aka the only people left in my actual immediate family per se, get to decide that I have a psychological issue and declare me depressed just because I go straight to my room from graduation and refuse to speak or move for a couple of days. In my opinion the very fact that I hate the way this place works just proves that I am the only one round here who isn't insane.

'You asked me how I feel and the honest truth is sometimes I think it would be better not to exist.' As soon as I've said this I know I shouldn't have done, I know that this has just pressed one of Dad's worst buttons and looking at him with this crease he gets above his top lip when he's upset I know I've Overstepped the Line.

'Seren, I am taking you to Med to see Dr Maddox, for your own good.' This is Dad, having run out of patience with me.

'No.' But I'm not angry any more, just sad, feeling like I have something as big and as hard as a coffee mug rammed in my throat where I will never be able to swallow it, let alone talk round it, and feeling that there is a crease above my top lip too, answering Dad's.

At a loss he sighs, and stretches his arms back so that they hit my shelf, where my only actual physical book, a copy of *Tender Is the Night* which belonged to Great Granny Bea, sits open, face down, gathering dark dust. After a moment of looking at it, he says, 'You used to read so much, Seren. And now I never see you reading.'

'Dad ...'

But he holds his hand up, has his say. 'I could never get you off your pod. You were working your way through the whole library at one point, and you loved it. Why don't you ever do that any more?'

'There just –' I shrug '– doesn't seem any point. I mean, what even is the point in reading about a real life in a world that for all we know doesn't even exist any more, when all there really is or will ever be is this place? These grey walls, grey ceiling, grey uniform ... this cold, this dark ...' I shake my head, regretting everything I say even as I say it. Not because it's not true, but because I know that every word that comes out of my mouth only makes it worse.

Dad pulls off his cap then and leans forward over his knees, rubbing his hair back and forth and back and forth so that when he stops it is all sticking up. There is a lacy patch of red along the side of his neck, spreeing he calls it, from the cold in the Production bay. I get so annoyed at him right then, letting himself get cold like that. I get so annoyed at him for being so lonely and so alone, and letting me be.

'I just can't see what the point of it all is,' I say.

He looks up at me, pushes his cap back on, tugs at his nose, looks at the floor, his face telling the story of how he's been here and done all this before.

'The point is: get up, do your work, come home, love your family, full stop. That's what the point is. Keep going. Keep going. We have to do that for our kids and for their kids and for those who come after. It's the same thing on Ventura as it would have been on a planet, Seren. You just think there's more to it than there is. You think there's something else that you're missing, but there isn't.'

'How do you know, though?'

'I just …' He shrugs, slumping forward again. 'I know, baby, trust me.'

I look up at the vent in my ceiling then, so desperate not to be as trapped in this room as I know I'm about to feel.

Dad puts his hand on my knee. 'Seren, the life path you have is a good one. I don't know why you can't see that. I don't know why you won't let it unfold in front of you with a happy heart.'

'What? Marrying Ezra Lomax, that arrogant pig, and squeezing out his evil babies, who are going to spend their whole lives stuck in this thing before getting flushed out into the vacuum along with the sewage?'

'You just can't see the good in anything at all, and the last person I heard talking like this was very unwell ...' Referencing my mother, of course, who made a point of getting herself sucked out of the airlock just after I was born.

'Are you sure she was unwell? Are you sure she wasn't just sick of all this? Sick of you?'

So, yeah, obviously this is where he just gets up and leaves, and I feel so horrible that it turns out he wins this one, by default.

I agree to go to Med but I put my foot down as far as Dad coming with me goes. So I'm here in the waiting room, and I guess everyone here knows that this is the evening for the mental health clinic, so we're all looking at each other out of the corner of our eyes, looking but pretending we're not looking, wondering which one of us is the craziest. Just about everyone else here is in pairs. There's a young guy from Cultural with his mother, a couple, and also two older women.

And then there's Domingo Suarez.

He's talking to those two older women the first time I see him, in Spanish, and because there aren't that many people who actually speak Spanish these days, seeing someone do it is impressive somehow, almost like a magic trick. He notices me watching him at one point and so he keeps sneaking his eyes over to me while he's talking, almost like he's including me in his conversation, the one I basically can't understand at all, when all of a sudden he's clearly said something pretty funny because both his aunties, or whoever they are, crease up laughing and so does he, and they're all slapping their knees and whatever else.

It's only after this that I notice his mouth. It's soft, full, dark against white teeth, beautiful. And when he smiles, runs a hand through shining hair that is as black as water at night, I am absolutely stopped, dead in my tracks, literally slack-jawed with astonishment at his never-before-noticed hotness in all its glory.

I don't know exactly how I look at that moment but I guess it's pretty weird, what with the way I don't manage to recover quick enough to hide the fact that I am essentially gaping right at him and, sure enough, he catches me and loses his smile right away. He looks back at the women but you can tell he's only fake-smiling, totally distracted, and then only a few seconds later he is excusing himself, getting up, and I think he's going to leave, but then he's next to me.

I don't look at him at first, in fact I'm so uncomfortable I am looking down at my pod, pretending to read even though all I'm doing is running my eyes over the same few words again and again. He watches me, watches the side of my face, then looks down at his hands where he clasps them loosely between his spread knees. Then he watches me some more. Finally he moves his elbow a little, just until it touches my side, so of course I have to look at him then, which I do, with as filthy a glare as I can muster even though I know I'm kind of smiling too. He meets my eye, smiling at first, then mocking my scowl by matching it, then smiling again.

'You don't remember me?' he says then, a question that throws me, because I was pretty sure that he would be the one not to remember me. 'I was in Education with your sister.'

'I ... You ...?' And so I just go back to staring at him.

'I ... You ...' he mocks, laughing at me, flashing those white teeth again.

And this is when the woman at the Med desk says, 'Seren Hemple?' because it's my turn, and right at the same time, *BLEEP*, there my name is, twenty centimetres tall on a screen on the wall, and I swallow hard.

Domingo looks from the screen back at me, then back at the screen, then me again, waiting for me to get up and go. When I don't he laughs, leans in to me, raises his hand to his mouth to stage-whisper behind it, 'Shall we get out of here, Seren?'

And I say, 'I don't know you.'

'You do. We just established that. I'm Domingo Suarez. I was in Education with your sister.'

BLEEP. My name flashes again and by now everyone is looking at me, including Domingo's aunties, who I had completely forgotten about. And all I am doing is sitting there and thinking that maybe I don't have to be this person, the person sitting in Med waiting to see her shrink, not if I don't want to be, and about how there was only this one possible outcome when I walked in this door, and now it seems like there are so many different ones, and all of them are better.

'Let's go,' he says then, and even though he gestures just the tiniest bit with his head and shoulder as he gets up, somehow irresistibly I am following him, up and out of the clinic, along the main Med corridor where I have to pass my name on another couple of screens before we make it out on to South Main and it is only once we have put a bit of distance between us and Med that we look at each other again, and then I stop.

'Your aunties!'

He laughs. 'My what?'

'You left your aunties, your family, whoever they were, back there in the clinic.'

He flaps his hand. 'No, I wasn't there with them. I just know them somewhat.'

He pushes his hands in his pockets and falls into step next to me, even though he is so much taller than me that each pace of his is two of mine. For the same reason when he looks at me he leans a little forward and peers back. Neither of us explains what we were doing at the mental health clinic, as if we agree on it silently. Instead he says, 'So, Seren Hemple, Pandora's sister, new friend of mine, what do you want to do now you've escaped the purgatory of the Med waiting room?'

And I shrug and say, 'No real plan, to be honest.'

'No real plan, huh?' he says. 'That's just how I like it.'

There's something so intense in it then, in the eye contact he won't let me break, in the way his arm is almost touching mine but not quite, that when he says, 'Want to see something cool?' I know there is no way I could ever say no.

He asks me to follow him and I do, all the way to the downwards transporters at the south-west corner of the plaza, where we stand looking at each other and while we're waiting I say, 'You speak Spanish?'

He smiles. 'It's true.'

'I didn't think anyone actually did that any more.'

'Some people do. Only the chosen ones.' I watch his Adam's apple move when he speaks, then he laughs. 'Nah, I guess it's like ... if both partners in a Union have grown up speaking it, it just passes on to their kids, you know? Probably won't last much longer, I guess.'

'Shame.' I give him a half smile. 'I like it. It's cool.'

'Good to know. Note to self: speak more Spanish.'

I laugh it off, even though it makes me want to fall into a thousand pieces at his feet. I have to change the subject. 'Where are we going?'

He leans against the wall and crosses his arms and says, 'Don't you like surprises, Seren?'

And I think about it and say, 'I don't actually have much experience with them.'

And I feel that slow, sweet smile spread from his face on to mine.

We get off in Production where he shakes hands with a guard before leading me into a space so freezing cold and dark I wonder for a moment if we have gone out an airlock, but that's when I realise we are in the Fisheries.

The thing is that Science base most of our food on fish and egg proteins; from these they can basically synthesise anything they like, which is why the only living creatures on Ventura, besides us, are like a million fish and laying chickens. They breed and keep the fish in a series of these huge tanks of water way in the bottom front of the ship where there are actual windows (which is more than we get in our quarters), portholes along the side wall, and through them comes the pale light of Huxley.

'This place is amazing; it's so cool. Why have I never come here?'

He grins, holds his hands out to the side and turns slowly. 'You could almost be on a real beach.'

I nod, even though it's so cold the air burns in my throat and chest. I squat, peer down into the darkness of the water, which is when a perfect silver sleek of fish and fin just barely breaks the surface and makes me nearly fall backwards.

'Wow,' I hear myself say.

'I know, right?' He laughs.

'What's it like working here?'

'It's cool; I like it more than Maintenance and stuff. Production's interesting. I like the fish.'

'How old are you?' I ask him.

'Eighteen. Graduated just after my fifteenth birthday. Youngest in Generation 81.'

I lay my hand on my chest. 'Fourth oldest in mine. I'm almost seventeen.'

He puts his hand up for a high five but I end up doing it kind of lamely, and then I think of something. 'My sister and I ... she's actually only two years older than me. Well, a little more. But due to the whole thing of being a generation apart she has managed to spend our lives acting like she's basically my mother. Like she has all this life experience I can only guess at.' I shake my head, flush a little in the realisation that it's not that cute to hate your sister. Whether things are cute or not has never mattered much to me before now. And suddenly, like an avalanche of solid rock, it matters.

'Older siblings are all the same.' He smiles. 'My brother busts me for stuff more than my dad ever has.'

'Well, then I guess you must be pretty naughty,' I say, feeling the afterburn of having said it in my cheeks.

'Nothing wrong with being a little naughty sometimes.' He winks, and I nearly die.

'Do … um … ' I shake my head; try to cover the fact that I am completely lost for words. 'Do you live in berths?'

'Yeah.'

'So you haven't married your life partner yet?'

'Not yet.' He smiles, shrugging it off.

I look back at him then, wondering why I never noticed the almost unspeakable beauty of him when he was in Pan's class, and in fact barely even remember noticing him at all. He has got to be the only person that has ever made the Ventura uniform that all of us are stuck wearing 24/7 look good: I hate the stupid caps but his suits him; the dumb grey overalls cling to his broad, lean shoulders in a way that wipes out logical thought, especially with the way that maybe one too many (or just the right amount?) of the snap buttons at his chest have come undone. Like most Production guys he carries his key fobs on a chain round his neck, but I've never spent as much time following the line of it down under anyone's overalls with my eyes as I am right now.

And all this time he is looking at me so intently,

with this shadow of a smile, like I am just about to say something incredibly interesting or amusing, like I am this amazing little oddity that he has just discovered, when in fact all I really am is someone flinching under an expectation I can't possibly fulfil.

'What?' I ask him.

'Tell me things,' he says, leaning back on his hands. 'I want to know things about you.'

I shrug. 'There isn't anything to say. Graduation, fulfilling my life's great purpose, all that.'

'Ah.' He grins. 'I see Father Seth hasn't lost his touch when it comes to inspiring the next generation. On the positive side, one glorious day, maybe you could be the best latrine operative West has ever seen.'

I laugh again, watching his lips as he speaks, trying not to think about them too much, and failing, as he adds, 'And, you know, you get used to the smell in the end, so just give it a chance.'

'You can talk, fish boy,' I say, smiling.

'Fish boy? Ouch.' He takes hold of the collar of his uniform and sniffs it. 'Is it that bad?'

I shake my head, nearly tell him he actually smells incredible, and stop myself just in time. 'I get my assignment Monday, so I guess I'll just have to hope for the best on the whole latrine thing.'

'Seriously, don't knock it.' He smiles. 'It could be worse. My first assignment was waste management.'

I feel myself make a face. 'Wow.'

He nods. 'I know. I've led an incredibly glamorous – and fragrant – life.' He spreads his hands, palms up. 'As you can tell.'

We both look up, watching through the portholes above, where we see the edge of Huxley-3, the planet that's been coming into view, the half of her that's in sun anyway. She's getting so big she's a little blue crescent now, a fingernail clipping.

'Why do fish need windows?' I ask him.

'They like to have a little sun.' He shrugs. 'When there is any. Which, right now, there is. Which is nice.'

'It is nice.' I nod, panning back down to the water and watching my feet as they dangle over the glossy darkness that's streaked with the slipping bodies of fish and flashing with the starlight that sneaks through the portholes. A fish is plying the surface with its lips just at that moment so that I almost feel it catching my eye, and I lean towards it and say, 'Can I touch it?'

Domingo pretends to be shocked. 'This is all so sudden!'

I roll my eyes and try not to smile. 'I meant the fish.'

And yeah, I mean, he makes a bunch more stupid jokes then but I take my trainers off and he helps me step down these couple of metal rungs into the water that is barely above the temperature of ice and totally black as oil but I hold my hand in and sure enough I don't have to wait long until one glides along my palm, so gloriously full of flickering energy and life that it makes me shiver a little; makes me scream. We laugh while he's pulling me back up the steps and telling me I need to be quiet or I'll get him busted by the guys and joking about how he should never have let me in here because he could tell I was trouble from the start, and all the time all I can do is think about his beautiful, sun-squinting eyes. And I can't explain it, because he is basically a stranger to me, as much as anyone can be in this place, but at the same time he feels more like a friend than anyone has in forever.

So much so that, after he walks me home, after he leaves me at the door, shaking my hand but then holding it until it slips out of his, then looking back until he goes out of sight, I am left wondering how I've ever lived without him, and how I ever will again.

The way I fall for him is that quick, that strong, that beautiful.

And it is also totally impossible.

Chapter Five

Pandora makes me go out with her to this Captain Kat thing, some kind of community meeting or briefing that's bound to be a waste of time, but Cain is out working and Dad has Put His Foot Down. Dad doesn't really do this a lot but when he does he generally gives you a heads-up by announcing that he's doing it. He'll actually say, 'I'm putting my foot down' and then go back to doing whatever it is he's doing, like watching something on the screens or whatever, and this is exactly what he's doing tonight and why he will absolutely not be drawn into what he calls Captain Kat's Propaganda Machine. Yeah, Dad's a real revolutionary for about five minutes until he goes back to playing *Football Manager* on his pod. Anyway, Pan is Captain Kat's number one fan so before I can say too much about it (and probably mostly because I'm in a crazy good mood for my own personal reasons) we're on our way to the drill hall.

While we're walking people keep stopping to paw at Pan, going on about her baby belly like it's the first time anyone ever got knocked up. People also make jokes about me being next and I swear I could retch; I could actually vomit to think of that being me. But anyway this isn't about any of that, it's about how when we get there the place is all dark and horribly cold and the only light is on the stage and there are a bunch of chairs that Maintenance have laid out in rows and we sit and shiver a little and wait for Captain Kat's pronouncements and there are cameras setting up and Pan waves at someone because he's a friend of Cain's, some dark-haired guy who works for Cultural. And then he starts coming over to us, grinning and coiling a cable round his hand and elbow and then I'm thinking, wait, maybe he's ... but then it's too late.

'Hey, Pandora,' he says, doing that thing some Spanish-speaking guys do with their Rs. They exchange pleasantries and just general sounds for a moment before he says, 'I don't suppose you've seen my brother?' before scanning the crowd.

And I feel my skin prickle while Pan says, 'No, not for ages actually. How is Domingo?'

He smiles. 'The same. Follows his own path. He missed band practice last night because apparently he felt sorry for some sick girl at Med and took her home.' He laughs, and I'm not quick enough to stop staring at him, and Pan clocks it in the corner of her eye. 'He's always playing the hero for someone or other,' he adds, and right at that moment I notice that he has the exact same teeth as his brother, strong and totally white but with one slightly turned the wrong way.

'You were in Med last night weren't you, Seren?' says Pan.

I think fast. 'Yeah, but I ... I didn't see anything strange.' After that the best tactic seems to be to ignore them both or act like I've suddenly become unbelievably interested in something over the far end of the hall where some people from West are just filing in, looking bored and cold. The fact of the matter is I'm actually thinking about Domingo, about how he obviously thought I was a freak and felt sorry for me, about who he plays the hero for and why, and all these other thoughts that kill my mood somewhat, to say the least.

Anyway, so Domingo's brother says a bit more and then takes the hint and goes back to his camera, and once he's gone Pan sets about staring at the side of my face until she realises I'm not going to look back at her and says, 'Well?'

And I'm like: 'Well what?'

'Why did you go all weird just then?'

'I didn't.'

She studies me through half-closed eyes, then says, 'You were with Domingo Suarez last night!'

43

'I wasn't!'

'And now you're denying it, which makes it even weirder.'

I shake my head. 'Whatever, man.' But I know I'm burning and no amount of turning away is going to hide it.

Pan takes this as a foregone conclusion and shakes her head, face screwed up like I just confirmed every bad thing she ever thought about me (which is a lot of bad things). 'What would Ezra think if he heard you'd been hanging around with another guy?'

'I have no idea, and I couldn't care less.'

'I don't understand you. I just don't. You got given one of the best Unions of anyone I know, and all you do is cause problems for yourself.'

And right now is when the music starts and everyone who's here, which is actually not that many people, slumped around the chairs in their jackets and hats, sits up a little and looks at the stage. Captain Kat walks out, holding her arms up for just a second until she hears the pretty pitiful patter of applause that goes around, and following her, sure enough, here comes Ezra, supposed love of my life, looking smug and full of it just like always, and Jonah, looking completely baffled by the world in general.

'Hey.' Emme arrives next to me, nudges me, waves at Pan. 'What'd I miss?'

'Nothing yet.'

It's not like there was even any reason at all to come down here when the whole thing is going out on every screen on board and echoing on every sound system too but look, whatever, Pan has this thing about being present for things, call it a sense of occasion or something. But in this particular instance she turns out to have made a good call.

'We are now very close to the planet known as Huxley-3,' says Captain Kat. 'It has two moons, circles K-dwarf star Huxley and seems to have some form of atmosphere. For this reason, we at Command have decided that we will have to make an unscheduled stop in its orbit so that it can be investigated.'

This is the point at which everyone who has bothered to make the trip down here starts shuffling around and looking at each other, and Pan makes this grab for my hand that kind of ends up on my elbow.

'Seren,' she says, and yeah, I guess I even feel a little something too, though I'm not entirely sure what. This has never happened before so there is no reference point, just a whole mass of confusing thoughts about how it will be to be so close to a planet and what it will all mean when my whole life has just been basically one huge status quo of vast black space.

'We will make ninety orbits while tests are carried out.' That's when Captain Kat temporarily crushes a lot

45

of the hopes most of us didn't even realise we had: 'For safety reasons there will be no non-essential excursions to the surface at present, but the viewing rooms will be open twenty-four hours a day during this period, so I suggest you make the most of this exhilarating opportunity to see a real planet first-hand.'

And here's the thing – make of this what you will, but even after all that, I'm still thinking about Domingo.

Chapter Six

This is me in Service. This is me working. And yeah, I know that basically Service is the two years of your life when you do all the jobs that no one wants to do, the real grunt work, and you're mainly stuck in Domestic or Maintenance or Production, but I am still glad of it because I am just so tired of Education, of being stuck in that little classroom with those same people and those same teachers telling us basically the same stuff over and over in different ways: you're stuck here; you're stuck with this; do what you do; don't complain; our whole existence is about keeping this thing going, for us, for Earth, for humanity, for the future, for God, whoever he is.

So even though I get to the board and find out my first posting is in Maintenance, refilling vending machines, and even though I have to wear a hairnet under my hat, I am more or less on a high that first day. I even get first session and that is a serious plus since I don't have to swap my sleep patterns or anything yet. Just as I'm checking the board one last time to figure out how to get to where I'm going, I hear someone, and when I look it's Ezra saying hey and standing in behind me super close so that he is reading the posting list over my shoulder and his breath is moving my hair. And for a second I am looking at his jawline and ear and hair at point-blank range.

'You really should think about going a little easier on the hair wax, you know.'

He breaks into a smile and puts his hand on my shoulder and says, 'Check you – looking after me already. The devoted wife.'

But I'm shrugging his hand off like it's diseased and walking away and wishing he wasn't following me but he is.

'I guess you noticed I got Engineering – straight into Flight Training. Don't hate me. They just know talent when they see it.'

'Sure, Ezra.'

'I mean, it'll be skivvy work at first, we all know that, but it's about getting your foot in the door, getting known. What did you get?'

'Maintenance. First session.'

'Well, of course first session.'

'Why of course?'

'You think they'd put a sixteen-year-old girl on nights

with everything that goes down in this place after hours? Seren, come on.' Before I even get a chance to ask him what he means by this he has his arm round me again, pulling me into his side where his hipbone drives into my rib and he is talking into my hair, making it wet, and he says, 'Whenever you want me to put a bun in your oven and take you away from all this, just let me know, baby.'

So I elbow him in the groin, not as hard as I could but it's enough to get him off me and have him rolling into the wall while I walk away and tell him he can keep his stinking buns.

I get to the Maintenance offices in North and buzz at the door even though it's open anyway and there's this girl I half recognise in there filling up a trolley with nut bars and packets of nachos and she doesn't really look at me before she says, 'Junior Technician Seren Hemple, Service starter, right?'

'Yeah.'

'Petty Officer Mariana Moreno. And you're late.'

'Sorry.'

'Stop wasting time – come in and help me with this trolley.'

For today Mariana makes me follow her around North on her circuit, learning the ropes.

'Basically the population of this ship have an insatiable appetite for synthesised junk so we can't refill these things fast enough. By the time you get to the last one on your circuit the first one will be empty again. It's the most colossally futile exercise the universe has ever known and for the next six months it is your life.' This is the kind of thing, I learn, that Mariana says a lot, so yeah, I pretty much like her right away. Not that she seems to like me very much.

The cool thing about doing the machines is the fact that they're all over the place, in a whole bunch of places you need clearance to get into so of course I've never actually been in them before. Mariana has this special Maintenance pass that she just scans on the door fobs and they open right up. So at one point we're up in Science and it's kind of quiet and smells weird and you pass doors that are open where people are talking quietly and looking at brightly coloured computer screens and saying things like: 'But where's that ferrous scan? Why can't we do the overlay?'

And man, they have the most awesome windows. Actual windows, not portholes, so they can just goggle the hell out of Huxley-3 in the most intense way. At one point Mariana tells me to get some paper towels and while I'm doing it I just stand there at the door to one of the labs that's empty and I edge in a little and to the left so that the sunlight is falling on my face and it is actually starting to maybe feel a little warm. And there she is, Huxley-3, a beautiful jade and aqua-blue, and she has clouds, CLOUDS, that move and swirl, slow but sure, a living thing as sure as I've ever seen one.

We even get to go down to Engineering, only about three bays away from flight deck, where the recons are leaving and arriving, and we hear them leave, hear them arrive, a sound like some type of explosion, combined with the grinding metal-on-metal of the bay doors. And in between times we see guys walking in ones or twos down the corridors in flight suits and harnesses, depressurisation masks under arms, on their way back from the recon, and I strain my ears like crazy but they are always talking quietly or even not talking at all, except for one and all I hear him say is, 'I don't know, man, that's how it looked to me.'

At this point Mariana says, 'Hey, recruit!' so shrilly at my back that it makes me jump. 'You going to stand there checking out the flyboys all day or are you actually going to do any work?'

So I come back over to her just as she hurls a box of protein bars at me and I fail to catch it.

'Look,' she says, standing and dabbing the black oil residue from the inside of the machine off her hands. 'You know, I'm not asking you to be in love with this job. I am simply asking you to not suck at it. All you need to do is not suck for long enough to make it to the end of the few shifts you last before you decide to marry your little boyfriend and get pregnant and go on leave for the next several years.'

I pick up the box of protein bars and pull it open on my way to the machine. 'Well, don't hold your breath on that one,' I tell her.

Chapter Seven

I am just running past the swimming pool on morning circuit when I see him, smiling at me so that I smile at him but still pass, having too much momentum to slow or stop fast enough.

Domingo Suarez.

I turn back and pull my earphones out. And then we are standing there and watching each other, covering the distance between us in a few short paces and I am thinking that here we are again next to water, almost like there is something elemental in it, in the way I draw him to me, me to him, however it works, but who cares anyway because he's standing there and I swear I am so busy looking at him that I can't think of a single thing to say. Especially because I am totally sweaty and gross in my rec uniform of standard-issue grey vest and shorts, and he is, well look, you have to know this guy always looks amazing, even when he's on his way home from shift and has the arms of his overalls tied round his waist and his T-shirt all dirty and whatever, he is just one of those people. So he is standing there and he is hitting every point on the spectrum of male beauty and I am sweaty as heck and yet in a weird way I am forgetting it more and more with every moment, what with the way he looks at me.

'It's you again,' he says, smiling on the side so that this one dimple appears.

'I could say the same thing.'

'You could indeed.'

'But I won't, because, you know, that would be boring.'

He nods. 'That would actually be incredibly boring.'

He watches me a minute, and neither of us stop smiling even a little, to the point that my ears almost start to ring.

'How are you?' he asks.

'Now who's being boring?'

He laughs. 'OK, you're right.' He pushes his hands into his hair before looking back up at me. 'I'm under pressure here.'

'True.' I laugh, still panting from the running and not doing that well at bringing it under control while I watch the way the blue light from under the pool plays across his skin and wish there weren't hundreds of people milling past on change of shift.

'I guess you need to get back to your run?' he says,

but it's a question, and so I'm left wondering whether I should say yes or no, and which answer he wants me to give. It must be all there on my face as I look at him, look at the flow of everyone passing, and back at him again and all I say is, 'Well, I ... maybe we could take a walk around the swimming pool?'

'A walk around the swimming pool?' he echoes, and we both look at it then, at the way the water puckers a little because of the vibration of the ship, something I guess we aren't even able to feel. 'Well ... um ... I guess ... yeah, we can do that.'

At first it's kind of awkward with the way we both walk super slow and it seems like there are so many things to say that neither of us even knows where to start. There's also this added complication in that when he looks at me I forget everything, like this wave of amnesia just washes everything away except him, and when he smiles I do too, completely against my will, and then he says, 'So I haven't seen you since the whole Huxley-3 thing.'

'I know, right?' I say, accidentally getting a little loud. 'Man, what I wouldn't give to be a flyboy right now.'

He makes a face. 'And most of them won't even appreciate it.'

'EXACTLY,' I say, turning to him and holding his eye. 'It is so utterly wasted on them, I can hardly even bear it.' As I am shaking my head I am suddenly becoming deeply, intensely aware of the eye contact, turning away a little so I can even out my breathing again. 'What about if it's safe though? Think they'll let us go down there?'

'Um, well ... maybe,' he says sadly. 'But I seriously doubt it.'

'But it's our only chance to see a real planet, probably ever in our lives. Why should we have to die without ever knowing what it's like?'

'Well, isn't it obvious?' he says, half smiling, turning to me. 'Because then we might find out what we're missing. And I guess they think that as long as we don't know, we'll be content with what we have. It's the theory behind a lot of things in this place.'

He leaves that in the air between us, something I always knew but never really knew I knew. Something I have always thought but never thought I thought. He says things like this – things that suddenly make all the messed-up ideas that have always been going round and round in my head come into focus and make sense. I find I'm squinting up at him, trying to figure him out, shaking my head a little. 'Some of the things you say ...' I begin, before realising this isn't something I can tell him and feeling a chill of regret steal through me.

'What?' He smiles. 'Some of the things I say what?'

But I am speeding up, flapping a hand at him. I won't

tell him, of course, I'll only shake my head, so after a few more metres he gives up, shrugs, changes the subject.

'Bet you're glad you won't have any more swimming lessons,' he says, nodding at the pool, saving me.

'Yeah, with Lieutenant Maria Fernanda yelling and jabbing at you with the pool brush if you weren't kicking your legs right.'

He laughs. 'I always wondered what the point was of teaching the inhabitants of an interstellar space traveller how to swim. Even though, actually, it's turned out to be kind of handy for me.'

'For you, sure, but for the rest of us – utterly pointless.'

'I know, right? I guess it was just to give us something to do, keep us active. Also I think people actually used to use the pool more, on days off, for fun.'

'Yeah, what happened to that?' I look at the rectangle of blue water, at the bolted-in seats around the edge that no one ever sits on any more.

'The ambient temperature on board was warmer back then. It's dropped over the years the ship has been in deep space, by just over two-point-four degrees.'

'I love it when you talk technical.' I smile, amazed by my own bravery.

'Noted,' he says, and then, 'Happy to be of service,' and he touches the peak of his cap and winks at me at the same time and I laugh and push at his elbow a little.

I guess I do it without thinking but the contact utterly throws me. There's this half second in which both of us flush and just generally lose our place in things before he makes a few random filler noises and then says, 'I actually remember Pandora being the best swimmer in my class.'

'Pan? Can't have been. You're thinking of someone else.'

'No, she was. She was really good. Why is that so hard to believe?'

I sigh. 'I guess because all she ever does these days is moon over Cain and talk about babies. She specialised in information systems in Science, just because she knew she'd only have to work first session and she wants to be there for her kids. That's so lame.'

He seems to think about it for a second, looking up at the ceiling. 'It's not THAT lame. Is it?'

'I guess I think anyone who's content with what Ventura has to offer is lame,' I say, wondering why I'm saying this when it will probably make him stop liking me at all, but I do this you know, I hit the self-destruct button from time to time.

And, sure enough, he doesn't say anything for this long moment and we slow to a stop and then stand, and I look down at our feet, his trainers and mine, almost toe to toe, grey with a blue stripe down the side, identical of course, except his make mine look tiny.

When I finally do get the courage to look up at him he is watching me, and so I start walking again and he follows me and then he says, 'Do you remember that we've had conversations? Before the other day, I mean.'

'Um,' I say, thinking, while he watches me carefully and sees no sign of it on my face and shakes his head.

'Don't worry, doesn't matter. It's not surprising. I guess you were still pretty young when my generation graduated.'

'Thirteen,' I say, squinting up at him, thinking about how much he must have changed in that time because I swear I never noticed him.

He laughs. 'I remember you from lunchtimes, when we used to go down to the cantina and Education B would be there finishing up and Pan used to say you were her sister and you were just this pretty little girl with pigtails and big brown eyes watching everybody. So calm and so, I don't know, serious, with all the other kids in your class going crazy and spilling food and you just pretty much rolling your eyes at them.'

'That sounds about right,' I say, feeling myself flush a little.

'You remember Pan's sweet sixteenth birthday party?'

I frown. 'A little.'

'You don't remember talking to me then?'

'What did we talk about?'

'Basically about how everything sucked.'

I laugh. 'That does sound like me, but I still don't believe you.'

'Why not?'

'Because there is no way I would forget spending time with you.' Like always I've said it without thinking, just being honest without thinking through what I'm actually saying until afterwards, so once it dawns on me I am way too embarrassed to face him. I turn, walk away, change the subject. 'So now the only reason anyone comes to the swimming pool is to drink stolen alcohol when they're underage because it's a camera black spot?'

He walks close behind me, laughing. 'You've been talking to Cain.'

'You were part of that too, I'm guessing,' I say, finally recovering enough to turn and face him.

'Sometimes.' He nods, smiles. 'Cain always was good at getting into trouble. He was a lot of fun.'

And just when I'm about to tell him what a major drag Cain is these days, he says, 'Well, here we are,' because, sure enough, we have gone all the way round three edges of the pool and are back at where West Main is passing, but quieter now with first session underway. 'Where do you need to be? Can I walk you somewhere?'

I think for a second, watch him bite his lip a little, and though it's hard to get it out, I say, 'I guess ... probably not, right?'

He laughs, looks down at his feet. 'We're allowed to

be friends, Seren.' He shrugs, sending this prickling heatwave of embarrassment through me so hard I almost shudder with it, because there I was assuming something when he hasn't actually given me any reason to think it, and so I say, 'Sure we are, of course. I'm sorry. I was only thinking ... never mind.'

And I start to walk away, shaking my head, talking to myself, winding my earphone cable around my pod and shoving it in my shorts pocket as he catches up to me. Then I feel his fingers touch my wrist for a moment, close to my side, and he says, super quiet, 'Seren, I don't want you to think that I—'

But I don't get to find out the rest because right then we hear: 'Dominguito!' echoing down West Main and then see this walking bunch of pink and purple flowers coming at us from behind, about twenty metres away but closing pretty fast.

'Hola, abuelita,' Dom yells back and as I start to walk away he says, 'I'll catch you up.'

I move fast but can't help looking back at how this little Spanish lady with a white streak at the front of her black hair hands him the flowers before yanking on his neck so that he has to bend all the way down, and even bend his knees a little too, to kiss her once on each cheek while she babbles on at him and he smiles and nods.

I'm so deep in thought that he scares me a little when he suddenly appears beside me with an armful of flowers.

'She gave you flowers?' I frown.

He laughs. 'What can I say? I have this effect on women.' And when I don't laugh, he says, 'No, they're for the drill hall, for la misa ... for Mass, church service, whatever you call it. She asked me to take them there for her. Smell them.'

He offers them to me and I lean into them but find that all the time I am looking at him, looking up at him while he looks down at me, and I breathe in the smell that is beautiful but always makes me sad since Production only seem to grow the flowers for Union ceremonies and funerals, and it's weird because this is the first time I've actually taken the time to smell them up close and when I try to describe it all I can say is, 'They're ... ' and then nothing else, and man, it is horribly embarrassing but I feel this burn in my eyes almost like I could shed a tear, and all the time he is watching me, smile fading, a little frown gathering, and I turn away, shake my head, and he says, 'I think you should have them.'

And I say, 'No way! They're for the church. I can't do that. And anyway, what would people think if I turned up at home with a bunch of flowers?'

He nods once, frowns down at the floor between us, and I notice right then that there are these ridiculously pretty moles on his face that almost form a line, a constellation, from cheekbone to earlobe to jawbone, down his throat and then under his clothes, like a route marked on a map. Each mole is so dark, so perfectly shaped, I realise now for the first time why people call them beauty marks.

There are voices at the end of the corridor, three Admin workers who are late for shift.

'I should ... um, I guess I should probably go,' Domingo says, pulling his pod out and checking the time.

'Yeah, right, of course.' And then, I don't know why, but something makes me say, 'You could call me sometime, I guess, on my pod. If you wanted to, that is.'

'It's not, um, I ...' He laughs, but doesn't finish, and so I say, 'No, of course, you're right. Not a good idea.'

'Seren, you know ... you're not ...' He smiles on one side. 'You're not making this easy for me.'

And just then as the Admin people are passing on either side of us, probably on their way to the offices on the far side of the plaza, I'm raising my hand and saying, 'OK, I'll see you around,' and then I'm running. I run and only look back once, just before I round a corner and go out of sight, and when I do he is standing there, legs apart, flowers upside down in his hand by his side, watching me, like someone who isn't quite sure what just happened.

It's only when I get home and am about to put my shorts in my laundry bag that I turn out the pockets and find the head of a perfect, beautiful purple flower, wilting just a little against the hot skin of my palm.

Chapter Eight

I'm on my way home after work one day, walking down North Main, when I find a hand on my arm and look up into pale eyes, and it is Ezra.

'I've been calling you,' he says. 'Didn't you get my messages?'

'No – I've been busy.'

'Busy?' He laughs and says, 'Seren, stop it, please ...' sliding his hand up on to my shoulder and then squeezing. 'It's me.'

Which just makes my skin crawl in the worst way, but by this point it seems like a few people passing are maybe looking at us while pretending not to be, so simply because I want to avoid a scene I walk on and let him follow me to the plaza where I stop and turn to him.

'What do you want?'

'Honey.' He laughs, looking around like he's checking no one heard me.

'Don't "honey" me.'

Which is when he gives up and gets to the point. 'Mum wants you and your family to come to dinner in our quarters tonight.'

'My family?' I don't even try to hide the look of horror I know I'm wearing. 'We can't, we're busy.' I turn to go, but there's his hand again, kind of hard this time. I turn and he's leaning down to me while looking around the plaza.

'Arrive at seven, OK?'

And even though I pull my arm away and leave without answering we both know I'll be there. It's just more trouble than it's worth to cause problems for Captain Kat or her evil spawn.

Fast forward to about eight minutes past seven that evening and we are sitting there like inanimate objects while Captain Kat finishes her call. Me, Dad, Pan and Cain (who is grinning like a dumbass), Grandpa, Ezra and Jonah. Literally sitting there utterly silent and barely breathing while we look at each other and listen to her voice slide out of the next room like a snake, all the right answers, all the right laughs, in all the right places.

'Listen, Van Hyden, seriously, I must go. Yes, it's a rather special evening.' She lowers her voice for the next bit, gets all cute while the rest of us cringe. 'I have my son's intended here with her family. It's a big moment for all of us, so let me call you in the morning.'

She appears then, arms open, beaming around at us. 'I am so sorry. So, so sorry. Urgent calls, you know how it is. Welcome, welcome to all. So happy to have you here.' And while she's saying all this she is walking around the table and kind of stroking everyone's shoulders before she stops at Cain.

'My goodness, is this Cain Keller from Engineering? For a moment I wondered what strange young man had wandered into my quarters without removing his hat first.'

And as he pulls it off and murmurs, 'Sorry,' Pan is looking daggers at him.

Captain Kat walks to her seat. 'Now, whatever has happened to catering?' she says, which is the exact moment that her door buzzer goes.

I've only ever eaten somewhere other than the cantina maybe twice in my life. Being Chief of Security, Grandpa has officer's quarters that he's allowed to entertain in but I think he basically gave up on it when my grandma died which is already more than ten years ago. In a way it's not like it's such a big deal, since you get the same food anyway and if anything it's colder by the time it gets to you, but it's still weird to be sitting here while these guys from Domestic come in pushing one of the Maintenance carts and start offloading pots of food on to the middle of the table. Meanwhile Captain Kat is pushing her pod into its dock on the wall so that this weird music starts and I look once at Ezra who scowls back and we are clearly all wondering who is going to be the first to speak.

It's my dad in the end. 'So, Jonah, you heard the calling?'

Jonah basically jumps out of his skin before recovering enough to speak. 'I did.' He nods. 'And I'm so honoured to be able to follow it.'

'Yeah,' says Dad. 'Great honour, of course.'

'Pretty convenient too.' It's out of my mouth before I can stop it, and suddenly they're all looking at me. 'Just ... you know ... we have this uneven-numbered generation and it just so happens that one of the guys decides to become a priest.' I shrug, not dwelling on the fact that it looks like Pan is planning to have me killed, but she needn't worry since Captain Kat doesn't even miss a beat.

'God does move in mysterious ways His wonders to perform.' She beams – so hard her lips make a sound as they move over her teeth. 'Now, who would like some chicken stew?'

So a bit later, Pan's going on about her belly and her baby and whatever else and even I can see that everyone's bored, and so I'm like: 'So ... Huxley-3,' because there is no way I am going to miss this opportunity to grill Captain Kat. I mean, I know one day she's going to be my mother-in-law but up until now I've never even spoken to her one-on-one. 'Will we get to go down there now we're in Service?'

She laughs then but it's basically an impression of someone laughing rather than someone actually laughing and it ends too fast and she drinks more wine. 'Oh, Seren, how sweet. Of course you won't, but I do wish life could be the way you see it.'

I ignore the fact that she's trying to make me feel stupid and take a breath in, then out. Once I'm over it, I say, 'OK so ... how does it work?'

'Well, we will enter orbit proper in about a week and will then spend about sixty-two of our days, ninety orbits, here surveying, studying, doing reconnaissance, and most importantly attempting contact.'

'I fly out tomorrow,' says Cain, grinning through a mouthful of food.

'And what about if there's life? What about if it's habitable?' I ask.

More of the fake laugh from Captain Kat, but this time she accompanies it with a glance at my grandpa as if she can't quite believe I'm related to him. 'Seren, we know the chances of it holding civilised life are millions to one.'

It's only now I look across at Jonah, at the way he's just staring at his food and hasn't even eaten any of it, and at Ezra and the way he's just tearing lazily at his bread roll before sighing. Only Pan seems to be listening. 'So what have they seen so far?' she says.

Grandpa leans forward, wiping his mouth on his napkin and looking at the ceiling as if he can think of twenty other places he'd rather be. 'First shuttle crews have seen absolutely nothing of any interest whatsoever.'

'Typical,' smirks Ezra, and Cain laughs, adding, 'I know, right?'

And I just stare at them in utter confusion.

'How does this not matter to you?' I ask, so loud that Jonah finally seems to wake up from whatever heavenly vision he's currently in and the others stop their lame sniggering too. In fact the whole place is silent, except for the tiny ringing noise of the cup where I just accidentally knocked it with my knife. 'This is the only thing that's ever actually happened and you don't even seem to want to be a part of it. You just want to let it happen to you the way everything else does.'

'Oh, Captain Lomax, did I mention that I just love what you've done with your quarters?' interrupts Pan, cheesy smile in place. 'This tablecloth is exquisite.'

And Captain Kat's all broad smile and slow blinks. 'Thank you so much, Pandora,' she says. 'An heirloom, of course, an Earth original, passed down to me by my grandmother, God rest her soul.'

But after everyone's looked at the tablecloth for a minute (it's this ugly green thing) and made noises like they like it, it's still awkward, which I guess is why my grandpa says, 'With your permission, Captain Lomax ... '

'Kat, please call me Kat. After all, we will soon be family.'

'Very well, *Kat* –' said like it's in quotes, '– I fear we've strayed a little off-topic.'

'Have we, Joshua? Why? Whatever did you want to talk about? Let's not talk shop now. This is a personal visit, and a happy one. You might even say joyous.'

'Indeed, which is the very reason I wondered if I might propose a toast.'

She simpers then, reaching for her wine. 'Why, of course, how remiss of me not to do it before. Whatever would I do without you, Joshua?' And they share this look which basically indicates that she means the exact opposite and they both know it.

Nevertheless, everyone lifts their cup then, even Cain (looking embarrassed that it's empty already).

'A toast to Seren and Ezra,' says Grandpa, pinning me in his grey gaze. 'Who have a life filled with love and happiness and the laughter of children ahead of them.'

And everyone says, 'Seren and Ezra,' and I think the only people that don't join in are me and Ezra. And then there's this whole scene where everyone's making a big deal about making sure they chink with everybody else so that we are all up out of our seats and knocking things over on the table and in the end I just sit down and watch it play out.

'I've said it before and I'll say it again,' says Captain Kat, still forcing this huge smile as she gets back to her seat. 'It couldn't be more perfect. A union between our two families.' She brings her hands together and leans her chin on them, shaking her head at Ezra and me like she can hardly believe her luck. 'It's perfection.'

'Or another thing that's suspiciously convenient,' I say, making her widen her eyes in horror, and bringing into being another epic silence that makes even me cringe.

Grandpa clears his throat. 'Seren, as you know, Science make the partnerships. Command have no control or say in it at all. Genetic combinations are mapped in order to ensure future viability of our population.'

I meet his eye across the table. 'I understand all that, of course I do. I'm not an idiot. I just don't understand, when it can all happen on a Petri dish, why they get to dictate who we spend our lives with, whether we like it or not.'

I feel Ezra staring at the side of my face for a few seconds until I look back and he's shaking his head at me, narrowing his eyes as he says, 'You really are a charmer, you know that?'

Dad drops his fork, but manages to say, 'Seren, honey, really, what are you talking about?'

But Captain Kat is patting his hand on the table and tucking the loose strands of her blonde hair back behind her ears as if about to go into battle.

'Jamie, in a way, there is no better time than now to discuss any doubts or reservations, don't you think?' And without waiting for his answer she says, 'Seren, it's not your fault that there are certain things about life on the Ventura that you have forgotten. Maybe in the last generation or so, life on this ship has become too ... easy ... comfortable. And the problem with that is that for some of us our true identity has become a little ... lost.' She stops then, frozen, smiling a half smile while she smooths the ugly tablecloth and I realise the music is some kind of whale sound compilation they used to play us during rest break in Education.

'Our true identity,' I echo. 'And that is?'

Her smile fades. 'We are undertaking the most ambitious, important project humanity has ever known. We are First Contact. Every man and woman that entered this vessel knew what they were signing up to and why. They swore to do their duty for their country, for their planet, for their species, for progress, for science, for the future ... and you and I and all of us are just a continuation of that. Don't you know that?' She laughs again, that weird, fake-flirty toss of the blonde hair.

'Whatever do they teach you over there in Education? Sounds like we need some new policies, Joshua.' This last bit being aimed at Grandpa like a little in-joke but one he doesn't seem to find funny.

'But I didn't choose this,' I counter. 'I didn't choose any of it.'

'That's completely irrelevant.' She beams, her smile and soft voice completely at odds with the blunt axe of her message. 'You only exist to be a part of this mission. You, and all of us, are the property of NASA, ESA and our sponsors Ventura Communications Incorporated, and as such you must fulfil the purpose for which you were created. Fulfilling your purpose isn't about choice. The original crew of this ship was eight hundred and eighty-eight people. Four hundred and forty-four breeding pairs. One birth cycle every three years and an unpredictable number of deaths. Our on-board population now totals two thousand, two hundred and twenty-three. We have a seven-hundred-year round trip to plan for. If we are going to keep creating viable, healthy children, if we are going to have a future on the Ventura at all, we all have to do what is asked of us. Stable Unions, planned family units, are the foundation upon which our entire civilisation is built. So whether you want to marry my son and bear him children and raise them until they are self-sufficient enough to replace you or not is absolutely none of my or his or

73

even your concern. It isn't anyone's business to consider. Because either way, it's just the way it IS, and that's the end of it.'

I stare at her, feel the curl in my lip. 'But what – we're all just supposed to live our lives pretending to be happy?'

'Such a firecracker,' interjects my dad, looking so sweaty and flustered I'm amazed he can still put words together. 'I was always full of questions at her age too.' He shakes his head, as if he's simply reminiscing rather than trying to belittle me totally.

Captain Kat laughs, lets it turn into a purr, as she narrows her eyes and flips into flirt mode. 'Oh, Jamie, you were always such a revolutionary. You know, I don't mind admitting, I always thought it was a little alluring.'

'Mum!' Ezra looks genuinely appalled.

'What? All the girls did. Especially Gracie, of course. Dear, sweet Gracie.' And she switches modes again, now doing a perfect impression of someone who gives a damn, a study in picturesque sadness. 'If only she was here now. Just imagine how happy she'd be. How proud.'

And even though I never really knew Mum I still have my doubts that that's what she'd be thinking, and I can see from the way my grandpa raises an eyebrow that he feels the same.

He clears his throat and says, his tone distant, 'Grace

was someone filled with questions about our society too. Indeed my dear friend Captain Lee was a fan of philosophical and ideological debate himself, and often found a worthy opponent in Grace.'

Captain Kat bursts into a half-crazed laugh. 'Really! Lee was such an eccentric!'

Grandpa doesn't crack a smile. 'He was a great man and an inspirational leader.'

Just as she opens her mouth to respond, his pod chimes and when he checks it he says, 'I'm afraid you'll have to excuse me. I'm needed downstairs. I'm terribly sorry. Thank you so much, Captain Lomax, for your hospitality,' and he does this little bow as he leaves.

She never takes her eyes off him as he walks out, watching him with her mouth half open as if there are all these things she wants to say but can't. Once the door closes she does another weird laugh, talking down at her plate almost like the rest of us aren't there. 'Lee and his ridiculous forums and think tanks and whatever else! People talking themselves in circles only to come to the conclusion that the way it has always been done is the only option available to us. Nothing ever changes. Nothing CAN change. All that kind of thing does is corrode at our civilisation and endanger our way of life. Whatever Joshua might believe, there was never so much chaos and division on this ship as there was in Captain Lee's tenure, you know that, Jamie.'

My dad seems to make a point of not reacting at all.

'The point is, since we lost contact with Earth we have been alone out here, and the chances are we will be for another two hundred and sixty-two years at least. We are responsible for our own survival, for the survival of our species. And it is our duty, every one of ours, to make that our priority.'

I'm silent then, letting it settle on me like falling dust. Duty. Property. Fulfilling the purpose you were created for. This is really what it comes down to in the end, despite all the time they spend programming you into believing you're the lucky ones, you're the ones who were specially picked for this amazing mission, you are honoured by this God-given assignment, you are the authors of a new, connected galaxy.

Almost like she hears my thoughts, she looks around her as if waking up from a dream, and slips right back into the old spiel, with that fake smile. 'We are the stewards of all of this, you see; we are a message to the beings of the universe. We are creating the people who will be the ones—'

But I've heard enough and I scrape my chair back and throw my napkin on the table. 'Thanks for dinner – I really must be going.'

'Seren!' my sister all but shrieks. 'You can't just leave!'

'I have to work,' I lie. 'I forgot.'

'Oh no, darling, please don't go,' yawns Ezra, tipping

his chair back and giving me the finger behind him where no one else can see.

Nobody else says anything, Pan and Cain stare at me and my dad shuffles his chair as if he's going to get up. Only Captain Kat actually speaks.

'There are those who don't survive this place, Seren, as you know, and they are usually the ones who have kicked the hardest against it.'

But I leave, regardless.

Chapter Nine

I'm there without really knowing how I got there. Production Bay 6, where I know he'll be working, and I see him and he sees me and there's this moment where he looks surprised and I wonder if I should have come, especially with the way he looks around a little as he walks over.

'Hey,' Dom says. 'What are you doing here?'

'I guess ... I just ... wanted to see you.'

It's weird how he takes this – he watches me, so serious for a moment, then he smiles a little, then he doesn't again, then he says, 'Oh man, Seren, it's ...' and shakes his head. Then he makes this weird growling noise to himself like he's completely, I don't know, frustrated, and just when I say, 'Look, I'll ... I'm just gonna head home. I shouldn't have come,' he takes hold of my sleeve and says, 'No, stay.'

And so I do.

He says he has a couple of things to do before he

finishes shift and so we walk over to this big set of double doors, he pushes this huge red button that opens them and we're inside where it is almost completely dark, smells vaguely like puke but sweeter, and is warmer than anything I've ever known. All around us there's this clucking, this soft sound. He answers a question I didn't need to ask:

'The chickens.'

We walk then, down the aisles between the cages with hundreds of thousands of them, packed in on both sides and there is just the tiniest amount of light, a dim bulb every hundred metres or so, and this is why we can see nothing at all of them really except the odd glimpse of light caught in their little round black eyes or glancing off their feathers. And it just seems so sad to me suddenly – so bottomlessly, achingly sad – that all they exist for is to lay eggs for us, to make meat, to occasionally breed and make more chickens, all just to float in a dark tin can in space at our whim. This is when I look at Dom and he has stopped next to a cage, opened it, reached a hand in, and picked one up so tenderly, holding her out towards me where I can touch her, touch the first bird I have ever touched, and she is amazing.

'So, I was watching Huxley-3 yesterday,' he says. 'At View. I wondered if I'd see you, actually.'

I smile. 'You did? You could have ... called me.'

'I don't know.' He laughs a little, shakes his head. 'Like I said, I guess I probably shouldn't do things like that. Call you, I mean.' He looks at me, watching my face while I can't keep a smile off it.

'Well, look, why not?' I say. 'We're friends, aren't we?'

He seems to think about this for a moment, then nods, shrugs. 'That's true. Why shouldn't I call my friend and see if she wants to come and check out our friendly neighbourhood planet with me?'

'No reason at all.' I smile.

'In that case, next time, maybe I will.'

'And, I mean, if I want to come and see my friend at the end of his shift once in a while, why shouldn't I just go ahead and do that?'

'Not a reason in the world.' He smiles and I realise how quickly he can make me forget everything, everything except him, even when it's all such a mess, and he must see something on my face, he must see the shadow that crosses it, because he says, 'Bad day?'

And I say, 'I've had better.'

And he says, 'Tell me.'

And I say, 'Sick of this place.'

And he says, 'Yeah, that happens,' and nods, and all this time he carries on stroking the chicken, moving it around in his hands a little so that we are both watching the way she keeps her head steady no matter how you move her body, which makes us both laugh a little bit.

'You just gotta be a bit more like this chicken,' he says. 'Just go with it.'

It's so warm here in the chicken bay. It smells so bad but feels so warm. It's the first time I remember feeling like this and it's all I can do not to just lie back and relax in it – the warmth, the soft clucking everywhere, a sound that makes me want to fall asleep. I reach for the chicken, find the silkiness of her feathers and want to drown in it. My fingers touch Dom's then, but just for a second before I pull them away.

I sigh, to cover up the fact that touching him has flustered me. 'I came here so mad at it all, but now I can hardly remember why I cared.'

He laughs and I feel, or imagine I feel, his breath on my lip. 'That's because it doesn't really matter right now. You can't change it anyway, so why worry?'

We walk back out to the Production bay.

'What's that?' I ask him, noticing the orange plastic sack he carries out with us.

'Nothing,' he says, and because he so obviously doesn't want to show me I slow, stop, knowing that he'll look back at me, and when he does I hold his eye. 'Really nothing,' he says, passing it to his other hand behind his back, but then, 'OK, it's the dead ones.'

I feel my lip curl. 'The dead ones?'

'Chickens.' He looks sad, apologetic almost. 'The dead chickens. There's a certain amount of ... by-product.'

'By-product?'

He shrugs, looks at the floor between us. 'Some just ... die.'

'Because they're old?'

'No.' He smiles sadly. 'Not always. We try, but the fact is it's not easy for them here.'

After that we get out into the vast dark space of Production Bay 6, and I am following him over to the waste carts and on the way he says, 'I love the echo in here, don't you?' and raises his eyebrows. 'Think it makes me sound sexy?'

I frown through the jolt of adrenaline. 'Why would an echo be sexy?'

'Yeah, I don't know.' And we both laugh, and I let myself bump into him a little as we walk, feel him do the same, almost sigh or collapse in the heat of him, which is when I hear: 'Hey, Seren.'

And when I turn it is Graham, who works with my dad, and he has just passed us but has stopped and is frowning and he says, 'You looking for Jamie?'

And I'm just getting totally stuck for an answer when Dom says, 'She was, but I told her he's got the night off so she's about to head home, isn't that right?' He looks at me, kind of nodding a little in this encouraging way.

And even though I am so mesmerised by him I almost miss it, I manage to say, 'Yeah, sure, that's right,' and I'm waving at Graham and we are walking away even though he's still standing there, still watching us, so much so that I feel the weight of it and peer back once before we get to the door and he is squinting at me through the dark, scratching at his jaw, frowning.

It turns out Dom lives in West, so we walk back there together but kind of not together because I guess we're both thinking about that whole thing with Graham and whether it's a good idea to be seen with each other. But once we get to his place, there's no one in the passage so I somehow, not so subtly, end up next to him and we're both looking up and down the empty passage while he is punching in his code and buzzing us into his berths. Inside, he picks a guitar up off the floor and as the door clunks closed he turns and smiles.

I look around then for the first time. It's a pretty usual kind of berths: grey bunks built into the walls, shelves between, all with recessed lights. There's this single slowly flapping metal bird, hanging from the air vent in the middle of the ceiling. There are another seven beds but all of them are empty.

'Working,' he says, answering my unasked question and then, 'Come and sit,' as he pulls clothes off the end of his bed.

I look around, but there really isn't anywhere else to sit except there on his bed, so I sit, slowly, still not sure I'm actually staying; my heart is pounding so hard it seems far more likely that I'll run away, or maybe just explode. He sits on the floor in front of me, starts tuning his guitar, and neither of us speaks for a while. This is how I end up leant back against the wall, watching him, listening to him starting to pick out a tune, listening to the way he sings super quiet but so sweet, just below the level where I can hear him properly, and just when I think I hear my name in the lyrics he stops and says, 'So you never told me what you were doing tonight.'

And I say, 'Oh just ... I don't know ... nothing ... nothing good, anyway.'

He sings again then: 'She's so mysterious.'

I laugh. 'It's not that. I just ... I hate my life. I hate our lives. I've been with Captain Kat.'

He stops. 'THE Captain Kat?'

I shrug. 'Is there another one? God, surely one is enough.'

'You know her?'

'Sure – her son is my ...'

'He's your life partner?'

I just look at the floor, making a face, while Dom laughs. 'You look so happy about this fact.'

'Would you be?'

He laughs. 'Um, he comes over a little ... smarmy, I guess.'

I nod. 'He's definitely smarmy, among other things.'

He laughs again, shakes his head, strums at the guitar.

We don't speak again for a while, and then I say, 'How do you even have a guitar?'

He smiles. 'There were forty-seven on board originally. I think something like thirteen are now beyond repair, leaving thirty-four, and I guess I just got lucky.'

'No, really – how?'

'My great-grandpa, grandpa, dad are all pretty good, and they passed it down. But as for me, like I said – lucky.' And he winks.

'Can I see it?' I ask, and he makes this face so that I laugh in this stupid way and then roll my eyes and add, 'The guitar.'

He hands it to me and it's a little lighter than I expected. I lay it across my lap and look at the beautiful amber rippled markings of its smooth surface, run my fingers along its ribbed strings, raise its hole to my face so I can take a deep breath of the fragrant air inside it.

'What's it made of?' I ask, and when I look up I realise he has been watching me the whole time.

'Wood,' he says. 'From trees.'

I run my hand over it a couple more times before I hand it back.

And after that I am just listening to him sing, mostly humming, a tune I've never heard before.

'What is that song?' I ask him.

'I don't know yet.'

'You don't . . .' I sit up. 'You don't know?'

'I'm still working on it.'

I don't know why it has never before occurred to me that people actually write their own songs, write their own music, but it hasn't. That is how messed up this place is. It isn't something we have ever been allowed to do, so I just assumed that people didn't do it.

Command calls it Cultural Preservation. The problem is what we might become, how much we might change floating out here a million miles from where we started and creating for ourselves. We're supposed to be envoys of Earth, not a whole new species. So that's why this moment is one of those you just know you will never forget – to watch him there, sat on the floor, running fingers over the strings of his guitar and tilting his head like he is listening to it, like it is the one making music no one has ever heard before and he just happens to be there. I feel myself shudder then.

'You're cold,' he says, and he takes his jacket off and hands it to me, and when I put it on it is (of course) exactly the same as mine but much too big, so it is SO NICE just pulling all the warmth of him around me and it smells like him, sweet and clean and as buttery as warm bread, like something that's mine but better. And as if his gaze had physical weight I feel it on me then – watching me, then the guitar, then me again. I watch him back, fighting a weird urge to kick my shoe off and slide my foot on to his shoulder, down his chest, into his lap, feeling the slow smile that creeps across my face to match his.

'Domingo?'

'Yeah?'

'Who's your life partner?'

He stops playing, but stays looking at the guitar. 'Annelise Gutchenmeyer,' he says.

Tall, blonde, specialising in Med, captain of the rec volleyball team I used to be a member of, before I realised I hated team games. 'Nice.' I nod.

He shrugs. 'I guess.'

Silence then.

'The thing is,' he says, playing one single chord, a sad one. 'No matter how hard I try I just can't believe it actually works that way. You know? The heart wants what it wants, doesn't it?'

I nod, wait for him to carry on, but he doesn't.

'And yours ... ' I say, 'doesn't want Annelise?'

He doesn't answer, just plays the saddest, prettiest little sequence of notes you could ever imagine, and both of us watch his fingers on the guitar. When he's done he frowns and says, 'I think ... maybe ... I wrote that for you.'

'For me?' Even though he won't meet my eye he nods. Something makes me speak quietly then, almost as if he is an animal that might be easily startled. 'Play it again.'

But just as he's about to, the door buzzes open and these two guys he berths with come in talking louder than anyone ever, and so this is when we both jump up and he introduces me as a friend and I say, 'I'm just leaving,' and these two guys just stand there watching us, all raised eyebrows, and so I wave my hand goodbye and when he follows me to the door and offers to walk me home I say no, because by now even I can see we're way too close to crossing a line.

I'm almost home when I realise I'm still wearing his jacket.

Chapter Ten

There's this one passage in West near a service transporter
where you can look down into the Production bays and
I find reasons to walk along there just in the hope that I
might catch sight of Dom. I do, a couple of times, way
down there in the dark, the shine of his hair as it flops
over his face when he pulls his hat off for a minute. The
way he laughs when someone cracks a joke. The way he
leans on the three-metre stack of egg crates to use his pod
and I wonder who he's writing to, wishing it was me.

Whenever I walk past the doors to the West cantina
during second session, which is when I guess he would
be eating, I pull myself up to the windows by my
fingertips, right on to my tiptoes, nose pressed, heart
literally flapping in my chest over the thought that I
might see him, before someone tries to pass me and
gives me a funny look as I walk away. Every time there
is any machine to fill anywhere near Production I get
these stupid, almost unmanageable adrenaline rushes

just because there's an off-chance that I'll see him, this shot in the dark that I'll happen to put in the nut bar that'll be his, that I'll touch the Cheeso snack that will be the one that touches his lips. Yeah, I know, it's lame; it is super lame. There are, in fact, almost no words for how lame it is. And nothing has ever felt so good.

Then this one day after work I get back to quarters and Pan is acting like some kind of brain-dead idiot and crying over a pile of socks. She's had way too much time on her hands since she went on her maternity leave and I guess it's a hormone thing too so I'm not all that surprised until it goes on longer than usual.

'What is it, Pan?' I ask her in the end, standing there and feeling that bone-tiredness of having been at work all day.

'Cain finished his shift three hours ago but he still hasn't come home.'

'OK,' I sigh. 'But if something was wrong with him Engineering would have told you by now.'

'I know, Seren. It's just that he used to rush home to me every night and now he just . . . ' She blows her nose on one of the socks, then gestures at the rest of them. 'I wanted him to come home to darned socks but I can't even get that right.'

'So . . . what? You think he's got someone else?'

She slams her hand down on the table and glares at

me. 'Well, I didn't until now! For God's sake, what is wrong with you?'

'What's wrong with ME? You're the one crying because your husband is avoiding coming home to you.'

She sobs then, really sobs, to the point that she's a total snotty mess and I actually start to feel a little bad.

'You know I always try to help you, Seren,' she sniffs. 'Every time you're having one of your bad times I try my hardest to help, even though you make it just about impossible. Can't you try being a little sensitive for once? I just want someone to listen to me.'

I shrug. 'OK, I'm sorry. Talk ... please.'

'It's just that I really need Cain to be there for me right now and instead I'm just so lonely and I have no idea what to do about it.'

And I don't know what it is, but something makes me actually feel for her a little then, something makes me ache. Maybe it's because I have just started to know, for the first time, what it's like to miss someone. So I take a step towards her and I say, 'Just tell him how you feel.'

She slams her hands on the table in front of her and rolls her eyes. 'Don't be so naive, Seren. I don't even know why I'm talking to you. You know nothing about relationships.'

I draw back, a little lost for words. 'I ... I know you start from a point when you love being together and you just make each other feel good and you just ... they

91

are the one person in the world you can rely on, who never lets you down.'

'No.' She shakes her head. 'You really have no idea what you're talking about.'

I make a face. 'Oh, don't I?'

'Of course not! You haven't even entered your Union yet!'

I shake my head at her. 'You're an idiot. I can't even believe we're related.'

I crash out of the galley and push past Dad as he steps into the passage. Pan follows me, yelling, 'You have no right to pass judgement on me, EVER, you pathetic little child.'

'Girls!' admonishes Dad, lamely.

I wheel round on her. 'You are so far away from knowing about love, about real love, that you don't even know it exists. That's how much you know about it. I never want to end up like you.'

'You WISH you could end up like me!' she shrieks while Dad stares. 'You wish! You're just an ignorant little girl who's miserable about the fact that she ended up with a life partner who hates her. But no wonder! No wonder he hates you! I hate you too and I'm your sister.'

Dad looks from her to me with a frown. 'Ezra hates you?'

I roll my eyes.

'Newsflash for the unobservant,' sneers Pan. 'They

hate each other, Dad. Lucky they don't have to breed the old-fashioned way or it would never happen.' She laughs then, tosses her hair, walks into her bedroom, making me so furious I go after her.

'You think I care what that idiot thinks of me? I couldn't care less what he thinks or what he does. And I certainly don't want his stupid children. Unlike you, I'm not interested in getting knocked up just so I've got something to do with my pathetic life.'

'Seren!' This is Dad, who has followed us and is now standing in Pan's open doorway, using the voice he uses when he is Not Kidding Around, but even though Pan spends a few seconds looking like I just slapped her across the face and I do feel a bit bad for my unborn niece, she has made me just too mad and I really don't care any more and so I say, 'Don't put it all on me just because your life partner is a loser who prefers to spend his evenings drinking in the plaza than with you.'

'He's working late!'

I snort. 'Sure he is.'

Dad stops me leaving when I try, landing his hand on my shoulder and holding the other in the air between us where it wavers uncertainly. 'Girls, what is all this about?'

This, ironically, is the first time either of us is silent. It is only when I say, 'I'm going out,' that Pan pins me with one of her evil looks and says, 'To see Domingo Suarez?'

Then she stands there with her arms folded, eyes daring me to speak. I guess I'm not hiding my shock very well so I go to leave but Dad doesn't step aside to let me by; in fact he lays his hand on my shoulder and says, 'Domingo Suarez? That kid in Farm and Fishery? What's he got to do with anything?'

And just then Pan passes us both on her way to my room.

'Hey!' I yell, turning to follow her, but she's already back.

Holding Dom's jacket.

She presses it to her front like she's trying it for size, sly smiling and managing to tap her fingertip where his name is stitched before I yank it out of her grasp.

'I found it when I was tidying her room, Dad,' she says. 'Under her pillow!'

He turns back to me slowly, then waits, watches for me to give myself away, while I look through every part of my brain for something to say and end up doing this weird kind of laugh. 'He ... I was cold, so he lent it to me. That's all.'

My dad frowns. 'When and where were you with him, exactly?'

I laugh again. 'Just ... ' I start, before turning back to Pan. 'Why are you even going in my room?'

'Maybe if you weren't such a slob and changed your own sheets I wouldn't have to!'

I've never been so glad to hear Cain at the door.

'Only me!' he yells. 'Yoo-hoo! Where is everyone?'

And this is when I duck under Dad's arm and slam into my room, but not before I hear Pan yelling, 'The sooner they move us out of here the better!'

Which is an understatement.

I have no idea how I get through work the next day, when it sits inside me the way it does: part fear, part nausea. I'm just leaving, stowing my trolley in the Maintenance office when Mariana says, 'Chief Sherbakov wants you to report to him in his office, Hemple.'

And it suddenly seems so predictable I laugh. 'Oh.'

She looks confused. 'Care to tell me what that could be about?'

'Um ... I guess ... probably not much,' I say, pulling off my hairnet and ruffling my hair before jamming my cap back on. 'He's my grandfather.'

The weird thing about Grandpa's quarters is that they are huge but they are just for him. He's been high up enough in Command to have these quarters for as long as I can remember so once upon a time he lived here with my grandma. Lianne, who has only ever been pictures and movies to me, died when I was little, of PEST. And look, don't ask me what PEST stands for because I don't know but evidently it's nothing too good because it is an autoimmune disorder that we have basically invented on Ventura by having crappy food and no actual air or sunlight and such like. It pretty much ends up with your body just turning on you and making it so you are destroying yourself from the inside out. To the observer all that happens is that the sufferer just gets thinner and thinner, no matter what they eat, almost like they were just smuggling themselves out of existence piece by piece. Then they start bleeding out and that's the end of it. And this, apparently, is what happened to this woman, the mother of my mother, who I never really knew.

Anyway I get up to Command deck where all the officers' quarters are and it is weirdly quiet and most of the lights outside the doors that tell you whether people are in or not are red. Only Grandpa's is green, way at the end of the corridor.

He buzzes me in and I walk through the place until I find him, right in the back, frowning at his screen and furrow-browed, and he doesn't even greet me, just comes straight out with, 'Who's Domingo Suarez?'

And after I cough and nearly choke and almost fall over, I cough some more and then say, 'God he's ... no one ... just a guy I know.'

He waits, letting a silence stretch out that I am expected to fill, but don't. He sighs. 'In what capacity do you know him?'

I shake my head. 'Man, it's a space traveller with a couple of thousand people on it – I pretty much know everyone! It's a small town, Grandpa.'

He studies me carefully, pulls his hat off, tosses it on the table where it slides.

'Here's what happens in this life of ours. You meet someone and maybe you spend a bit of time wishing things were different, but they're not, and you learn that fast. You both move on,' he sighs. 'This is no time to be taking your eye off the ball, Seren.'

'No? Why's that?' I go to his porthole then, gaze out of it, struggling to control the guilty smile on my face.

He comes to me and I feel his hands, one on each shoulder, heavy and pushing down, dense as a collapsed star.

'You are my granddaughter. You are marrying the son of the captain. Seren, in so many ways you could be seen as the figurehead of the whole mission.'

'Figurehead? Jesus.'

He frowns at me in our reflection in the glass of the porthole.

'I'm sorry – it's just … I am not a figurehead of anything. And certainly not of the stupid mission.'

He ignores me. 'You, your husband, your children – whether you like it or not, you will inevitably come to be the very symbol of the Ventura's journey into the future.'

I turn and look at him then, the way his eyes are gleaming, the way his jacket isn't done up and underneath his T-shirt is stained with sweat rings. 'Are you OK?' I ask him.

'Of course,' he says, scrubbing at his bald head with his fingertips. 'It's just that now, more than ever, we need to hold firm.'

'Why now more than ever?'

And he doesn't answer; of course he doesn't. Joshua Sherbakov, the Ventura's Chief of Security, my grandfather, has never been a sharer, even at the best of times. But you know, I can tell, I can tell from the way he goes to his desk and stares at it, stares at it without seeing it, touching the skin above his eyebrows and peering through his fingers in this gesture I feel like I have never seen him do before, I can just tell that something about all this, something about me and I don't even know what else have got him rattled.

'Listen to me, Seren. You've known Ezra Lomax all your life. Whatever you may think of him, at least there can be no surprises, surely?'

I sigh hard, a sound that almost becomes a growl. 'Exactly! That's part of the problem! Don't you get it?' I check my pod for the time, because, you know, at this point I am in dire need of an excuse to get out of here and I'm like: 'Listen, Grandpa, I really have to get going.'

And he looks at me, waits a beat, then nods, but sad

somehow in a way that is strange for him, and then he says, 'Just take some time to reflect on things, will you, Seren? You need to work at it with Ezra. You need to do what you were born to do. You are making your father unhappy – what would your mother say if she knew you were doing that? Hmm? There is such a thing as duty, Seren. There are the things you have to do for your family, for your race. Don't force me to ...' He stops then, checks himself, and even though I'm almost at the door I stop; I turn back.

'Don't force you to what?' I ask him.

He picks his hat back up, pushes it on, giving me my cue to leave. 'I know you'll do what's right, Seren.'

'Do you?' I ask him then.

Because I don't.

Chapter Eleven

This is the night for phase one of Dad and Grandpa's campaign to get Ezra and me to like each other. I've agreed to it under duress but I've never known anything so doomed to fail.

Buzzer and it's him.

'Honey,' he sneers, sliding past me.

'Get out of my room!' I yell, horrified by just the sight of him there. It's only now I notice the crisp creases in his just-pressed grey overalls and the way his hair isn't artfully messed up and waxed to heck like usual but is combed back, wet-looking.

He notices me looking but just says, 'Get ready. This is our date,' and then stands looking bored while I get my stuff together. 'Chop-chop,' he says after less than ten seconds, just as a call comes through on his pod. 'Hey,' he answers in a voice I don't recognise, stepping out of the door and making it slide closed behind him.

I'm just about ready by this point so I go to the door

and stand next to it, straining my ears and cursing its density. All I hear is his tone, the softness of it, how totally unfamiliar it is, and this is when I realise that I actually don't even slightly care who he talks to or how he does it or why, and I pull my hood up, release the door and catch him looking like someone doing something he shouldn't and saying, 'OK, I'll speak to you later,' and hanging it up.

'Who was that?' I ask, more to wind him up than out of genuine curiosity, but he doesn't answer, just takes hold of the back of my neck and steers me into the galley to Dad.

'Thanks for letting me borrow her, Mr H,' he simpers, as Dad pauses *Football Manager* to nod and look startled.

Out on the passageway he switches into walking three metres ahead of me and checking messages on his pod as if I'm not there at all. I follow along behind and check my own pod, find a video message there from Dom and, as you can imagine, I can't resist playing it (super quiet).

'Hey,' he says. 'Just … I don't know … you said I should call and I guess I just thought I might.' He's almost lost in the darkness of the Production bays. 'Anyway, since you're a music fan I find myself wondering if you want to come and see my band. Not because we're good or anything, because we're not. In fact we basically suck, but, you know, maybe you have really bad taste.' He laughs. 'Anyway I'll message you the details and it's up to you but, you know, it's always good to see a friendly face in the crowd when you're making an idiot of yourself. And by the way I hope that you're appreciating this whole echo thing I got happening.' And just before he hangs up he looks right into the pod's camera in a way that ... I don't even know what it does, but for a second I wonder if I might die of just how cool he is. And then Ezra is dropping back.

'Give me your hand,' he barks.

'What? No way!'

'Just give me your stupid hand and keep quiet for once in your life.'

'You're not the king, Ezra – you do realise that?'

'As far as you're concerned I am the king, so you may as well get used to it.'

At which point all I can do is stop dead in my tracks and laugh at him. 'Man, you actually are nuts!'

He storms back towards me and raises his hand so that for a moment I'm sure he's going to hit me and in spite of myself I flinch, but all he does in the end is point. 'You, Seren Hemple –' he says my name like it's in quotes, '– are luckier than you can even imagine to get me – ME, EZRA LOMAX – as your life partner. And all you do is bitch and moan. And I am sick of it. I am so sick of it I can hardly even speak.'

But, you know, there really isn't anything I can do

except laugh at that, which annoys him, but it's not like I care.

We are on our way to the plaza obviously, because that's basically the only place to go. The plaza is this big cavernous hole that's right in the middle of the ship where they put a bunch of bars and places that serve coffee and stuff and there are weird synthesised trees in tubs and tables and chairs all around. Basically, VCI was a Spanish company originally and so I think they based the whole plan of the ship on this kind of town square concept, as if the Ventura was this village and this is where everyone would come together and get all warm and fuzzy. The entrance to the drill hall is here at one end (where they have all the briefings and the church services and weddings) and there's a bunch of other stuff on this level too that you get to from the plaza, like the cinema and the offices for Cultural. And all the four different sections of the ship – North, East, South and West – are defined by their position in relation to the plaza, like the dingiest set of suburbs you could ever imagine.

Anyway, we take an upward transporter from the residential decks and even when we get to the plaza and sit at a table, we carry on playing with our pods and sometimes looking around at all the people who are out for whatever reason pretending that life is great; like life, here on this ship, would ever really be like that.

'What do you want?' he says, fanning himself with his drinks menu.

'Whatever,' I say. 'Coffee.'

'Coffee?' He says it like I just said something that could be found down a toilet, while I look at him once then ignore him. It hasn't ever been worth listening to most of what he has to say but I never used to find him as annoying as I do now. Before, he was just there; now that I'm being told to spend the rest of my life with him he is incredibly offensive in every way. There's this thing he does with his hair and I guess he's always done it (pulling it over to the side and messing with it) and now I swear it's all I can think about, and every time he does it, it takes every bit of willpower I have not to scream.

And then it gets worse.

My gaze gets pulled over like something in me sensed him there. Dom. And the moment I see him is the same moment he sees me; it's this completely spontaneous meeting of eyes. And there is this split second where we acknowledge each other, or surprise each other, or something, before we both look away.

Because here's the thing: he's with her. I can't see her face but I know enough to know it's Annelise. Blonde hair in a thick plait down her back, glimpses of a profile that is sharp-lined and lightly freckled and pretty. She's talking, using her hands a lot, laughing. He looks like he would be laughing too if he couldn't feel me watching him, but because he can he's only smiling at her, pulling on the front of his cap so that it shifts up and down on his head, something I've never actually seen him do before but which I feel instinctively he does when he's uncomfortable.

They're three bars over, sat at a table under a screen with a nature documentary on it that's playing on silent while miserably bad karaoke blares from inside. I try not to look over but it's almost impossible not to. My eyes just keep going back to him, maybe partly because every now and then I notice his gaze shift from hers to meet mine, and when it does there is something so sad in it that I feel matched in my own. Luckily Ezra is either in the middle of a monologue or checking his pod and so basically notices nothing, right up until the point that I see Annelise get up and go, probably to the bathroom, and I take the chance to watch Dom fully, thinking he'll do the same, and when he just pulls his pod out of his pocket, I feel something lodge in my throat like a blade. Then my pod chimes, and I check it, and it's from him:

Nice to see you.

And when I look back up to meet his eye, Ezra clocks it and follows my gaze over his shoulder. Dom realises and sets about scratching his jaw and looking round the plaza but I guess Ezra must get the idea because when he turns back to me he is scowling harder than he usually does.

'Did you even hear what I just said?' he asks.

'I . . .' But I haven't even got a guess so I just say, 'Not really, no.'

And he sighs.

We manage to get through another hour or so somehow, without having to talk too much; mostly the karaoke is too loud to hear anything else anyway. I only dare to look for Dom again once Ezra goes to the bathroom, by which time I can't see him anywhere, and then I spend so long wondering what to answer to his pod message that I don't end up saying anything at all. Then Ezra walks me home, and it's nearly, so very nearly over, and I am literally at the door to quarters and punching in the code when he says, 'I'm coming in,' and my mouth is open to tell him no way when I turn to him and he is standing there, leaning against the wall, S-shaped and pale-eyed and something makes me hesitate, only for a second, but it's too late – he sees it. 'You nearly said yes.' He grins, pointing in my face gleefully. 'Wow. One coffee and you're putty in my hands.'

I just shake my head. 'Goodnight, Ezra.'

But he takes hold of my arm, his other hand on my neck. 'I'm having my kiss, Seren,' he says, moving right into me so that I'm trapped by the wall on one side, him on the other.

'Man, Ezra, WHAT are you doing?' I yell, planting my hands on his chest and shoving him so that he has to step backwards, but his expression doesn't change: half a smile, something dark in his eyes.

'Look, Seren, I'm not going to force you but I think we both agree we need to just bite the bullet on this one.'

'Bite the bullet?'

'Why do you have to make everything so hard?' And this is the point at which he takes hold of my face, angles it upwards and pushes his lips into mine, hard enough so that he mashes our noses together and I feel his teeth. Because neither of us closes our eyes we see into each other, eyes merging into one, into a big black hole, and we are staring each other down, while at the same time our breathing is noisy in our crushed noses and I don't know why but I let my mouth open just a little, feel his tongue on mine, horribly wet. This is when I shove him again, hard this time, punching at his chest, and he grunts but is laughing by the time I'm through the door and making it close on him. And I lean there for a little while, up against the inside of the door, and I don't know what I'm thinking, but whatever it is Cain is waving his hand once, then twice in front of my face before I realise he is there, asking me how my evening was, not getting any answer.

Chapter Twelve

Domingo sends me the details about his band and I spend two days thinking about whether I will go or not, while basically knowing the whole time that I will. So on the night itself I rock up at Emme's quarters and ask her to go there with me. Even though we're legal now I'm pretty sure her mum isn't going to be that keen on the idea of us going to a bar, so we tell her we're going to look at Huxley-3 for a while and, I mean, it's what everyone is doing at the moment so she doesn't even seem a little bit surprised.

Because of the whole Huxley-3 thing and the fact that everyone is in View it's pretty much dead at this bar when we get there, so we get an iced tea and sit around talking and all the while I am looking at the stage where they are setting up for the band and wondering about Dom.

I tell Emme about Ezra kissing me almost like I would tell her about some annoying thing at work or something that happened to someone else.

'Oh dude, you don't even know how lucky you are,' is what she says in response.

'Didn't you even hear the story?' I ask her. 'He basically attacked me.'

'It sounds hot.'

'Then I didn't tell it right.'

'He's a passionate guy.'

'I don't know, Em. I think of the two of us you lucked out.'

'You're crazy. Ezra's a total fox. You have no idea how good you've got it.'

I give her a look. 'Do you remember how he was to me when I came back after I was ill last year? Or do you have selective amnesia?'

'OK,' she concedes. 'He was a little insensitive.'

'Calling somebody a nutjob is more than a little insensitive.'

'Oh Seren, your cup is always half empty! It could be worse, you could have got Leon.'

'Em, Leon's OK.'

She's already shaking her head. 'He's so weird. I swear, he is TERRIFIED of me. He won't come near me. He's a million miles from throwing me up against a wall to make out.'

I laugh. 'He's all right; man, just give him a chance to get used to it.'

She rolls her eyes, throws a coaster at me. 'So what are we doing here? Whose band is this?'

'Just this guy I know.'

'From work?'

'Yeah. No.'

She frowns. 'You're being weird.'

And yeah, I don't tell her anything about Dom, I don't tell her that actually half the reason I brought her here is because I didn't trust myself to come alone, because I know that one word from him is all it would take right now for me to be gone, so gone. And this is when I see him, going up the steps to the stage two at a time and walking around checking things, smiling at someone who's setting up, then seeing me over the guy's shoulder.

'Hey,' he says, arriving and sliding in next to me. 'You're here.'

'This is Emme,' I say, and I point at her across the table and watch him shake her hand while her face is all What the Heck Is This.

'Glad you came,' he says, and then to me, quiet but not that quiet, 'It ... um ... it was weird the other day. I was going to come over and say hi but it just seemed like maybe ... '

I smile and shrug it off. 'It's cool. We were both ... you know ... busy, so ... '

He's nodding. 'Exactly. Right. We were busy.' He smiles, looks relieved. 'And you've been OK?'

'I've been OK,' I say, which makes me sound like a weird parrot but at this point his hand is on the seat between us, so close to my leg that I am just completely distracted; it's borderline out-of-body, the effect he has on me.

'That's good,' he says, slow smiling, and then, 'We'll talk after, yeah?'

And just as he gets up to go he taps my leg goodbye with the back of his fingers and even though it's such a little thing it's almost more than I can bear, looking up at him and the way his hair is so black, a little bit over-long, eyelashes so dark, that mouth. It's the kind of beauty you just want to roll in, like fresh sheets. And it's while I'm thinking all this and he's walking away that Emme is looking at me, basically just open-mouthed, and then she's like: 'Seren, what was THAT?'

But thank whatever God there might be that the band start to play right at this moment and so I don't need to answer, especially because they're loud, and I am just watching him. I swear I don't even hear what they play at first because I am just watching the way he hunches over his guitar, his T-shirt riding up a little at the back so you can see the sleeves of his Production uniform overalls tied round his hips and a little skin above them. And they're good, him and his band: his brother, one of his berth mates, some other guy he knows from Education, just playing and kind of looking at each other sometimes, and most of the time his brother sings, but then after a few songs it's Dom. And if I thought seeing him speak Spanish was like watching a magic trick, that was nothing on this. His voice is like something that makes you want to die, just because you know you'll never hear anything like it again. He sings a song I know, something that I think is usually sung by a girl and usually sounds happy, but the way he does it is the saddest thing ever and I sit there like someone hypnotised until he catches my eye and smiles and it's like something just happened to me for the first time in my life.

That song ends and he starts another one and I know it but I don't know it, and it's only when the lyrics start that I realise it is the one he was working on the other night and I start wondering whether people will realise because, you know, as I said, it just isn't done, you're not supposed to do it; we're not supposed to write our own stuff or make our own songs or movies or whatever on the Ventura. And it's only now I hear it, hear it properly for the first time, that I realise just how much we've lost.

Of course most people just assume this is some obscure album track they've never heard before so they don't think much of it but Emme is a lot more on the ball than most people so she isn't fooled. It takes a while for me to notice that she is standing, leaning down to me, saying something.

'Seren, let's go. This is a Cultural Preservation Infraction.'

'What?'

'New material – contraband.' She shakes her head. 'You know I want a career in Science. I can't have a CPI on my record. You shouldn't want one either. It'll hold you back.'

I laugh, but then see that she's serious. 'You go,' I tell her.

'Seren, I don't want to leave you here.'

'Em, I think I can handle a bit of music.'

'The music's only half the problem,' she says, glancing over at Dom. 'Promise me you won't stay too long?'

And, you know, I do promise and everything, but I guess I don't really intend to keep it and obviously I don't. I stay right until they're done and just when I'm leaving Dom jumps off the stage, jogs over to me, stands so close I can't meet his eye.

'You were so good,' I tell him.

He laughs. 'I doubt we were, but thanks anyway.'

'I, um … I need to get back,' I say. 'Or I am going to be so busted. My dad thinks I'm at View.'

'It's late. Want me to see you get home safe?' He tilts his head at me with his hair a little sweat-damp at the front and this slight heat flush on his cheekbones, a wave of sweet warmth coming off him that I just want to drown in. And, you know, I should say no, but I can't, not to him, not that I even try, especially when he does this thing he does where he bites the inside of his lower lip a little and it just makes me think about his mouth too much.

So even though he shouldn't, and I know he shouldn't, and he knows he shouldn't, he follows me. And I let him. Or maybe I make him. Whatever you call it when your heart is calling someone on with all it is, all it has, and so is your body, and so is every part of you, even though you know, you actually know in your head, that it's wrong.

Once we are almost back and there is nobody around he catches up to me and starts asking me what I've been doing and I can hardly think of anything to say, all because of the whole thing with Ezra. Even though I can't explain it, it already feels so wrong to keep secrets from him.

At the door to quarters, he leans against the door jamb, draped there, so long and lean, cheek on hand, watching me while I watch him. And I guess it's the fact that it's the same exact piece of wall where Ezra stood last night that makes me say, 'Want to come in?'

He doesn't answer right away but the way he looks at me then, so steady and serious and right in the eyes, is almost too much to take, and then he looks away, looks at the floor. 'Ah man,' he says, pinching the top of his nose. 'I can't. I just . . . can't.'

And I start messing with the keypad again as I'm saying, 'Of course – you're right. You're totally right.'

'No, Seren, it's—'

'It's OK, I understand.'

But then he takes my hand, just the tips of my fingers, and when I turn a little to look up at him there is this long moment where both of us are completely still and I feel like he is leafing through the pages of me like I was a book written in a language only he can understand. Then he nods at the keypad, takes this deep breath and says, 'Well are we going in or not?'

As I suspected, my dad is asleep in front of the screens on the bench in the galley, blue light on his face from the images of Huxley-3's surface that they show almost all the time at the moment, so we move fast, through to my room, and I let us in, hear Dom close the door after us.

'Jamie Hemple is your dad?' he hisses, making this face like he can't quite believe it as he leans on the inside of the door. 'I realised you were related but . . . man, he's your dad? I mean, we work together.'

'I know.' I frown. 'And?'

He laughs under his breath as he takes a few steps towards me. 'And?! And I'm sneaking into his daughter's room in the middle of third session.'

And just the way he says that, and how it sounds, what it means when all's said and done, fills the air around us with something hot to the touch. And suddenly just standing there looking at each other an arm's length apart is the most intimate thing I've ever done with anyone.

Maybe this is what makes me turn away, moving to the wall where I click my pod into its dock and look through my music for something to play.

'Do you ever sing in Spanish?' I ask him.

'No, not really. I guess I don't know many Spanish songs. What with it basically getting phased out.'

'You don't even have an accent when you speak English.'

'Don't we all just sound the same now? Aren't we all just, pretty much, *Ventura*, at this point?'

I find the perfect song and press play. 'You can be Ventura if you want but I'm going to give it a miss.'

He laughs. 'Fair enough.' And then, 'Man, how do you know this song? I love this song.'

And I smile, and it is right then that I feel him behind me, close and warm. Then he slides his hand on to my shoulder and across, until his arm lies along my front, pulling me into him.

'I ...' I try to speak, can't, start again. 'I thought your singing was amazing, by the way. It was ...' But I'm not sure how to describe it and anyway his breath in my hair is making it impossible to think, let alone talk.

'Seren,' he whispers. 'There's something I want you to know.'

It makes me so dizzy, the proximity to him, that I almost don't even manage a response. 'What is it?'

But he never tells me, he doesn't have to; all that happens is that I turn to him and he moves his hand to the side of my face, runs his thumb across my lips, once, watching them, twice, and it is almost like he is asking me a silent question, asking me if I want him to kiss me. And all the time I am thinking, *YES*, thinking it so hard that surely he can almost hear it, surely he can feel it pulsing under my skin. So I smile at him and I think he's going to too but he doesn't; he just goes on looking at me super serious and insanely beautiful in the half-light of my room, like he's still checking with me. And even after he seems sure, because he's tall and I'm short there is this long moment where he leans down and I stretch up and arch back, and it just isn't possible to want something more than I want him right then.

And then it's happening: we're kissing. And right then I know that I am his and always will be. Always was.

It's like we're in this world where none of it, nothing else, exists. There's just us in the vacuum of our own space. There's just kissing him. There's just the taste of him, like the first sip I've waited all my life to taste, only to realise I have always known how sweet it would be.

There's just his thumb tracing my jawline and knowing that this is something I was born to do.

Then he pulls back a little and all but kills me, just by looking in my eyes, before leaning his forehead against mine and saying, 'I'm sorry, my fault – I shouldn't have done that.'

And I swallow the pulsing in my throat and say, 'Why?'

And he says, 'Because we can't get into this, Seren, you know we can't.'

And I say, 'Then how come I want to so much?' as I run my hand down the front of his sweat-damp T-shirt, hearing the heaviness in his breathing and knowing I am the reason.

'Oh man, have you actually got any idea how difficult you're making this for me?' is what he says, voice hoarse, and he is shaking his head.

It's only now I notice the gooseflesh breaking out all along his arms, even as he is watching me slide my hands up under his T-shirt sleeves.

'I still have your jacket. Do you want it?' I watch him nod, but when it comes to me getting it, there's this moment where he doesn't let me go (and I don't want him to), which we laugh off. 'It got me into trouble actually,' I tell him once I tear myself away, while I'm looking for it in the back of the cupboard.

'It did?' He almost raises his voice, then covers his mouth for a second, remembering to whisper again. 'How?'

I find the jacket right at the back of my cupboard and bring it to him, bundling it against his chest while we look into each other's eyes.

'My sister told my dad about it,' I say. 'It's no big deal.'

He sits on the edge of my desk and raises his thumb to his mouth as if he might bite his nail, which is not something I've ever seen him do and though in the end all he does is touch the knuckle of it to his teeth it still makes me feel bad. 'You sure about that?'

I shrug. 'I guess . . . as much as I can be.'

He's in the middle of pulling on his jacket but once I can see his face again he laughs a little through his nose, but without making eye contact. 'You know what, the moment I saw you I knew you were more trouble than I could handle.'

I pretend like I'm going to punch him then but he grabs my swinging fist and laughs, taking hold of my other wrist too, and then he kisses me again, so gentle and so soft and so long that I forget everything, or forget that any of it matters anyway. When we stop he holds me, close against his chest where I hear his heart, hear him breathing, feel warmer than ever before, look up at him while he looks down at me, smile to smile.

'Have you done this before?' I ask him, super quiet, not sure I actually want to know the answer.

His smile fades, eyebrows gathering a little into this

frown I haven't seen before, and he says, 'Something similar maybe, but it wasn't anything like this.'

That's when everything shifts. There's a rending, almost like our entire world sighs, or maybe groans. It unsteadies us, sends us both lurching into the wall. My couple of sets of folded clothes slide off my shelves and puddle on the floor. We both listen to the distant sounds, like the far-off call of some animal, or a set of giant footsteps moving through the ship.

'What was that?' he says, eyes wide.

But somehow, without even thinking about it, I know. 'It's the orbit. We're entering the orbit around Huxley-3.'

He nods, smiling. 'It must be. You're totally right.'

My door buzzes, startling us both. We look at each other, but there aren't any better ideas so I press the intercom. 'Yes?'

Dad: 'Oh OK, you're home; I was worried. Did you feel that?'

I pause for a second, and then, 'Yeah I did. The orbit, right?'

'The gravity shift, yeah, it's all over the screens.' He sounds excited. 'You gonna let me in?'

Dom and I stare at each other, eyes wide. 'Erm, no, Dad, I'm … I'm undressed. I'm going to bed. Can we talk tomorrow?'

And even though I leave the channel open there's a silence, him listening to me listening to him, before he sighs. 'Well, OK.' He sounds so disappointed it makes me a little sad. 'But Grandpa and I wanted to talk to you about something tonight. He's coming over tomorrow.'

I don't miss a beat. 'Yep fine. Night, Dad.'

'Goodnight then.'

Once I've cut him off Dom goes to speak but I lay my finger over his lips and shake my head. I know Dad is still standing there, just on the other side; I can feel him there. It's only after about another ten seconds that we hear his cabin door slide closed, know that we're alone and turn to each other, meshing fingers.

'What do you think your grandpa wants?' Dom asks.

I have a few ideas but I just shrug. 'Who cares?'

'But . . . isn't he the Chief of Security?'

'And?'

He laughs. 'I'll admit I'm a little scared.'

'Don't be.' I shrug.

'Seren,' he says then, 'you know I don't want to cause problems for you, right?'

'I know you don't,' I say, leaning into him, knowing that it's true.

But even so, all that night we talk, watch the feed of Huxley-3 as it runs on my screen and kiss until it hurts. It is almost the beginning of first session when we finally accept that he should leave, and once he does I go to my bunk and fall asleep, curled into a comma, knowing suddenly what it feels like to be in love.

Chapter Thirteen

'Sure, yeah, it was only a matter of time I guess.' This is all I can think of as a response when I am sitting in the galley and Dad delivers The News, which is, of course, that we have been reassigned and we have to move out of our quarters. He's an SA (single adult) now and so am I, and Pan and Cain are getting moved into their own quarters for when the baby comes.

'You know, you could consider . . .' he starts, but since I know what he's about to say I am shaking my head already by the time he looks at me.

'Seren, don't throw the baby out with the bathwater.' This is my grandfather now, his hat under his arm as a concession to the fact that he's dealing with his family rather than his subordinates.

'What does that even mean?' I ask him, which earns me one of his Looks.

'What I'm saying is that in your situation, the prudent thing would be to expedite the Union situation and get married sooner rather than later. It was good enough for your mother, indeed for many of the women on this ship. Seren, you don't want to live in berths for too long at your age.'

'Because?'

He tugs at his cuffs, walks the length of the tiny galley, then back, caged I guess, looking for escape. 'Because … well, there's a certain culture … Let's just say the single life isn't great for morale. Here on the Ventura we favour family life, as you know.' He puts one hand on the back of my father's chair, one on the table. 'Lot of happy memories here, Jamie – I know it will be hard.'

Dad nods, pinches the bridge of his nose in such a way that for a moment I get a little scared he might cry, but he doesn't, because actually all he's doing is figuring out how to give me the next part of The News. I guess I realise this because I hear myself asking, 'And what about you, Dad? Where will you go?'

They share a look then, the two of them, both knowing something I'm about to know and obviously not like.

'Well,' he says, studying his hands. 'You know that a while ago we were talking about me applying to be reallocated?'

'You did it?'

He nods. 'I applied with Olivia Wren, and we got approved.'

'Olivia Wren?' She's this woman who works in Cultural who has these two little kids and a husband dead from PEST, who I guess I had noticed Dad was spending time with. Maybe I was just too busy with my own stuff to put it all together before now. 'OK, so you and her are like a thing now?'

'Yes.' He smiles. 'We're a thing, and I'm moving into her quarters.'

'So – one question – how is that fair? How come you get options and I don't?'

'Because ...' He laughs, pinches his nose again. 'Because I've played my part in the breeding programme, Seren, and Olivia has played her part too, and we're both ... widowed, and so ...'

'So marrying Mum, having us – it was all just you "playing your part"?'

'Seren, don't talk nonsense.' This is Grandpa, putting his hat on and getting ready to leave.

Dad looks pained and says, 'Baby, please—'

'Don't you "baby" me.' I leave him in the galley and go to my room, locking the door behind me, maybe for the last time. He sounds the buzzer almost right away. I push the intercom, say, 'Go away, Dad,' and cut it off. He buzzes again. I ignore it. He buzzes again. I try to ignore it and lie on my bed but he does it so many times that in the end I give up and press the com.

'What?'

'Let me in, Seren. I want to finish this conversation.'

'No, I'm done talking.'

I hear him sigh. 'I know it's hard for you to think of me with someone else when –' he sighs again, '– when Mum should still be here. But she's not. And meanwhile I'm only thirty-eight and I've just got too much time left on the clock to believe my life is over.'

'Your life was over the day you were born, Dad,' I say, and I release the switch even though I can hear that he comes back at me, slamming his fist against the door when he realises I've cut him off. I wait for him to buzz again then, but he doesn't.

I lie on my bunk and roll over towards the wall, and even though I know I could I don't cry. I refuse to do that; crying is just so lame. Instead I look at my great-grandma's pictures, unfolding the corners where they are curling up a bit. Great Granny Bea, five years old in a little dress, freckled sandy legs. One of the things she remembered most about Earth was the beach; she used to say it was the one place she really felt at home.

It's lunchtime, and we are sitting in the North cantina which stinks right now, because Day 22 is fish stew day and no one likes it but, you know, there isn't an awful lot you can do about it since we all eat in one of the four cantinas every day depending on where we work, where we live, and they all have the same structured menus anyway, have done since the start, will do until the end. The only thing that's different about North, as opposed to East where I've always eaten before, is that maybe the tables that are bolted into the floor aren't quite so caked in crusty old food because Education and most of the family quarters are in East whereas North is mainly SAs who don't make such a point of spreading their food around the place as kids do.

Anyway we're there, slurping at our gross slop and hoping no one weird sits with us when Mariana says to me, 'Come to a party with me tonight,' almost like it's an order.

I blink in surprise before shrugging. 'Sure.'

'Don't need to ask your dad?' she sneers, and then, shaking her head, 'I don't know how you still live in family quarters.'

'I don't. Not for much longer anyway.'

'Good – it's the only way to do it.'

'What about your life partner?' I ask her, realising I never have before.

'He's on ice.'

'Dead?'

She laughs, pulls the rubber band out of her dark hair and runs a hand through it, and I notice a blue streak for the first time. 'No. Not dead. We just … still aren't ready. And I'm sorry if this offends you, but the whole system is a sham anyway.'

'You think you're the only person who thinks that? Come on, man.' And while I'm chewing on a forkful of fish stew she's laughing at me.

We finish up and go to the party straight from shift, taking a sideways transporter as it's a bit of a haul down there to this rec room shared by a bunch of berths in South. Having been in family quarters I haven't seen that many rec rooms, but to be honest it doesn't seem all that different to our galley with its bolted-in tables and chairs and the screens on the walls, except that obviously it's bigger, and right now is so full of people that you can hardly even get through the door. The party is loud, which Mariana assures me is quite normal, since these berths are mostly Medical personnel and everyone knows they're nuts. They've got several kegs of beer and we're drinking out of a couple of metal cups, slick with foam, and talking to these two guys I half know when Mariana says, 'Hola, primo,' and pulls someone tall out of the crowd before saying, 'Seren, meet my favourite cousin, Domingo,' and while she gets into a debate with some guy about whether she wants to dance or not, Dom and I stand there face-to-face and both amazed.

'Man, what are you doing here?' he says.

'I came with Mariana. I can't believe you're cousins – how crazy is that? And how about you? Whose party is this?'

He looks weird then. 'Oh I don't know. No one's I guess.'

I feel myself frown. 'Why are you being weird?'

'I'm not.' And then, taking my hand where nobody can see and lowering his voice, 'OK, maybe I am. It's just that—'

'Seren,' says Mariana from behind me, touching my shoulder. 'Here's the birthday girl, Annelise.'

I turn around and there she is – one of those freckle-faced natural beauties who manage to pull off the feat (as she is right now) of looking good in her standard issue undershirt and a light sheen of sweat, and not only that but she's smiling and kissing my cheek and being really sweet, and also even smells good.

'Happy birthday,' I manage to squeak out.

'Thanks!' she says. 'I see Dommy's looking after you.'

'I …' Not having a clue who she's talking about I don't really answer but Dom manages to say, 'Seren is Pandora's sister, you know.'

'Yeah – we know each other from volleyball, right? OK, I'm going to get some beer. Come get some!'

'I will.' I nod, watching her go, and then to him I say, 'Dommy?' making a face, but all he does is look back at me, pained.

'Look, don't go anywhere, OK? Promise me?' He touches his fingertips to my cheek and it almost seems like he's going to kiss me then but of course he can't, so he doesn't, and I'm just left there, feeling the ghost of the kiss he never gave me resting on my lips, like unspoken words.

I don't know how much beer I drink. Too much, I guess, but you never know how much is too much until it's too late. It's not as if I particularly like the way it tastes or anything but it's just a case of cups keeping arriving in my hands and me feeling so much like I wish I wasn't there but also not wanting to leave, so in the absence of anything approaching a better idea I stand with Mariana and drink. I meet her life partner at one point and he is this super-tall guy with cornrows called Michael who works in Engineering but with computers, and he seems really nice if maybe a little vague. But maybe that's just me because I am not really paying much attention to him or anyone because, you know, I am mostly just watching Dom. Dom playing half a song with his band before the mess officer comes and pulls the plug; Dom standing next to Annelise while she tells a joke that everybody laughs at, including him; Dom refilling Annelise's drink; Dom changing the music when she says she wants something different; Dom killing the lights when one of her friends walks into the rec room with a cake and candles.

It's her twentieth you see, a semi-big deal, so once everyone has sung she makes a speech and it's all thanks to this person and thanks to that and the most important thing is thanks so much to my life partner, Dommy Suarez, for understanding that for now I have to put my career first but I couldn't be more excited about our life together when we finally get time to start it. And afterwards she reaches her hand towards him and he takes it and she pulls him towards her and she kisses him.

And yeah, so I suppose you can guess that this is the point at which something pretty awful happens to me, and it's not quite clear whether it's the excess of beer or whether it's a literal physical aversion to it all, but suddenly I can't see straight and all I can do is get out of there before I fall on my face. So then I'm out in the corridor with this awful noise of wolf whistles and cheers behind me, and I'm clinging on to the wall like it was the floor and wondering if they switched off the gravity. Somehow I make it to the door at the end of the passage even though it feels like I walk in several swirling spirals on my way there, ceiling wall floor wall ceiling wall floor, and I grab at the handle and miss it once and miss it again and by this time, God knows how he managed it, but he's standing there, standing in right behind me with his hands on my wrists and saying, 'I . . . I had no idea she was going to do that.'

And I turn to him, and I get ready to say all these things and instead when I open my mouth all that comes out is, 'You're not hers. You're mine.' It's just as whiny and childish and lame as it sounds and it's amazing that he doesn't laugh, but he doesn't, not even a little. I turn away and hide my face in my hands. 'Is what she said true?' I say into my own palms.

'Not any more, no.'

'Not any more?'

He pries my hands off my face and makes me look at him. 'Don't you know yet that everything changed the moment I saw you that day in Med? I just ... it's like I suddenly knew what it would be like to have a real life.'

Which makes me forget to breathe for a moment, but then I think of something. 'Wait ... what were you doing there?'

'What?'

'Why were you in Med that day?'

'I ...' He grips my hands tighter but doesn't answer.

'You were waiting for her to finish work, weren't you?'

He blinks, shifts his gaze. 'Why does it matter? I left with you. And it was the best move I ever made.'

It's the first time that he's spoken to me this way, looked at me this way, frowning and lips a little parted and leaning into me, and all of a sudden I realise I don't want there to be anything he doesn't know about me.

'Well, do you want to know what I was doing there?' I ask.

'Only if you want to tell me.'

'The fact is I have a mental health issue. I'm crazy. My mum was, and now I am too. So what do you think of that?'

He smiles, his hands as warm and damp as mine are. 'I think I really, really like whatever it is that makes you you, even if other people call it crazy.'

People spill down the passage then, throwing beer at each other. We hear Mariana yelling at them just in time to move apart before she gets to us, but she still stands for a few seconds looking between us with a frown before she says, 'Hemple, you're drunk – I'm taking you home,' and slams open the door release.

'I'll come with you,' says Dom. 'Walk you back.'

Mariana scowls at him. 'Primo, what're you talking about? Why would you do that? It's Annelise's party.'

He laughs. 'Right, of course ...'

It's only because she steps out first that Dom has a chance to grab my hand then, pull me back and speak against the hair near my ear: 'Nothing's going to change the way I feel about you, estrellita, OK?' before Mariana pulls my arm again and we're gone, and on the way home I ask her, 'What does "estrellita" mean?'

And she says, 'Little star. You know, like the twinkle, twinkle song?' and looks at me funny, but I guess she must be a little drunk because she doesn't ask me anything about that, or about the stupid smile I know I have on my face.

Chapter Fourteen

Mariana and I are checking stock in the storeroom and even though I've managed to resist the urge for days, I suddenly can't help myself grilling her about Dom.

'So are your dads brothers?'

'No, Domingo's mum, Tia Lola, is my mum's sister.'

'What's she like?'

'Super guapa. That's where Dom gets his looks. She used to act in the Cultural programme shows, so you've probably seen her.' She smiles to herself.

'And his dad? What's he like?'

'Tio Fernando can sing like a ...' She frowns. 'Wait, why are you asking all these questions?'

I shrug, turn away, pretend to be absorbed in protein shakes. 'Just taking an interest in you.'

She lowers a box to the floor and I feel her gaze on me. 'In me? Or in my hot cousin?'

'Mariana, that's not what this is. I did think he seemed interesting, but as a friend. We're allowed to be friends, right?' I turn to meet her watchful eyes in the half-light of the storeroom.

'To be on the safe side I'd probably advise against it,' she says.

But I just laugh, because she has no idea how right she is.

Whatever Dom and I are, we're not just friends. Every moment we've found to be alone together has only made it clearer that we could never have been just friends. Not with how when we talk it unspools everything in my head and rearranges it in a way that suddenly makes sense. Not with how when he looks at me it feels like I have always known him, like he's the other half of me that has been missing my whole life. Not with how when he touches me I feel him in my bones, my flesh, in each breath, in every racing beat of my heart.

For weeks, I've been dreaming about Huxley-3 almost every night. I am there. I am the one flying over her surface. It feels like I don't exist any more and all of it is happening through me, flowing through my soul. She is beautiful, she is a whole, beautiful, perfect world. She is music, a sweet, sad sound that plays in my ears and in my heart. She is mountains covered in snow, she is endless forests of green, she is orange deserts bathed in setting sun, she is bluest seas, she is beaches. And she is ours.

And then one day, I have this feeling when I wake up

that there is this other life I was born for – that we were born for – Dom and me. I can hardly make it through my shift that day – every hour is a week – especially when some half-cut off-duty engineers decide I'm their sport and start giving me hassle about there not being enough energy drinks in the machines on their mess deck. I'm in a good mood but no mood is good enough to put up with much of what they have to dish out, especially since they have their hats on backwards and overalls undone and are like: 'You're Lomax's woman, aren't you? The feisty one.'

I just shrug.

'What are you doing working Maintenance?'

'Why wouldn't I be?' I heft a box of muesli bars.

One of them shrugs then. 'Can't he get you out of it? Pull strings? Knock you up or something?'

'I'm ignoring you now,' I say, so at least he knows the situation, not that he seems to care.

'There are rumours about you, hot stuff.'

'OK, move along,' I tell them.

'Why don't you come keep my berth warm tonight?'

'In your dreams, loser,' I tell him, and they're gone, sniggering like a couple of kids, shoving each other around, and yeah, the whole thing is weird, it makes me think, I guess, but I don't let it get to me, not too much anyway, because maybe I feel like there's a way out of this for the first time.

After shift I get to Dom's berths and he is waiting for me, damp-haired and holding his guitar by the neck, undershirt riding up at the back so that I can't help but touch the skin there on the way over to his bunk, which makes him turn and pull me in against him, stooping down, parting his lips as he presses them to mine.

Dom and I have lost hours like this, but it only ever feels like minutes, when it's me and him on his bunk, when it's that part of second session when there's no one else in his berths. Sometimes we listen to music, an earphone each. Sometimes I trace the line of his name where it is stitched into the front of his overalls, just over his heart, while he kisses me, kisses me and kisses me for so long that we almost forget we could be walked in on at any moment, and only remember just in time.

By the time I'm done on my shift he's been asleep for hours so he's always a bit slow and full of sighs at first, talking through yawns and smoothing the skin on my arms while I gabble on at him. He's always wet-haired too, smells of toothpaste and shampoo, and today is the first time I ask him why.

'I get in the shower; wake myself up.'

'How long have you been asleep?'

He squints at his pod. 'Three hours.'

'Is that enough?'

'Sure,' he says, yawning.

'It's not, is it?'

'Who cares? This is our time together.' And he pushes my cap off and kisses me once, quick but tasting it afterwards, like someone eating a sweet. 'So tell me what you were talking about in that message you left.' He grins, watching my lips as I speak.

'I keep dreaming about Huxley-3.'

He raises his eyebrows. 'Huxley-3?'

'Yeah ... I just ... I don't know. I guess you're going to think it's weird.'

He smiles. 'Try me.'

'I dream about it every night. It's like ... I don't know ... like this is something huge. Like this is something bigger than us, than all of us.' I shake my head. 'I know it sounds dumb but sometimes it just seems like this could be it. This could be the thing that changes everything. And it could be our chance, our chance to live a real life. Together. Somehow.'

And though he doesn't speak, I can tell in the way he kisses me that he feels it like I do; that it's all there waiting for us.

And this is probably why on this particular afternoon we get to the point that we are both way more undressed than we should be, and he is breathing deep against me, and I hear this sound way back in my own throat that I have never made before, and I am sliding my hands across his shoulders, his chest, down to his hips, tasting the salt along his collarbone and pulling him to me, and I couldn't, absolutely couldn't, care less who walks in on us, because he is MINE. He is mine right then in a way that no one ever belonged to anyone. And then he shifts, moves on top of me, holding himself over me on his elbows, completely still but trembling just a little, and looking into my eyes, killing me, utterly killing me, and then he says, 'Oh man, we can't do this,' and he kisses the end of my nose, my head, my hairline, sighs there, sits up and away from me, feet on the floor, holding his head in his hands for a moment before looking back at me and forcing this sad smile. 'You will probably never know how much I want to, but there is a world of trouble right there that we can't get into now. Believe me.'

'You know when I'm with you I don't care about any of that,' I say, curling my body around him as he sits there, laying my cheek against his leg as I look up at his face.

He touches my mouth then with his thumb, and I can see his resolve going, going, and then coming back, as he bites his lip on one side.

'Come with me somewhere later?' Asked like a question but he knows I would never say no to him, certainly not with his eyes the way they are.

When we get to the Fisheries for his shift he buzzes us all the way through with his fob and we see absolutely zero people, then we're there in Tank Four which is one I haven't been in before. It's weirdly quiet, the water utterly still like a mirror, bouncing Huxley-3 back up at itself.

'We're here,' he says.

I look around. 'We are?'

He walks along the metal decking, kicking off his shoes on the way, turns to look at me, walking backwards. 'Spawning,' is all he says.

'What?'

'Let's swim,' he says, pulling open the buttons of his overalls and shucking them down, then crossing his arms, taking hold of the bottom hem of his undershirt and pulling it up in one movement, covering his face, dropping it to the floor.

And I mean, yeah, I won't get into the way I feel right then, noticing the way that pretty constellation of beauty marks continues on to his body, punctuating the smooth muscles of his torso as if by design. I can't think sensible thoughts so I follow my instincts instead; I slide my overalls down, pull off my vest, eyes locked with his all the time.

'Won't we get eaten by the fish?' I ask, fighting the thudding heartbeat I feel in my throat.

'There aren't any,' he says, taking a step towards me, eyes only leaving mine briefly even though I know both of us are basically only thinking about the fact that we are standing there in our underwear. Then suddenly he is taking my hand and my heart is beating so hard, and just when I think I might actually be about to die, he is pulling me in with him as he jumps into the water, down, and it's FREEZING and we're deep, deeper, bubbles, then he's surfacing with me, both of us a shower of spray and sucked-in breath.

And I am yelling, 'Oh my God it's cold!'

And he is laughing at me.

'It's just eggs in here at the moment,' he says, wiping water off his face, looking around, arm circling my waist. 'All at the bottom, waiting to be born.' He raises his eyebrows. 'So it's just you and me.'

There's a noise then, a hiss, growing. 'What's that?' I ask him, and then suddenly it's raining, raining, heavier, dripping down our faces, drips forming in our eyebrows, growing on our noses, chins.

'Keeps the water fresh,' he yells, over the roar of it all. 'Needs to be fresh for the hatching.'

He pushes away from me, arcs over backwards, doing a full somersault before moving up the skin of my stomach, his face now close to mine, so close I can see the water trapped in his eyelashes, clumping them together and making them shine. And just then, right at the moment when I am pretty much Completely Lost, he looks away from me, squints up through the spray at the skylight above us and points. 'Look,' he says, and he swims behind me, tucking his shoulder under my head so that I rest it there, my ear close to his mouth, my body completely buoyant, weightless, his fingers on my spine, rain falling, and there above us Huxley-3 is a deep and brilliant blue and white, filling our window, just like sky.

'She's amazing, isn't she?' he says, his breath close to my earlobe, his fingers finding mine and meshing, and even though I'm shivering I am not cold.

So we watch her, watch the way she swoops in under us now and there is music, actual music, in my head when I look and see her clouds, see the way her two moons are pink and lilac in the dying light. Our life is down there waiting for us, somewhere we can touch the earth, feel it between our toes.

And you know what? You know when people tell you that love isn't like in the movies, that that kind of amazing moment never happens in real life? Well, they're only saying that because it never happened to them. It doesn't happen for most people. But it does happen for some, and this is one of those times. I turn in the water, turn to him, and I reach my hand through it to touch his chest right where his heart is, and we just look into each other's eyes and see everything, know everything, he is mine and I am his, and I say, 'I never really wanted anything until I met you.'

And he smiles a crooked smile and says, 'That's the coolest thing anyone has ever said.'

Chapter Fifteen

I move into berths two orbits later. Dad is working when I pack up my stuff so there isn't any kind of lame scene with him, but Pan manages to come out of her room at just the right moment, so big she barely fits through the door.

'You make some really stupid decisions, you know that, right?' is how she decides to bid me farewell, followed by, 'I just hope you won't make even more dumb moves without us there to keep an eye on you.'

'I'm pretty sure I'll live up to your expectations,' I say, shouldering my bag and heading for the door, where Cain is standing, arms outstretched for a hug. I oblige him since he's probably the one who's been the least awful to live with out of them all.

'Ready to tell me anything about that planet down there yet?' I say, into his shoulder.

He kisses my forehead and smiles.

'Classified,' we both say together, since this is the only

answer he's given anyone who's asked about his recons to Huxley-3 this whole time, the idiot.

'Seren,' he says, just as I'm stepping out of the door. 'Where's your berths? Where can we find you?'

'That, my friend, is classified,' I say, but I throw him a smile over my shoulder.

Of course, because I'm in North for Maintenance I get berths there too. Mariana manages to swing it so that I'm with her, in this berths of only six of us in a room for ten so I get to choose a bunk in the corner and, you know, for the first little while it's kind of exciting, it's kind of cool that I'm out on my own. The other girls in the berths are mostly OK and I can believe, or maybe kid myself, that this is the right thing for me. Mariana's all for heading to the plaza to get a drink and I'm just getting ready when my pod rings and it's Dom, and I guess because we're both a little overexcited by my new freedom and not actually thinking things through a whole lot, he says he'll come and meet us.

So the other girls from the berths and I get to the plaza and sit around a little, talking. Here's the thing: I've kind of always been led to believe that there aren't that many young single people on Ventura, but now I'm finding out that's not really the case. There are more than you would think. They've got a whole bunch of different stories, usually involving one or other of the life partners having a career they want to concentrate on, which in my mind probably just translates to them taking a while to come to terms with the fact that this is the person they're going to have to spend their life with and it's not what they would have chosen. No matter what platitudes they trot out, this is what it comes down to. The other story you tend to hear involves somebody dying. This is just one out of the whole host of flaws there are in the Ventura plan. Make people in pairs. For every boy make a girl. And if one of them dies, that's just hard luck. Because death is something not even the great scientific minds of the Ventura are able to prevent.

There's a bunch of Engineering guys over at the bar and after a while one of them comes over and puts his hands over the eyes of Jen, this girl I'm talking to, so that there is this long awkward moment where Jen's trying to think who it could be and I am just sitting there looking at him and slowly realising that it is one of the guys who was hassling me at the vending machine the other day. The one who works with Ezra. I'm not quite sure at this point whether he recognises me back because all he does is wink and listen to Jen frantically guessing who it could be so that the whole thing can be over. I sigh and look away; I really hate people who play this game.

When she tells him she gives up she twists in her seat to look at him and looks pretty genuinely disappointed with the truth. 'Oh it's you,' she says. 'This is Arnold Witney, my brother-in-law.'

And he stands there waving dumbly. 'What's happening, ladies? Little session?'

'Sure, Arnold,' she sighs. 'I would ask you to join us but I can see you have company.'

So in the end he takes the hint and leaves, and as he does she says, 'Idiot,' and rolls her eyes.

Dom arrives when I'm still talking to Jen and for a while he is talking to the others, all of whom he seems to know through Mariana or, in fact, through Annelise, which is, you know, obvious really, but that doesn't mean it doesn't freak me out a bit. But watching him makes me forget about any of that, seeing how funny and easy he is with everyone, how he doesn't even get how cute and cool he is, which only makes it better. Mariana laughs so hard when he tells a joke that I realise something I haven't fully clocked before: she loves him, she loves her cousin in a real way, in a way that doesn't always present itself just because you happen to be related to a person, but when it does it's something precious.

I don't even get to speak to him at all until half an hour later when I am on my way to the bathroom and he follows me, a fact I'm not aware of until I feel him close behind me when I'm crossing the busy dance floor and he says, 'Dance with me.'

And I'm saying, 'I don't dance.'

'*I don't dance*,' he mimics, in a voice that I guess is supposed to be me and then he apologises by running his thumb over my lower lip and I end up actually, physically, light-headed. So, you know, in the immediate aftermath of this wipeout, he is holding my hands, watching me, and I can feel his warmth, the smell of him, and I almost manage to forget that I am standing there, ridiculous and stiff, hands lost in mid-air. But I am shaking my head, trying to turn and walk away before he pulls me in against him, speaks into my hair, something in Spanish that I can't even hear, and I turn to him and raise my face towards the skin of his neck and then he is twirling me, showing me what to do, moving like it's something he does that's as natural as breathing or walking. And after a while, I don't know, it's not like I'm into it, into the dancing, but I am into HIM. God, I am more into him than anything ever, and so I watch the way his face is so moody, so serious, and I want so badly to run my hand along his cheek, his jaw, the softness of his mouth and he moves into me, says, 'I told you you could dance,' and there are no words for how much I want to kiss him right then.

And this is why I turn to leave, turn to go, but hold his fingertips low down as I do, so that he follows me. We get to the back passage that leads to the bathroom and there is nobody there so he falls into me as I lean back on the wall and I pull him even closer and he breathes against me and I sigh and we are kissing, me with a fistful of the front of his overalls, him with his hands on the back of my thighs. It is right now that the door from the men's room slides open and though we stand apart and try to play it off it is beyond obvious, and (even worse) the guy standing there is Arnold Witney.

'So it's true what they say about you, hot stuff!' he yells, clearly drunk, an arm suddenly heavy on my shoulder. 'Lomax has got himself a wild one,' he says, shaking his head at the floor. 'Poor sap.'

Dom grabs at the front of Witney's flight suit then, hard. 'Get your hands off her now.'

'Hey hombre, que pasa?' He laughs, raising pale palms between them. 'I'm just talking, man.'

'Well don't.'

'Or what?'

'Or you and me have a problem.'

And right now I am watching Dom, watching the way the anger burns in his eyes and he bares his teeth a little, and it is not something I have seen before or even suspected in him, someone who always seems so calm, so sure of everything being OK, and I'm thinking about how it's weird that you can get so close to someone and then they can surprise you, and all of this is there on my face, I guess, when he glances at me and looks away and then looks back. Which is when this Witney guy looks from Dom to me and back again, and then opens his stupid mouth.

'This isn't your woman – you realise that? This is not something you do – comprende muchacho?'

'Did anybody ask for your opinion?' snarls Dom.

'You realise it's my duty to report infractions? Yours too, even though you're only a grunt. But I doubt you'll report on your own lanky ass. Or hers. You can probably think of better things to do with it. I know I can.' He turns to walk away from us then, but Dom follows him and shoves him so hard he goes down, falling forward out of the doorway on to the dance floor and taking out this couple and their drinks on the way, which of course means that two of the guys who work behind the bar arrive almost instantly and one takes hold of Dom's arms.

'Unless you want me to call Security, let's go,' he tells him, while Dom looks at me.

They both get dragged towards the doors, and though Witney yells and lunges at Dom, all Dom does is look over his shoulder at me and call out something I can't hear. I follow him, of course, right up until the point that I feel someone yank on my elbow and when I turn it is Mariana, wide-eyed, appearing out of the crowd and saying, 'Don't, amiga, please. You'll only make it worse.'

I just stop dead then, watch him disappear, and he is looking at me and I am looking at him and suddenly it feels like there is no air at all in the room, no blood in me, and so much to fear. I'm about to go to him when Mariana grabs my arm again. 'You leave with him now and everyone's going to be talking about it.'

And when I look at her she is making this face so I let her bring me over to the bar where she orders something, and I keep looking over my shoulder to where I can still see him just outside with Arnold Witney pointing in his face before Dom shakes his head and walks away.

Mariana follows my gaze and says, 'Care to tell me what all that was about?'

But I just look at her, look down, shake my head.

She sighs. 'Seren, I love my cousin. And I care somewhat about you too. And I guess you already know that things don't generally go well for people who mess around with other people's life partners.'

I say nothing, look away, though now there is a fear in me that I don't recognise, can't even name. To cover it, I chink the shot glass she hands me against hers, throw the alcohol down my neck where it sears, makes me retch, makes my eyes tear, but when I blink it away, she is still studying me hard.

'So, like, what is this with you and him – is this ...' She looks at the ceiling as if the right words might be written there. 'Is it an actual thing that is actually … happening?'

I force this strange sound that's supposed to be a laugh, but is more like choking than anything. 'I don't know what you're talking about. What thing?'

But she just looks at me. 'Seren, if you think you're managing to hide it, you're more of an idiot than I thought you were, and that's saying something.'

Since this is the first time anyone has come out and asked me about it, I take my time to frame my answer and just as I'm about to speak I feel as if I might cry and then I say, 'It's the first real thing that has ever happened to me in my life.'

She does her shot then, swallowing it neatly like it's water and ordering another round. Looking back at me again while the guy behind the bar is refilling our glasses, she squints in a way that reminds me of Dom.

'And, what – you, like, you're in love with him?' After she watches me nod, she says, 'Dios mío, what a mess.'

And even though it's not funny at all I laugh, laugh through the tears in my eyes, and this is when we do our second round of shots, and it is only once we've stopped coughing that she says, 'Whatever you may think you feel, Seren, you need to stop it, man – I mean it.'

I feel the smile fade from my own face just as it has from hers.

'You don't even know,' she says, shaking her head. 'You have no idea what you're getting into, on so many levels. Seriously.' There is this anger in her eyes now, even more than usual. 'Messing with the order on Ventura is nothing but a world of pain. Truly. It's not something you want to do. Get found out and you're talking about time in Correctional at least, maybe worse. Take it from me. And jeez, if you won't take it from me, take it from Dom. I suppose he told you why he isn't in his Union yet?'

I feel myself frown, feel myself blink a few times and then I say, 'Annelise's medical training had to take precedence, and, I mean, I guess, apart from anything else, his heart isn't in it.'

Mariana is watching me, her eyes darker than ever. 'That's what he said?'

And I search back, think back, all the while nodding though I can't actually be that sure, and then she says, 'I think you guys need to talk. There are things you need to know about him, things he should have told you.'

'Like what?'

She doesn't answer me, just slides off the stool like she's getting ready to leave. 'I know you don't want advice from me. Man, I wouldn't even take advice from me. But I've been where you are, and it didn't end well for anyone involved, OK? And it's not something you can just leave behind either; it's not something you can ever forget.' She looks so pained I take her elbow in my hands for a moment before she pulls it away.

'Mariana, what are you talking about? Please tell me.'

And though she looks at me for a long time then, holds my eye, all she says is, 'Just don't make the mistake I did, Seren. It's not worth it,' and then she's gone.

Chapter Sixteen

I've never seen the drill hall like this. Never. I guess none of us had actually noticed how many of us there are until now when we're all in here and there are about five or six people for every seat. Briefings are non-obligatory so mostly people don't come, but today, for the mid-orbit update, anyone who can be here is here, and that doesn't even account for all the people who are on shift and haven't been able to get away. There are kids and old people and everything in between and I swear for a while we are all just standing there and looking at each other and thinking how mad it is. I even see my dad and Olivia and the two little boys she has and my dad is carrying one of them, but none of them see me.

This is how much everybody cares; this is how desperate everyone is for something to actually happen to them for once in their life, something that's real, something that has meaning. We were basically born to die, and I guess we were all just pretending to be OK about it up until now.

I haven't seen Dom since the whole thing at the bar because he was working and then I was, but he's right where I arranged to meet him and at first we both talk at the same time and then we stop and then we start again and he says, 'I'm so sorry, estrellita. The other night, all of it, should never have happened.'

I shake my head. 'It was ... I was so worried about you. I wanted to follow you but Mariana wouldn't let me. She ...' I study his face then, the way he bites his lip, wondering if it can be true that he's hiding something from me, and I'm just about to ask him when Ezra edges in behind us and takes hold of my ponytail.

'Hey,' he says, before looking sideways at Dom, then back at me. 'You're up there with me. Mum's orders. First family and all that.'

'I don't ... I'm not ...' I say, but Dom nudges me a little.

'You should go,' he says.

'I want to stay here with you.' Down near my hip I hook his index finger with mine.

'You should do what you need to do, Seren.'

And though we're whispering all of this, the look of horror on Ezra's face when I turn around says it all, and for a while he doesn't move, just stares at Dom; stares at Dom who stares back.

'I know who you are,' says Ezra then, through clamped teeth.

'That makes two of us,' says Dom.

And right then I am so afraid of what could happen next that I say, 'OK, Ezra, let's go,' and though he stays there staring for a second, he grabs my arm suddenly and we're gone, me looking back at Dom watching me getting pulled away.

'Are you ever going to get tired of embarrassing me?' Ezra says, hauling me through the crowd with his fixed smile in place.

'Probably not,' I tell him, matching his grimace with one of my own.

'I mean, what the hell WAS that?'

'You wouldn't understand.'

'What does that mean?'

'Never mind.'

He pulls me up next to him but doesn't look at me. It's only now I notice the way he is sweating a little, shining with it, an actual drip appearing at his hairline and, I mean, it's not hot in the drill hall; it's never hot anywhere on this ship.

'Well, look, whatever it is with that guy, you had better start saying your goodbyes.'

'My goodbyes?' Fear passes over me then, steals down my neck.

'People are about to get some bad news, so Mum

155

wants them to have something good to look forward to, to soften the blow.'

I don't even hear a lot of what happens next because everything is slowly draining around me, the colour, the life, all of it, twisting and melting and falling and sliding down a hole. I look for Dom then; I look for him in the crowd and I can't find him. It seems like there are a million faces and none of them are him. And there's nothing then except Ezra's hand pulling me on to the stage behind Captain Kat and we are following her, following her through a world of noise and chaos to the centre of the stage where she stops and we stop but we are in the wrong place so her two Security guys come back and position us. Jonah is there too.

Then she is talking and at first I'm not listening, and this is why. I know, you see, I know by this point that she's telling us that Huxley-3 is just another dead planet. It's only partly formed, riddled with dangerous microbes, not a safe atmosphere and no signs of intelligent life. All this time the screens are showing images the recon missions captured – black rocks and dark water and lonely mountains with lava streams and steam. Even though there's no real hope in these images I can't stop watching them, can't stop feasting my eyes on them, because they are still the closest thing to a real planet we have ever seen, and it is almost hard to believe there is no life.

We are a First Contact vessel, so all we are looking for is signs of life. Failing to find it, we move on – that is our mission. And that is all that has happened, for eighty-four years. And it will probably continue to happen for another two hundred and sixty-two or more. This is what we are learning – our universe is mostly lifeless, mostly full of vast dead planets, and this is just another one of those. Big surprise. And the truth is I don't even look for Dom any more, because this is what I should have known would happen to my dreams, to everything we hoped. This is how I should have known it would turn out. It feels like this marks the end of so much, maybe even everything, when it comes to me and the only things I ever wanted.

'As you can see, this is a planet that is still in its very early stages, still terraforming, so it has a highly hazardous and hostile environment,' says Captain Kat, glancing back at the screens while she talks. 'We will gather whatever useful data we can before exiting Huxley-3's orbit on schedule and continuing on our direct route to Epsilon, from where we continue to receive our signal, our beacon. Don't think the time we are spending here will have been wasted. We hope that the knowledge gained here will, in the fullness of time, go on to enrich all of our lives in one way or another.'

There's a shuffling, a muttering, and I look around at what we have become, at who we are, at these few thousand men and women and children, all of us in our grey uniform overalls and trapped in the drill hall, the down-at-heel gunmetal grey drill hall with its sagging half-forgotten flags. Some people gather up children then, hoist them up on hips and start to head to the doors with their shoulders slumped, and this is when Captain Kat says, 'While we are all gathered here I would like to make a happy and very welcome announcement,' and even though she doesn't look at me I sense it. I sense it in the way Ezra tenses up beside me, hisses out his breath all at once. When I look at Jonah he just stares at the stage about a metre in front of him. Almost as if there's something I could do to stop it I look for Dom again then, look and look and look, and then just want to scream that he is not there, not anywhere in the vicinity that I left him. There is this kid with his tongue out, this old guy with a drooping face, this grinning woman, but there is no Dom. And now it is happening, HAPPENING, and I cannot run away from it.

'As you know,' says Captain Kat, sweeping at us with her hard-nailed hand. 'My two sons are new graduates in the latest rising generation. And as a passionate believer in our mission, in everything we are trying to achieve on the Ventura, my son Ezra has decided to begin his life, his purpose, as soon as possible. Therefore as the first family we would like to cordially invite you

158

all to join us to celebrate his Union with his new bride in two weeks' time.'

'What?' I can't help myself, though luckily it's only Ezra who hears me, looks at me, shushes me by scissoring my hand between his and clamping it there, fake-smiling at me in such a way that it forces my face into it too. And there is applause, not exactly rapturous but pattering, like rain.

'Here in the drill hall we will gather to celebrate the beginning of these young lives as a symbol, a symbol of our quest, our ongoing mission to communicate with the beings of the universe, and I hope you will join us. I hope you will pledge your support, for this and for all the Unions which are essential to our way of life.'

All this time I am heavy breathing, all this time I am saying *no no no no*, all this time Ezra is squeezing my hand tighter and tighter and willing me, basically willing me not to screw this up for him, for her, for all of us. But I can't look at him, the reason being I can't guarantee anything yet, right now it could still go either way, what with the heavy breathing and the wheezing and the full-blown panic attack and the way everyone, everyone, is disappearing down a tunnel that I am at the end of, or a hole that I am at the bottom of.

Chapter Seventeen

I have a mess duty that afternoon but obviously I don't go, obviously I just stay in my berth and lie there and pretend I don't exist. I open my eyes at one point and Grandpa is standing there, hat in his hands, looking at me, then up at the ceiling, then down at me again.

I don't know what he says. Stuff. Things. Blah, blah, blah. I only really tune in when I hear him say, 'You've never been very good at hiding your feelings, Seren,' and as he sits on my bed he sighs, clasping his hands between his knees. It seems like for ever until he carries on, 'Our reality is we don't have the luxury of leaving these things to chance, of living like animals. We are not animals. We are essentially a military operation and we must run like one, whether you like it or not. And the breeding programme is just a duty that we have to fulfil, like any other.' He sighs. 'That being said, I feel it pertinent to point out that, while I appreciate you're upset, you should know that your own choice for yourself would have been highly unsuitable in any case.'

I wake up then. 'What does that mean?'

'Did Technician Suarez ever tell you why, having completed his Service more than a year ago, he still hasn't married his life partner?'

'Annelise wanted to do her medical training first.'

He smiles. 'Seren, there is no reason for a married woman to put her career on hold, until she decides she is ready to join an appropriate breeding cycle. That's not the reason.'

I swallow the tightness in my throat. 'So what is?'

'Technician Suarez is not permitted to marry, until he finishes his Correctional programme. He was involved in an incident of grievous violence, two years ago. He has not yet completed his rehabilitation.'

'An incident of grievous violence?'

'So he didn't tell you?'

And I cover up for him: 'Yeah, no – he did. Of course he did.'

To which he just raises an eyebrow. Then, after sighing through his nose, hard, 'You know, I look at you sometimes and all I see is Grace.'

He very rarely talks about my mum, if ever, so I hold my breath, wait, watch the way he frowns down at his clasped hands and stammers a bit before he starts to speak, in a way that is utterly unlike him. 'You ...

you …' He clears his throat. 'You're just like her, in so many ways, and I don't want you to go down the same road she did – unable to accept things the way they were, questioning everything to the point that she couldn't even see all the precious blessings she had.' He touches my cheek with the side of his thumb then, just once, and I swear it's the first time I remember him touching me in forever.

And it is right then that my pod chimes in a call and when I check the screen it is Dom, and my grandpa just watches the way I check it and don't answer and of course he knows, and so he says, 'You have to put this behind you now, Seren,' taking the pod from me and squinting at it before clearing the call. 'I suppose I hardly need remind you that, apart from anything else, interference with the breeding programme is a criminal offence. And it carries particularly severe penalties for those with a previous transgression on their record.'

He stands then, pushing on his hat.

'I am telling you this because I love you, and I don't want you to get hurt.'

He leaves my pod on my shelf as he walks out.

Dom is working second session at the moment so I message him to tell him I'll meet him at View after he's finished and eaten. I set my alarm to wake me up but as it turns out I am not asleep anyway when it buzzes under my pillow. I'm still awake, have been for hours, even though it's some way into third session by now, when I'm supposed to be asleep. I pull my clothes on in the dark and sneak out of my berths. All the passages are pretty much empty except for people in ones or twos heading to or from their shifts. At one point the night shift of circuit runners drum past me and a few raise a hand. Funny how quickly things can seem like they belong to a different life.

View is utterly silent and empty and desolate. It couldn't be more changed from the way it was back when the whole world was different and all everyone wanted to do was watch Huxley-3 and Dom hadn't lied. When I get there he is right up front, gazing out of the glass at the way the view seems like it has already shifted slightly, now beginning to take in more distant stars, and darkness.

And I'll tell you what's really weird is that he looks different to me now. The beautiful curl in his lip is now a little bit sly in a way I never noticed before. Isn't it, I don't know, maybe a little bit too self-confident, domineering (maybe even sleazy?), the way he winks at me and lays his hand on the side of my throat?

'So I hear congratulations are in order?' He smiles, trying to make light of it, realising right away that it has fallen flat, then going to pull me into his arms. He senses it though, that something is wrong, that I am resisting him, leans down so that he can see my face even though I'm looking at the floor. And I realise I can't speak; I cannot say a single word until I know.

'Talk to me,' he says, lips close to my temple, while he squeezes my shoulders in once, then again.

And for a moment I wonder if I will ever speak, if I will ever speak again, but somehow, no idea how, I manage to get the words out. 'Why didn't you tell me?' is all I say, and he only hesitates a second, only long enough to lean back a little and frown and then I see it, I see that he knows and I wait, not even breathing, to hear what he will say.

'I wanted to tell you so badly, estrellita.'

'Don't call me that.'

And he flinches a little then, as if I had raised a fist, and then he takes my hands, both of them, or tries to, before I pull them away, and he gives up on it, pulling his cap off instead and sighing.

'Who told you?'

'My grandfather.'

'Look, I don't know what he told you but it's not the way it sounds. You know me, Seren – you know me better than anyone ever has. I was sixteen and the truth is this guy ... well, I don't want to get into it right now, but he had done something unforgivable. Unforgivable and horrible and hurtful and miserable and ugly and cowardly in the worst way, and then he just ... wasn't sorry. He wasn't sorry and he didn't care and it was made worse by the fact that we had actually been pretty good friends before, and I just ... I couldn't stand it any more. I couldn't bear to be around him. I couldn't look at his face and the way he just ... and he got hurt a little worse than I intended. It went further than I meant it to, that's all.'

He gets so upset just talking about it that I almost want to hold him, I almost want to tell him it doesn't matter. But this is a version of him I don't know and in some way it scares me and I feel myself drawing away. He sees it too and he comes to me, reaches his hands to me across the space between us and then lets them fall. 'Estrellita, please, believe me; it just happened. And once you do something, it's done and that's it. You can't undo it. You can't take it back, no matter how hard you wish you could. And I do. I've wished it every day from that to this. But never so much as I do right now, now I see the way you're looking at me, and the thought that you'll never feel the same way about me scares me more than anything ever has.' For this horrible, vertiginous moment it looks almost like he's going to cry, and I just know that would be more than I could bear.

I take a deep breath. 'What happened to him? This guy?'

'He just ... he ended up in Med. It was just unlucky that he caught his head against a bench on the way down. They thought he was brain-damaged but he wasn't in the end. He's fine. It wouldn't have been such a big deal if he had defended himself a little but he didn't. He knew how it would end; he wanted his hands clean; he was all about keeping himself out of trouble no matter the cost to others; he ... Look, it doesn't matter, none of it. Not any more.'

'Why were you so angry at him? What did he do?'

'I can't ...' He shakes his head sadly at the floor between us. 'It isn't my story to tell. Just believe me when I tell you that what he did was low. The lowest.'

And I do – I do believe him. God knows there are things that happen on this ship that come from the very darkest places in the hearts of our kind, whatever our kind even is. But it doesn't matter. I know what I have to do, for both our sakes, so I press down on my heart where it is trying to escape and I say, 'I came here to tell you that it's over.'

He freezes, utterly still, looking at me hard for several beats before he takes it in. 'Seren, you don't mean this. You can't mean this.' This is when he comes to me and I let him, his hands on my shoulders, the tops of my arms, my wrists, my hands, repeating in a whisper, 'You can't mean this.'

I hear myself let out a weird sound, a sob, something that was stuck in my throat without me even knowing it was there, and I hear myself speak as if I am far away from it all. 'What do you want me to say? You know what happens to people who don't obey the rules. They'll put one or both of us in Correctional. Or maybe even worse.'

'No, that won't happen. We'll be clever about it. We'll make it work. Somehow.'

But I'm shaking my head, rubbing my thumb along the back of his hand and biting down on my lip like there's any way to stop the tears that keep growing on the end of my nose, dropping off. 'It was never real, Dom. It was just … My grandpa says this happens to everybody. Everybody does this. They … spend a while wishing things were different. Then they realise. They just realise that things are as they are. They are the way they have to be.'

He holds my face between his palms, tries to make me look at him, but I keep pulling away, right up until he leans his forehead against mine. 'This is not you talking; I don't hear you in this at all.'

I close my eyes then; let the tears keep falling, our heads together, his breath against my lips.

'Dom, if we don't do what they tell us, they'll make life hell for us. And you know how weak I am. I'm not strong. I don't want to end up like my mum – so sick I can't even go on living.'

'Seren, that isn't right. That can't be what happened to her. I don't believe it. Don't listen to them.'

I pull away from him then, walk to the viewing window, touch the glass, as cold as something dead. The planet is setting for us now, a semicircle in the bottom of the window, but you can still see that the surface is green, aqua-blue, marbled, surging slowly. I used to see endless forests and beaches when I looked at her, used to feel sure I could SEE them no matter how impossible that might sound. Maybe I could even see people down there; maybe I could even see me, me and Dom, tiny as little fleas. Crazy. But anyway, now I don't; now I see poisonous gas and hot rocks and things that are dying or dead or on their way to being. Now I only see things that are burned up and sucked dry.

He takes my hand, presses it between his. 'We can still find a way to be together, just the way we planned, I know we can.'

But I shake my head and he watches me. 'I wish we could,' I manage to say, even though it hurts, physically, to get the words out, even though I am pushing them out around a big lump of pain, the like of which I have never known. Turns out I was wrong when I thought I knew all there was to know about being sad.

Chapter Eighteen

I don't want to go to the cinema with Ezra; it's always been my place. I even used to go by myself sometimes when Dad or Pan or Em or someone didn't want to go. It was always something I loved to do: escape for a while; get out of here. I've never been with Dom. I guess once I knew him I stopped wanting to escape.

The thing with the movies here is that there's no choice – they just play what they play – and though I can't prove it I have a significant hunch that it's all been cherry-picked to match up to whatever they're wanting you to feel about life, in a version of propaganda that isn't even particularly subtle if you ask me. Like if everyone's really down on on-board life and wishing they were never born they start playing something really feel-good or they pick something that's really pessimistic about life on Earth so that you end up thinking the Ventura isn't so bad. If I had to guess I would imagine that tonight it's going to be something Christmas-related since they're always pretty hot on getting everyone in the mood for it when it rolls around, every arbitrary 365-day cycle, which it will do in about a month.

Anyway, Ezra is getting popcorn and eying me since even though I am thinking all of this, and thinking a lot of things, I am not actually saying anything, and then, waiting for the popcorn still, he says, 'Do you have a favourite film?'

When I feel like this, I am not good at pretending that I'm not. I struggle to even get words out, so I am stuck for a while, not actually able to form sounds, until I say, '*Eternal Sunshine of the Spotless Mind.*'

He leans back, looking relieved that I've said something, anything, but after a little while of looking off to the side, thinking, I guess, he says, 'I don't know that one. What's it about?'

While I'm thinking about it, while I'm figuring out which words I can be bothered to say, he is turning around and getting handed the popcorn by the girl who works the counter, giving her one of these awful half winks he does when he is flirting, and the way she looks back at him makes me feel even more like I wish I wasn't there so I am walking away by the time he catches up with me.

'Where are you going? Tell me about the film. Your

favourite film? Tell me.' He throws a handful of popcorn in his mouth and smiles, holding the little plastic bucket of it out towards me and I shake my head.

'It's about a guy, who breaks up with a girl, and she gets her memory wiped, just basically because she doesn't want to think about him any more – she can't bear to spend every single minute thinking about him because it hurts too much.'

He stops munching then, watches me, watches me watching him, nods. 'OK, and then what happens?'

'She ... I guess she ...' But in the end I can't keep pretending I want to talk to him about it so I say, 'Are we going in or not?'

It turns out I'm wrong about it being a Christmas movie because it's not, and in fact it's one I've seen before and it always used to make me yearn for its sunsets and lakes and long grass and summer and ducks and clapboard houses, but this time I can barely watch it, can barely stay focused on the screen. Instead of losing myself, all I feel is stuck in my itchy uncomfortable seat in the cold, in the dark, in the horrible reverberation through the floor because down here we're close to the engine rooms.

So when it ends I go to the toilet to cry, and maybe that's why when he asks me afterwards I agree to go to View because, somehow, going back to the place I last saw Dom is the closest thing I have to actually being with him, and that seems like the only thing that'll make me feel any better.

There's a few people on View now, unlike the last time I was here, but still not that many. Back when the recons were happening there was so much laughter and buzz in the air; now it's almost like the few people that are here are just going through the motions, or maybe that's just me. Anyway, Ezra's steering me back to a couple of seats in the third row when I see him, right up front but to the right of the main window. Dom. Where we were that night, right in the exact place I last saw him, as if he never left it, but next to him, just finishing off laughing, is Annelise.

It's weird how much it feels like fear – how much I panic, can't breathe, can't speak, only want to run. I turn to Ezra and I am panting, actually fighting for breath and holding the front of his overalls, trying not to look but looking anyway to where she is pushing blonde hair behind her ears while he watches, watches in a way he used to watch me, and I want him to see me then, no I don't, yes I do, and then I want to speak to him, no I don't, yes I do, and was he – has he always been that beautiful?

Ezra has hold of my wrists and when I look at him his lips are moving silently and it is only once I really, really concentrate that I am able to hear him say, 'What is it? What's wrong?'

But all I can do is shake my head and, evidently, breathe so hard that by this time everyone is looking at me, so that I turn to check and yes, they've seen me too. 'Want to go,' I manage to gasp out. 'Get me out of here.'

He does; he tucks me into the curve of his arm and we go.

Out on Main, which is busy, and I'm still not breathing right, Ezra holds on to me, steadies me, makes me look at him and says, 'Breathe with me,' and so I do, following the steady in, pause, out, pause, of the movements of his chest, until I bring my own into line with his, and then he's nodding at me.

'Want me to take you home?'

And because actually I can't stand the idea of being alone with my own thoughts right now I shake my head against his chest and say, 'I want to be somewhere far away.'

And he says, 'OK,' and then, 'Well, I think I know just the place.'

We walk along Main, along to where the lift shafts are, and we stand at one of the access transporters which go straight down to the docks and Ezra swipes his fob and calls it, peeling me off the place on his chest where I seem to be welded and looking at me.

'Where are we going?' I ask, but he just smiles.

We go down so far my ears pop, and it is just us and these two flyboys that get on in Lower West and slap hands with Ezra before standing in the far corner and watching us.

In the docks it is cold as hell, and Ezra waves at a couple of guys before this massive access door opens and we are in this long narrow tube that I can't see the end of. As the lights flick on down its length in sequence I see that there are hatches spaced along it at intervals and it is only now I realise what this must be. Taking my cold hand in his, which is colder, he releases one of the hatches, pulling me through to the inside.

It's this incredibly tight little space, and as he pushes on the lights I start to see that it is white inside, two rows of two seats each, walls, floor and ceiling covered with control panels and the doors of storage lockers. He clambers through and calls me from the front so that I follow him, slide into the co-pilot seat and gaze out of the big front window screen and, because we're on the offside here, facing away from Huxley-3, all we see is space.

'Welcome to Explorer 37.'

'You've flown this?' I ask him.

'Well, no. I just, you know, like to come and sit.'

I nod, look at him sideways while he messes around with one of the screens and puts music on.

'But you know how to fly it?'

'I'm in Flight Training.' He laughs. 'So yeah. Shuttles, utility craft, even the Ventura itself – they all use the same operating system, so it's just a case of learning it.' The music starts then, something I recognise, something we've listened to before somewhere but I don't know when, but really it could have been on any number of occasions seeing as how we've actually been around each other all our lives.

'Have you ever flown for real?' I ask him.

'I'm still learning in the simulators; I won't be qualified in time for any of the final Huxley-3 recons. I have crewed on one, though.'

'You actually went there?'

He laughs, watching my amazement.

'What was it like?'

'It was ... what do you want me to say? You've seen the images; you've heard the reports.'

'I know, but ... tell me, just tell me what it was like to be there, to see a real planet.'

He picks up the control screen and starts swiping at it again, changing the music, infuriating me.

'It had ... ' He shrugs. 'Mass.'

'Mass?' I parrot. 'It had mass?'

'Look, I'm not good at describing things,' he says. 'But since you're now talking to me – how about you tell me something? What upset you so much before? Upstairs?'

'Nothing,' I sigh. 'Nothing worth talking about anyway.'

'Nothing to do with the fish guy, Suarez, who happened to be there with his hot wife?'

My scalp shifts under my hair but I manage to stay calm and, probably because I have no real idea how to deal with it, I only say, 'She's not his wife.'

Which Ezra just laughs at. 'OK, well, look, whoever she is, she probably didn't appreciate hearing about you being seen together in bars, and leaving each other's berths on several occasions, any more than I did.'

I look at him while he pretends to be busy with the screen in his lap.

'Have you told anyone about this?' I ask him, swallowing fear.

'Of course not,' he says. 'I've got a reputation to think about and, whether I like it or not, you're a part of that now. It's better all round if we put this whole fish guy episode behind us as if it never happened. Besides, I guess we've all done a couple of things we shouldn't have.'

Something sits in the silence then but I ignore it; if I actually cared about the answer I guess I would ask him what he means but I don't. Instead I watch the stillness outside, the long galaxy that stretches ahead like a road, like so much road still to travel.

'Haven't you ever sat here and been tempted to just launch?' I ask him.

'No.' He laughs, frowns at me. 'Why would I do that? Why would anyone do that? Where would I go? That would be crazy. And besides, deserters are shot to kill. It would be a ridiculous thing to do.' He studies me for a moment, then says, 'You're not turning into a nutjob on me again, are you, Hemple?'

Which is when I wonder if I might punch him, but instead settle for: 'Shut up, Ezra – you're an idiot.'

And I mean, God, I just feel so tired then, so tired in my bones. I blink, let my head drop back against the plastic seat rest, and just to stop myself from falling asleep I ask, 'Is this where you bring your girls then?'

He thinks about that for a second, then looks at me. 'No idea what you're talking about.'

'Whatever, Lomax.'

And he leans over, touches my jaw, goes as if to kiss me and, though I turn my face away at first, when he goes for it again I let him, but I'm pretty sure it's only because I'm kind of grateful to him, and also so sad.

All of this is why later, once I'm back in North, in the shower room, washing my face, I catch sight of myself in the mirror and for a moment think I'm someone else.

Chapter Nineteen

It's the next morning, a day off, and I'm doing my breakfast mess duty which is basically fine because it's just dishing out eggs for a while followed by a lot of loading up the dishwashers and is all over by ten. When I get out to head back to the berths to get some more sleep Dom is standing there. He is sad and beautiful and leaning the way he does, standing straight slowly when he sees me, pulling his cap off, looking like he's getting ready to say something but when I stop in front of him, watching him, he opens his mouth and nothing comes out. I'm walking away when he takes my hand.

'What are you doing here?' I say, not looking at him.

'I wanted . . .' he starts, but doesn't finish, and when I look at him he is just shaking his head, passing his thumb back and forth across the back of my hand in a way that feels like it will wear a hole. 'I would have done anything to be with you, Seren, remember that. You're the one who said it couldn't happen.'

'We're moving on with our lives,' I say, quoting Captain Kat I think, and regretting it instantly. All the same he pulls on my arm until I am close to him, not touching but almost, the heat of his arm warming mine, cool breath on my neck and he says, 'Te extraño, estrellita,' and then, 'All I do is miss you, do you know that?'

'Yeah.' I laugh. 'I can tell. It's really obvious when I see you out with her that all you're really doing is missing me.'

'Seren, you were there with HIM.'

'I know that.'

'So that's OK, but it's not OK for me?'

'I'm not the one standing here saying I miss you.'

'I could see you were upset last night, Seren. You expect me not to come to you?'

'Yes, I do expect that. I'm fine. I don't want you coming to me, OK?' And my voice gets all dumb and warbly and I try to wipe away the stupid tears that are burning my eyeballs, unstoppable, without him noticing, but I guess that never really works, does it? And while I'm standing there, shaking hard, he runs his hand down the back of my hair, picks up my ponytail, holds it to his lips, breathes in once slowly – all of this I know without looking at him; all of this I know because it's something he's done before – then he smooths it back into place, trails his hand down my back then up again, takes hold of my shoulder.

'I keep wanting to ask you whether you kissed her last night,' I say to the floor just in front of me. 'And then I realise I don't ever want to hear you lying to me again.' I try to walk away, just as he pulls me into him, closes his arms around me, stops my shaking or makes it worse, I'm not sure which, and we are right in the corner, up against the cold side of a vending machine, in one of the places where the sound from the engine rooms resonates, alone it seems, and I wonder why it is that we can't just stay here for ever.

'Just tell me he'll be good to you,' he says then, his mouth against my ear, his voice cracked in a way that makes me ache inside, that makes me blink a stream of hot tears on to the front of my overalls. 'All I need to know is that he knows how lucky he is to have you.'

I struggle then, elbow him, and he releases me; he doesn't make it difficult, just lets me go and then watches me turn back to him, looking back like it's the last time, and he is just horribly beautiful right then, draped into the corner with the flush along his jaw and cheekbone that shows even through the darkness of his skin, with a shine in his eyes that threatens to make me lose it.

'Just so you know,' I say, struggling to form words. 'It was NOT me that said it couldn't happen. It was life. It was this place. It was the system. So don't ever say or even THINK that it was me, because it wasn't.'

Then, just when I'm walking away, I stop. 'Please will you promise me something?' Out of the corner of my eye I see him nod, and I swallow, press my hand against my stomach, breathe, wonder if I'm really going to be able to say this and then I do. 'Don't come to me again; don't even speak to me. We just can't be characters in each other's lives right now, Dom, maybe not ever. Will you … can you … I need … please will you do that for me?'

And though actually all he says is, 'Seren, don't, please,' I know that what he's really doing is agreeing, I know it by the tone in his voice, I know it by the way he pinches his nose and doesn't look at me again, I know it by the way I walk away and all I hear is the hyperdrive sound as it echoes in the vents while Tamerlan, the guy who does my route on Saturdays, passes me to refill the vending machine with Nutso bars and watches both of us, me and then Dom, leave in opposite directions.

Chapter Twenty

I'm out at this bar with Ezra, double-dating with Emme and Leon, and basically all four of us are ignoring each other and just sitting under red and green flashing Christmas lights and watching everyone take it in turns on the karaoke. At some point Ezra and Leon go to get drinks and Emme takes my hand, too hard.

'I'm so excited,' she tells me.

'What about?' I say, blankly.

She looks shocked. 'Your wedding of course!'

'Oh right.'

She doesn't seem sure what to do with my lack of reaction, but ploughs on. 'I know you have Pan, but just let me know if you need another bridesmaid, OK?'

I blink at her, say nothing. What is there to say? I feel like I've lived a whole life she knows nothing about, like I'm a new person that she wouldn't recognise, like our friendship belongs to this whole other time that no longer exists. Maybe some of all this is on my face because she draws back, moves away, curling her lip a little as they arrive back.

Leon talks about his Service, which sounds an awful lot like waste management, and this makes me think of Dom and so it takes me a while to tune the conversation back in but when I do they are talking about the wedding again. Just because I can't go down that road, I interrupt.

'When will you guys get married?' I ask, turning the tables, watching them both shift a little and glance at each other before Leon says, 'I think we'll stick with tradition and do it at the end of our Service. I know a lot of people like to do it a little later or earlier these days but – what can I say? – I'm a conventional guy.' He reaches for Emme's hand then and squeezes it while she does this cheesy smile and pats at his fingers awkwardly. 'We're not as desperate to get baby-making as you two lovebirds!' And he does this stupid laugh and everyone joins in except me because I'm too busy cringing.

It turns out Leon put his and Emme's names down for the karaoke and when they come up she screams and spends like half a minute pretending she doesn't want to go, before bounding up there and duetting that Christmas song everyone loves about giving hearts as gifts with him. I watch them awkwardly stepping from foot to foot and looking in each other's eyes and messing up their harmonies and laughing it all off for a while before I say, 'I can imagine them being happy together in the end. They're as corny as each other,' while Ezra makes a face, and then I add, 'By the way, I hate these karaoke places. I can never get over how futile it is. It's depressing.'

He shakes his head. 'Hemple, you think everything's depressing.'

Which is when my pod beeps in a call, and after listening to the person on the other end, I tell him, 'I have to go.'

When I get to Med, I have no idea where I'm going. I go to the waiting room, which is the only bit I've ever really seen except for the inside of Dr Mad's office but I am so freaked out I guess the girl at the desk there thinks I'm having one of my episodes and doesn't actually listen to what I'm trying to say. Just then Emme's dad, Doc Wong, comes striding down the orange-lit passageway to the left and he sees me through the round window of the double doors, sees me just in the split second that I am deciding not to be here, that I am turning to go. Like he knows what's going through my mind he comes to the door and pushes it open gently, watches me duck under his arm and then nods up the corridor.

'I know you must be scared,' he says to my back as I head towards the door he's pointed out. 'But I'm pretty sure you're not as scared as she is.'

As I get close I hear Pandora – yelling, hissing, shouting – keeping up this steady *herrrr herrr herrr* sound like it's some kind of mantra, and suddenly it seems like opening these doors is going to spark off a chain of events that I will be completely unable to control. But I don't even know if it's the thought of that that stops me, or whether it's just fear: fear of blood, fear of pain, fear of death, fear of suddenly realising that we can be broken and smashed to pieces and destroyed. Lucky then, really, that a nurse chooses that exact moment to come out looking for something and sees me.

'Are you her sister? Good, then get these on and come in.'

So a few minutes later I am in these hideous green pyjamas and a mask and I am standing there next to Pan while she yells and sweats and swears and doesn't even know it's me until she quietens down for a minute and I take her hand and she squeezes.

'Oh my God; thank God you're here.' A sentence I've never heard from her and never expected to and at the same time she is fighting tears, her pretty lips stretched over too-dry teeth. 'They keep making me listen to the heartbeat and it keeps slowing down so I told them I don't want to hear it any more but all I can think about is that she's going to die and … *herrr herrr herrr* …' This is the point at which she is having another contraction and she turns away from me, and her gaze is kind of middle-distance but not looking at anything and she is squeezing my hand so hard I wonder if it might break but all I feel is relief.

As soon as it subsides she starts gabbling again as if it never happened. 'Because, you see, there's this woman, another woman in the bay next door, and they just had to pull the baby out and she was screaming so loud and I just don't want that to happen to me, because—'

'OK, Pandora,' says the nurse then, all business. 'You are nearly fully dilated. Not much longer and it will be time to push.'

'Time to push?' says Pan, so pale her lips are almost blue, so wide-eyed, sweat puddling at the base of her neck.

'Yes, time to push,' I say, trying to sound cheerful. 'That's good, right? That means it's almost over. You're nearly there!'

'Nearly there?' she repeats, stunned. 'But where is Cain? Where is he?' And this, of course, is the whole reason that I am here, since no one has been able to even raise him on his pod these past few hours and none of us can account for him, so my dad is currently scouring the plaza and anywhere else we can think of to look, and this is when the pain starts again and she is gripping my hand, and when it's over again she yells, 'I don't want to do this any more!' and starts to cry.

And I should say something encouraging but all I can think is that if I were her I wouldn't want to do it either.

'Something's going to go wrong,' she wails, after the next contraction nearly kills us both. 'I'm so scared the baby's going to be deformed.'

I almost laugh. 'The baby's not going to be deformed – why would she be?'

'I never told you.' She grimaces, fat tears spilling down her cheeks. 'I never told anyone, except Cain.'

'You never told me what?'

'I was too ashamed.' And then it starts again, and she hisses through this one, never taking her eyes off mine, and when it's over she says, 'The baby was a natural.'

'Natural? What, like . . . ?'

She carries on crying, spitting a bit when she talks. 'When we went to do our implantation they scanned me to check I was ready and stuff and I was . . . already pregnant.'

I frown. 'Well, but, they checked her and stuff, right? They only let you go through with it if they scan and test the baby and everything's cool, right?'

She nods just before another contraction grips her, takes her like a wave crashing.

'Then everything's going to be fine,' I tell her afterwards, squeezing her hand between both of mine, then laughing a little. 'Why would you be ashamed about that? I think it's nice.'

She laughs too, through tears. 'You would,' she says, and then, 'Please don't tell Dad or Grandpa.'

I don't recognise Doc Wong when he steps in in his green pyjamas, until he speaks. 'Seren, your dad's here. No luck finding Cain but he's asking if you would like him or Olivia to take over here.'

And I am just about to say yes when Pan grabs at the front of my scrubs and hauls me in against her. 'NO!' she shrieks. 'No, Seren, I want it to be you. Don't leave me, please.'

So of course I nod, of course I say, 'I won't – I'm staying.'

A little later, after a period that seems simultaneously like a matter of seconds and a thousand years, the nurse is pushing one of Pan's legs up and telling me to do the same, telling me to pull one of her legs over my shoulder and force it up towards her, supposedly to help the baby come out, and I mean, I do it, because what else am I going to do? And it seems like way too much pain and pushing as I watch the veins that pulse out on Pan's forehead and throat, and it takes so long, so long, to get to the point where the baby's head is even out to the extent that I am begging them to make it stop because she is getting so tired, and I am thinking that there is no way this is right, no way this is how it's meant to be, and then, nuts as it is, suddenly, amazingly, magically, she is here. She is here.

My niece is long and thin, purple and pink and streaked in red and white, laid out on Pan's chest, where Pan clings to her, pulls her in, plants kisses on her dark, damp hair, and she keeps saying, 'Hello, my darling. Hello, my darling.'

And I know now why people think this moment is amazing, because here we are meeting this person who is going to be a part of our lives, who is going to continue our family, and right now we know nothing at all about her except the fact that she is this little bloody being with this full head of hair and she is ... not crying. And this is the point at which they scoop her up and take her away and we start to wonder.

'Is she OK?' says Pan, and I nod without even thinking, but she says again, 'Is she OK?' and when I look unsure, she yells, 'Well go to her!'

And so suddenly I am with her, the baby, watching while they suck at her little mouth and nose, while she squirms and is slimy on a white towel and still doesn't cry, at which point Pan says, 'Seren, talk to me – just tell me!'

And, totally unsure, I say, 'She's fine, Pan, she's fine!' and I look at the nurse who manages to nod even though I'm pretty sure it's still touch and go, but anyway, look, things get better. This woman, this tiny, brand-new Hemple woman is NOT someone who is going to give up without a fight. And when they finally wrap her up and put her in my arms I am looking at her gorgeous mouth, her long elegant fingers, and I am thinking she is someone I know already, someone who is part of me, of the fabric of me in ways I don't understand. Then I take her to her mother, and I lay her in Pan's arms, and I see why people do this, why people want to do this, even when it has become something so detached from the way it's supposed to be, because this is something that is infinite, so lasting, and you can tell from the way she pulls her close and says, 'Oh my baby girl, oh my darling baby girl,' that even though she doesn't know her at all yet, she already loves her.

A little while later they let Dad and Olivia in, and they stand there making noises down at the new baby, who has her dark fluffy hair all sticking up and perfect little lips and who my sister calls Deborah. Dad is all overcome; well, what passes for overcome with my dad, which is to say that you can tell he's feeling something and he's maybe a little wet-eyed, but it's Olivia who holds Deborah and also Olivia who looks into Pan's face and asks her all this stuff about how the birth went. And then later, just when she's about to go, Olivia takes hold of my arm and asks me if I know anything about where Cain is and when I say he must be out on a utility flight or something (more likely something) she says, 'We must all take good care of her in these early days,

Seren – we must support her. We must bear in mind what happened to your mum, OK?'

And even though part of me thinks it's weird that she would say that, to me of all people, in some ways I am relieved that someone just went ahead and said it.

Later, after Pan has fed her and the lights in the room are low and Deborah is in this plastic cot thing they've given her and making these little sucky movements with her mouth in her sleep, the door sighs open and someone says, 'Knock, knock,' which I always think is the dumbest thing anyone could ever do. When I turn, it's Ezra.

'Ezra, come in.' Pan reaches her hand out to him and he takes it, kisses it, and says, 'Congratulations, Mama, amazing news.'

She practically purrs. And then he goes to the cot, stares down at Deborah, moves the blanket a little to see her face and manages to wake her so that she is making fists, making this little struggly noise, and I'm just thinking about what a total idiot he is when he picks her up like it is something he's done a million times before and she lies there against his arm, all calm while he talks to her, saying things like, 'There you are then. There you are, little girl,' and stuff that makes zero sense while all the time she lies along his arm and watches his face like it's a screen.

'You've done this before,' coos Pan, raising her

eyebrows at me, and like it's something they've planned and rehearsed he comes to me, puts his free arm across my shoulders. And it's only because he happens to ask me if I'm OK then that I look up at him, which means he can kiss me just once in this casual way but it's like, man, I don't know, there's this moment that I feel myself lean into him a little, melt almost, thinking that I can see in some ways that he is right for me, that I can feel the ways our bodies seem to fit. Dom was always too tall for me, thirty centimetres taller at least, everything in the wrong place and a literal pain in the neck for both of us as I pulled him down to me and he hunched over, bent his knees, whatever else, to get down to my level. Like something that didn't fit.

Cain calls finally and Pan cries even talking to him on the pod so we get out of the way, but just when I'm leaving she pulls me into a hug, and it is maybe the first in four or five years.

'I love you,' she says, another first in forever, and then, 'Thank you.' And because I hear tears I head out of the door, and straight into Ezra who slides his hand around my waist, kisses my neck, rubs my back and says, 'Well done, Hemple.'

'Yeah, that was ...' But of course I can't think how to finish; I just shake my head, stunned into silence. And this is why when he kisses me, I kiss him, and I am thinking: at least I like this about him. I like the way he moves. I like his skin, pliant as plastic. I like the cool, heavy lay of his hair against my palms. I do want him; it's not that I don't want him. And that means something, right?

Which is when someone passes us, saying, 'Excuse me,' as she goes, double-taking a little, which I guess is hardly surprising, and it's only as she gets to the end of the Med corridor and turns one last time that I realise it is Annelise and on her face is this tight little smile, and then she is gone.

Chapter Twenty-One

'You're coming tomorrow, right?' I ask Mariana, the day before my wedding, ignoring the sick feeling I have to swallow down.

She stops scrubbing at the dirty flap on the machine we're cleaning, which is up in Command, near the decryption office, and studies my face. 'You want me to?' she asks.

'Of course. You're my friend.'

She raises an eyebrow. 'In that case, I'll be there.' After she gets back to scrubbing the machine she asks, 'You looking forward to it?'

And I don't answer; I just study the wiry side of the sponge I'm supposed to be using until she says, 'You're doing the right thing, amiga. Toe the line. Anything else is just more trouble than you can handle.'

More silence, in which I notice the sound of the Epsilon signal that seeps out from under the nearest door and think about the people who sit in there for year after year of their lives wondering what it's trying to tell us.

'How is he?' I ask her.

She stops her scrubbing again, sighs, puts the sponge on the floor, then looks at me. 'What do you want me to say?'

I shake my head because I don't even know. 'That he's fine,' I tell the floor.

She pulls her hat off, swipes the sweat off her forehead with her arm. 'Then he's fine,' she says.

'I need to go,' I tell her, hearing the break in my voice. 'Remember I said I need to go early today.'

'Oh right, yeah - why?'

'I need to ... it's my egg harvest.'

We watch each other in silence.

'You want me to come with you?' she asks.

I shake my head, force a smile. 'Thanks, though.'

Waiting outside the Fertility laboratory up in Science, a floor above Med, I watch the instructional video that plays on a loop, while this couple I've seen around sit next to me, hands loosely linked. The video's all a smiling woman and her two perfect smiling kids and there's this music and it keeps going on about how your optimum eggs will be selected and kept for you until the time that's right for you and how it takes all the risk and danger and pain out of the whole thing. And then there's this sleazy bit with the couple getting all frisky in their quarters and I guess the general vibe is that you get to pair bond with your husband now that you have a low risk of natural pregnancy. Not that it's a hundred per cent because they actually have to leave some of your eggs, which mean it's more like eighty-five. People do get pregnant with naturals from time to time, which means your foetus will be screened and deleted if necessary. And apart from anything else it's a pretty great way to make sure there's no way you'll ever think about sleeping with someone you're not supposed to.

I guess I think about Ezra then, and I realise that I am gradually getting over the idea of hating him. It's only when I start thinking about talking to him, about spending the rest of my life with him, that I feel all the oxygen rush out of the room.

BEEP. My name appears in red letters. Like something that once happened in a dream.

Inside, cold, colder than ever maybe, in a flapped-open Med-issue night dress and with my legs in glacial metal stirrups and blinded by this big round light, I am suddenly hopelessly and full-on crying, heaving sobs, while this nurse watches me, just two dead eyes over a surgical mask.

'Don't you want to get married?'

She is stroking at my ankle in a way that is just corrosive, and this is when the doctor walks in and says,

'OK, Miss Hemple, let's set you on the road to life as a happily married woman,' before watching me cry some more.

I am spending tonight at Pan's and when I get back there she is staring at me, holding these two glasses of the fizzy wine we use for celebrations midway between us and letting her shoulders slump. 'Why do you look so sad? It's all part of getting married! Let's celebrate!'

'Where's Cain?'

'With the guys from Flight, taking Ezra out of course! Last night of freedom and everything.'

'Right.' I nod. 'That figures.'

'He swore he wouldn't keep him out too late – don't worry!'

'I'm not worried.'

'Yeah right!' She laughs, being an idiot, drunk on a sip after nine months of no drinking at all, which is probably why she says, 'So, Seren, off the record, what was really going on with you and Domingo Suarez?'

'Off the record?' I raise my eyebrows. 'So you won't be going straight to Grandpa this time?'

'I never did that!'

'Whatever, Pan.'

'You know that was Dad,' she says, sliding in next to me on the galley bench and lowering her voice. 'He was worried about you. So, what was really going on?'

I look at her and for this long moment I wonder if she is asking me an honest question, one that I can actually give an honest answer to, but she isn't, not really, so in the end I sigh and say, 'Nothing. What do you mean?'

And because we both know I'm lying she just looks at me, and then says, 'Well, I'm glad to hear you say that, because he is so not worth it anyway.'

'In whose opinion?'

'Mine. Mine and probably just about anyone else's you care to mention.'

'Because?'

'Because ...' She looks thrown by this, and it's no wonder really, considering the fact that if I was dead set on covering this up I shouldn't even be asking these questions, but I just can't help it. She tucks her hair behind her ears and widens her eyes at me. 'Because trouble follows him, it always has. Even just after we left Education there was some massive deal with him, I can't remember what, but it definitely wasn't good. Something to do with that weird cousin of his. I remember he was in a lot of trouble with Security over it for quite a while. You don't want to be associated with that, Seren, even as a friend.'

'Listen, Pan, if I want your advice I'll ask for it, OK?'

She laughs. 'I mean, I'm not blind, of course I can see the appeal, but he really hasn't got a lot going for him other than that.'

198

I shouldn't, but I lose it. 'Don't you dare talk about him that way. You know nothing about him!'

She looks shocked but manages to laugh. 'If this is the best you can do at pretending it never happened, you've got problems.'

She's right of course, so there isn't a lot to say; all I can do is avoid her eyes, burning into me as they are, while the silence grows.

'Just tell me you didn't sleep with him,' she says, messing with the little puddle of spilt wine around her glass.

'Of course not!'

'You sure about that?'

'I said no!' I leave a pause, just a little too long, before I add, 'I hardly know him, remember?'

She just laughs, and falls asleep in her bed with Deborah about an hour later, and I am left to sit in her galley and shiver even though I'm wearing my jacket and one of her big pregnancy smocks over the top. I find the outside view channel on her screen and sit down in front of it, watching this one star that sits right in the centre of the screen, knowing that it is Eridani, still two hundred and sixty-two years distant, and feeling like I am dust already, just so much dust. Fizzy wine does this to me. It makes other people happy; it makes me feel like dust.

The door buzzes just as I am pushing a tear off my

cheek. Assuming that Cain is struggling to punch in his key code I go to it, open it, and am in the middle of telling him he's an idiot when I realise it isn't him.

It's Dom.

'I know you told me not to come to you, but ... ' He shrugs, apologetic, leaning against the door jamb, face on the back of his hand. 'I had to,' he says, and then just looks at me, looks at me looking at him, looks at me starting to cry. He shakes his head. 'I'm so sorry. I shouldn't have come. It was selfish.' And he turns to go.

'Please don't go,' I say, my voice an ugly wail that echoes down the outside corridor as he comes back to me, and catches me just before my knees give out.

Once the door is closed we stand there together, watching each other's faces, listening to all the words we aren't saying. I realise I am holding his hand and lift it up in front of me, his one in both of mine, his large and strong, pale under his short nails. So beautiful. I raise it to my lips and he slides it along my cheek, my jaw, the back of my neck, into my hair, pulling me into his chest and resting his mouth on my hairline, sighing there.

'Are you here to tell me not to marry him?' I ask, my voice still broken.

'No,' he says, and I hear the strain in his voice through his chest. 'I'm here to tell you that you marrying him isn't going to stop me loving you. Or missing you. Or spending the rest of my life wishing you were mine.'

And I look up at him and say, 'I am yours; I'll always be yours,' and he kisses me then, long and steady and strong, and I pull him into me, against me, like I could make him a part of me somehow, and in between kisses I say, 'I'm sorry.'

And picking me up, carrying me to the galley bench, he shakes his head. 'Don't be sorry.'

'I can't live without you.'

'Me neither.'

'I don't know why I thought I could.'

And he smiles, sliding on to the bench next to me and pulling my legs across his lap. 'I don't know either.'

'Stop copying what I say.' I laugh, stroking his dark hair down over his ears, running my fingers along his eyelashes, suddenly so happy to have him near me.

'I'm not copying you, I just … I feel the same way. You're saying everything I'm thinking, just like you always do.' And after that, after trying really hard, we finally stop kissing each other long enough for me to say, 'Do you know how many times I think of things I want to tell you? You're the only person I want to talk to. On any day. On every day. I have this, like, long list of things to talk to you about I've been keeping on my pod.'

He laughs. 'What, it's an actual list?'

'Yeah – is that weird?' I make a face and he leans in to kiss me, hums against my lips.

'No,' he says. 'It's lovely. Show it to me. I want to see it.'

'You tell me things first. Tell me what you've been doing,' I say, with my head leant back over his arm where it lies along the back of the bench.

He shakes his head. 'Nothing. Nothing but missing you, estrellita. I heard about your new niece.'

I smile at him then, but feel it fade. It's just like it always was, except it isn't. 'How did you know I was here?'

'Mariana told me.'

I nod, then realise how hard my heart is beating and try to swallow, breathe through it. 'Dom, what are we going to do?'

And right now is when the door goes again and we look at each other, wide-eyed, before I get up and go to it, holding the com and saying, 'Who is it?' before hearing Cain reply, 'Let me in, Seren, jeez.' He's obviously wasted.

So I buzz him in while Dom is getting up from the bench and coming over and as soon as the door opens Cain basically falls into the room on his face.

'I'm fine,' is what he says then, into the floor.

'You should go,' I tell Dom.

'No way,' he says, shaking his head. 'I'm not letting you deal with this alone.'

So we struggle with Cain for a bit until we get him

sat on the bench, then we get some water out of the dispenser and try to convince him to drink it while he rolls his eyes and talks too loud and we shush him so he doesn't wake Deborah and it is only after a while that he slings his arm around Dom's neck and says, 'Suarez, what are you doing here, man? You've been told about this! You're crazy, man! I've always known you were crazy! This guy,' he continues, pulling Dom's head into a lock, 'this guy and I are the same generation, you know that? Like hermanos! Generation 81, man! Lo mejor, am I right? I love this guy. So it does NOT surprise me AT ALL that you do too, sis. Not at all. I just wish, I only wish, that things were different. If only, huh? Or if only everyone struck pay dirt like I did with Pan. You know, hermano, you know she was always the only one for me, the one I wanted, the one I secretly prayed for every night. And I was the lucky one. How many people get lucky the way I did? The girl of my dreams, man!' And this is when he just slumps down over the table in front of him, rubbing his face along his forearms.

I watch him and decide that, since he seems to be in the mood for truth-telling, I may as well do a little of my own. 'Cain, if that's the way you feel, why are you such a terrible husband?' To which Dom laughs but I carry on. 'It's true! You suck! You missed your own baby being born because you were getting drunk in some rec room!'

Cain is rolling his head against his arms. 'You don't get it, man – you have no idea how hard it is to just lie. Lie and lie and lie some more. And all because you have to keep some pointless secret and you have no real idea why. I can't look at her, this beautiful woman I have loved all my life and never lied to, never even wanted to lie to, and just … LIE.' He sits up, makes a face like he is tasting something bad, shakes his head. 'Can't do it.'

And all this time Dom and I are sitting on either side of him but watching each other until, even though I'm scared to know the truth, I say, 'What were you lying about, Cain?'

And he says, 'It's … she's beautiful.'

And I say, 'Who is?'

And he says, 'Huxley-3.'

And even though, obviously, there's this big stunned silence then, and this moment where Dom and I just look at each other, the first thing that comes to my mind is to say, 'Sure, Cain, whatever,' because, surely, I mean, there's no way. I was thinking affair, drink problem, I don't know what, but this is … too big to even think about.

'No, no, I mean it,' he says. 'I'm tired of the lies. It's true. She is like everything you ever dreamed of and more. Beaches, turquoise seas like you wouldn't believe, forest even; I saw forest, trees, everything. She's it. She's what we've only heard about, and always longed for.'

'But ... but we were told ...' I manage.

'I know. I know what you were told. That's what we were told to tell you. You know the spiel: First Contact, communication with Epsilon Eridani, blah, blah, blah, that whole thing. Nothing can get in the way, schedule to keep and whatever. It was like ... I don't know ... they told us it was too dangerous for anyone to know that there was this, like, crazy beautiful place down there. Because like, OBVIOUSLY, everyone would want to go see it and then there'd probably be people getting sick and, you know, deaths and stuff.'

'Deaths?'

'Yeah, they reckon there could be microbes and chemicals and whatnot that Science have never seen before down there which could basically kill you.'

'Microbes that could kill you?'

'Yeah.' He licks his lips, looks around, drops his voice, suddenly seems more focused than he has in a long time, skinful of alcohol notwithstanding. 'But, here's the thing: they don't know. Science don't KNOW, not really. So what if it's not the way they say? They can only guess at any of this stuff, and meanwhile here we are, steaming back into the DARK, and back there, back there ...' He waves his hand somewhere behind us before it hits the wall. 'Ah man, seriously, I saw it. I flew over this beach.' His voice actually breaks then like he might cry and he has this squinched up face like someone in pain. 'You should have seen it. Sand so white, like salt, blue sea … it was … it just … it made me want to be there, even if it was going to kill me. It made me want to go down there just to die on it. It would … ah man, you know, it actually made me feel like it might have been worth it.' And with this he falls forward again, face against the table, completely out.

Dom and I look at each other and I say, 'We have to tell everyone.'

He shakes his head, smiles, but sadly. 'We can't.'

'Why?'

He indicates Cain with a nod of his head. 'They'd know it was him who told us.'

'But this is … this is HUGE. People need to … they need to know.'

Dom sighs. 'Do they?'

I feel my jaw drop. 'Of course they do! Dom, this is our life. This is the only life we're ever going to get, and they lied to us. They stopped us from experiencing something amazing just so we wouldn't expect more. More than this darkness and this cold. We could make them stop; we could make them turn around.'

He gets up, comes to me, pulls me up into his arms and rests his chin on my head. 'And then what?'

'They'd have to … they'd have to let us visit.'

I feel him shake his head. 'Seren, all they'd do is make everyone think they were risking their lives and the majority of people on this ship wouldn't chance it.' He kisses the side of my hair, my ear, my neck. 'Most people on Ventura are pretty comfortable with their lives. I know you don't get it, but that's because you're different. You're not like other people.'

I pull away and look at him then, look at him for so long that something shifts.

'It wouldn't be enough,' I say.

'What wouldn't?' He tilts his head.

'Visiting wouldn't be enough, anyway. Even if we did risk it, knowing what we're missing would probably just make it harder to live without, wouldn't it?'

He sighs, looks so sad it makes me ache. 'I guess it might,' he says, and we watch each other, tangling our fingers, and he leans down to me and when he kisses me then I pull him in, hard, harder, tears forming in my eyes which fall when I close them against all the things we can't control, all the things we can't say, all the things we can't do, all the things we've known that we'll have to give up, all the things we'll never be able to forget, all the things we've felt that mean we'll never be able to settle for less.

Chapter Twenty-Two

I guess on the morning of the wedding I fall asleep for maybe an hour on the bench in the galley, my face against Dom's neck, and when I open my eyes he turns his face to me, puts his lips on mine, whispers, 'Good morning,' and I realise that I have been dreaming, dreaming about flying, flying along over water, over water that is as flat as glass and bouncing sky back up at me. And in the dream I am scared, but breathless with possibility.

I know he is about to leave when he carefully smooths my hair before kissing me, resting his nose against mine and looking straight into my eyes. He asks me whether I know what I have to do and I don't have to answer because we both know I do, but all the same I don't let go of his hand, can't, even when he is standing by the door with his other hand on the button that opens it. I am holding his hand still and looking at it and just thinking about how beautiful it is, how it is literally the most beautiful hand I have ever seen, how much I want it on me, always, and I feel my eyes fill with tears, and so I make him go then, even push him a little because getting like this will only make me more afraid. The stakes are suddenly so high, you see, higher than they've ever been in my life. I am about to have to lose him again, and I'm not sure I can bear it.

Cultural have sent someone to do my hair and she plaits it first, plaits it before wrapping it round my head like a rope and all the time I am shaking, shaking so hard that in the end Pan tells me I'm more nervous than she was. My dress arrives and it is white and heavy and looks like all the others but, regardless, when I put it on Pan cries and then my dad appears in his full-dress uniform. Tucking one of the orchids he has brought from Production into my hair and handing me the other one for his lapel he acts like, I don't know what, like this is the best – or maybe worst – day of his life. Whichever it is, he has actual tears in his eyes, which just makes it worse.

We walk there, to the drill hall, a cameraman from Cultural following us and Pan trailing in her blue dress on bridesmaid duty while Cain carries Deborah behind. And it's OK, I can do it, I can keep walking, I can keep putting one foot in front of the other until I get to the door and I see Dom, the back of him as he stands next to Mariana in the last row, turning only slightly as I come in, but it is that split second of eye contact we make that makes me falter, makes me freeze, makes me turn back to Pan and say, 'I just need a minute,' because even though I asked him to be there, even though I told him I couldn't go through with it without him, suddenly the idea of standing there in front of him and telling our whole world that I love someone else seems impossible. And now I'm here and there is the music and bile rising in my throat and this cramp gripping me and suddenly Mariana is next to me, holding my arm in her cold hand, tiny but strong.

'Are you OK?'

'No.'

I can tell from the way she looks at me that she knows and she says to Pan, 'Let me talk to her, OK?' and it is only because Deborah is just starting to cry that we are able to walk away without her saying much.

Ten metres away from the drill hall door, Mariana eases me against the wall for support and peers into my eyes like there might be something written there. 'What's wrong?'

And all I can do is shake my head and say, 'I can't do this.'

Even though it looks like she knew what I was going to say before I did, she grips my arms, looks around, shifts position and sighs. Then she says, 'What are you thinking? You know you're not the only one who ever felt this way, you know that, but you also know that trying to fight the way things are will only bring trouble to you, and to the people you love. Amiga, I have been where you are, I've loved someone for real, and I paid for it, and I don't want that to happen to you. Or to my cousin. Please do what you have to do, Seren, for all of us. We're stuck here, you know, whether we like it or not. We have nowhere else to go.'

'You're saying this like you think it's the right thing to do. But you don't. You didn't do it. So why are you telling me to?' I study her then, the violet skin beneath her dark eyes, the way she bites down on her lip while she thinks about what to say.

'Because I've spent most of my life since then wishing I hadn't made the choices I did. Maybe if I hadn't, I wouldn't have to carry so much sadness around with me.'

I shake my head. 'Your life doesn't seem so bad. It's better to be alone than to spend your life with someone you don't want to be with.'

There are people, latecomers, moving past us then, all happy until they see us and their smiles fade, turning into backwards glances over their shoulder as they head inside.

'If it worked for you ...' I take her hands in mine. 'Why wouldn't it work for me?'

She shakes her head. 'You actually think it worked for

me? Well where is he, then? The guy I loved – where is he? I'll tell you where – he did what was expected of him and now he's married and has kids and is living his life and I'm just . . . ' She shakes her head.

Right then I notice this strip bulb above us and the way it ticks on off on off, and it makes me think of Pete, this guy we know in Maintenance, and how his whole job, all day every day for the last thirty-something years, has basically been changing light bulbs, walking around the Ventura changing the light bulbs as they go out, using them up just as quick as Production can make them, and there aren't even words for how pointless that is.

Her cold hand is on my forearm again and she makes me look at her. 'Look, Seren, just go in there and do what you have to do. Please. I care about you and I care about Domingo, and I'm begging you to do what's right for now and the rest of it can be worked out later.'

And I can't explain it, but somehow the way she is looking at me makes me breathe, makes me stand back up, stand straight, and after a minute more I am somehow able to walk back to where Pan is jiggling Deborah and questioning me with her eyes, and when we get there I nod and so she hands Deborah to Cain and we go.

I walk up to the front with the music playing and Jonah's standing there in his cassock because, of course,

Captain Kat couldn't resist wangling it to be him in charge of the ceremony, and though he's smiling there's this fear in his eyes like even he's not too sure I'm going to make it. Then I look at where Ezra is standing, and he doesn't look back at me. I only see the back of his head until I am standing there and he turns to me once in a sly side glance and I know it makes no sense but this is when I KNOW what I am going to do, no matter what anyone thinks, no matter what Dom and I agreed, no matter what hell might rain down on us. I refuse to spend my life wishing I was somewhere else. I refuse to spend my entire life missing him.

So this is when I say, 'I'm not doing this,' and although Ezra turns to me right away and says, 'What?' it seems to take a lot longer than that for people to really believe what's actually happening, and by this time I have turned to Dom, I have found him in the crowd and, though his face is frozen with fear and also this expression like he's just about to say something, just knowing he is there with me makes me feel calm, and so I turn to Ezra and I say, 'I just can't stand here and lie. You might be OK with it, but I'm not.'

'What do you ... what?' And he does look genuinely confused, and for a moment I almost feel bad for him.

Cultural are getting all this on camera and Captain Kat is sitting in the front row with her smile slipping and her eyes shifting to the side, and most of the people watching are stunned in this O-mouthed, slapped-fish way and, seeing Emme's wide eyes over Ezra's shoulder, I almost falter.

By this time Captain Kat is standing, the irises of her eyes ghoulishly pale and her mouth struggling to make words, but not for long, as she spins and addresses the congregation. 'Unfortunately, my son's bride is suffering from a bad case of the jitters and we will have to postpone their vows. Please forgive her this wobble; it's very overwhelming beginning your Union, as many of us will recall.'

And so this is how, even though in the early hours of this very morning we agreed that the only thing we could do was go along with it, go along with it and do what we were supposed to do and bide our time until we could make a plan for how to be together, I do everything Dom told me not to do, I do just the thing he said would only bring us pain and trouble, and it's already obvious that he was right.

So now I am in this little side room, the place where the priests get ready for mass which they hold in the drill hall every Sunday, and it's this pretty standard grey office, really, apart from the hanging cassocks and crosses on the wall, but it's where Jonah brought me once he realised he ought to do something. There's this moment when we first get in there when I am hyperventilating so hard that I start not being able to see straight and Jonah has his hand on my arm, patting it, patting it while he is clearly so annoyed with me that he can't meet my eye.

'I didn't have any choice,' I manage to tell him through my heaving breaths.

He glances at me. 'OK, Seren, if that's what you think,' he says, taking a step away from me and parting the curtain a little so he can peer out at the seething mass of general murmur outside.

'And what do YOU think?' I manage to ask him through my rising nausea.

He sighs, and suddenly it's completely eerie, standing there with the double of Ezra while he does and says things that Ezra wouldn't. 'I think if you pretend to be happy about something long enough, you'll find in the end that you are. But it's a bit late for advice at this point, don't you think?'

As I look at him then, there is this shifting in my ears that means suddenly all I can hear is the engines and everything else is quiet, and just as I am realising that I am going to either pass out or be sick, Dom appears through the purple curtains, only pausing a second to double-take at Jonah before he comes to me.

'Why did you do that?' He has my face between his palms, his thumbs on my chin and he is shaking me just a little, soft mouth bunched and eyebrows together, anger and pain mixed. 'We agreed you would go through with it. Why did you do that, Seren?'

I hook my hands into the crook in his elbows and find myself yelling, 'Because I don't want to live a life without you in it. I can't do that again!'

He pulls me against him, and all I can hear is this groan that comes from right inside him all the way out through his chest wall, into my skin, his teeth and lips wet against my hairline, and he is holding my head between his hands, clamped tight and precious, kissing me, kissing my tears, trying not to add his own to mine, failing.

I know they have come for us now, know they are here, know there's nothing we can do about it. It was always going to be this way.

When Captain Kat appears through the curtains and sees us she draws back, visibly horror-stuck, before stepping forward again, looming. Ezra appears behind her, sees me and Dom, then leans against the wall with his face in his hands.

'I don't want to play this game, by these rules,' I tell them. 'I'm not going to marry someone just because it's what's expected of me. Especially when he isn't the man I love.'

'Love?' She looks from me to Dom. 'Seren, do you realise that you're admitting to a criminal offence?'

'At least someone in this place tells the truth!' I yell at her, before Dom pulls at my arms and simultaneously I turn cold, watching her raise an eyebrow. So instead of everything I want to make her answer for I only say, 'I can't marry you, Ezra,' and when I look at him, he is snarling a little, as if the words on his lips are something too awful to hear. I go to him and try to take his hand but he snatches it away, and I say, 'Maybe if I'd never known real love it would have worked. I'm not saying I can't understand why people do it, because I can. But once you know how the real thing feels, everything changes, and you can never go back.'

'You don't have to listen to this, Ezra,' Captain Kat tells him, but he's already gone and all she needs to do is look daggers at me before striding out after him, manoeuvring past my grandfather and making weighty eye contact with him as she does.

'Seren,' my grandfather says, as if the word in itself is some kind of command to the darkness, a magic word that should not be uttered, a signal for hell to rain down, and I feel his hand on my shoulder, shrug it off instantly.

'No!'

'Seren, you need to go with Dr Maddox. We're all concerned about you. You're not well.'

'She's not going anywhere,' says Dom, keeping me against his chest in a place where I only hear his heartbeat, a place I want to stay and never leave.

'Technician Suarez, unhand my granddaughter now, before I am forced to take immediate action. You are not authorised to make decisions on her behalf, not now or at any point in the future.'

'I don't want to make decisions on her behalf!' he says. 'She doesn't need me or you or any of us to decide what she does. She's cleverer and more capable than all of us put together. I'm the only one here who isn't trying to tell her what to do!'

'Nevertheless, you are in breach of the regulations of the Ventura Communications Incorporated and Euro-American Space Agencies Fleet. You have taken advantage of a young girl in a delicate mental state—'

'In a delicate mental state? She's the only sane person I know!'

'You have taken advantage of a young girl in a delicate mental state and interfered with the mission's breeding programme. Added to your previous offences, you are now extremely likely to lose your commission and are probably looking at time in Correctional.'

I lose it then, lose it like rope slipping through fingers. I turn to my grandfather and find his eyes on me, grey and profoundly cold.

'What makes you think you can destroy everyone? Who made you God?' I ask him, quieter than I thought I'd be, but with ten times the fury.

He frowns. 'Seren, I am under no delusion that I am God, but as Chief of Security on the Ventura I have a responsibility to make arrests when regulations are breached by personnel who I believe to be endangering other crewmembers. As far as you are concerned, I am your grandfather and as such I am responsible for your welfare. You are unwell and you must be treated. Come in, Dr Maddox, please.'

He appears then, stepping out from my grandfather's shadow in his formal, eyebrows knitted, his weird beard neater cut and squarer than ever, like someone pixelated. 'Come with me, Seren; I can make you safe.'

'I am safe!' I shout, twisting my arm around Dom's like I'm lashing myself to a boat caught on a rising wall of water. 'Just leave us alone! Dom is the only person who has ever made me feel safe.'

My grandfather steps to the side and five Security come in, looking worse than ever in their full-dress, which is completely black with metal bits that shine too hard, like chips of ice. And it's caving in on me now, the way it does, and just at this point I see my dad's face where he stands in the doorway, looking away from me, looking at the floor.

'Dad?' I plead, and he winces, looks at me for a second, looks away.

Security are taking hold of Dom's arms by now and I go to fight them, to stop them until he says, 'Amor, don't – it's OK.'

I take his head in my arms and pull it down against mine, kiss him while they pull him away and he says,

'There's a way through this, OK? Don't worry. I love you. Just do as they say, please.'

In the end I am just standing there, his eyes on my eyes and the rest of it unclear, and then he is gone and I am pushing my fist against my lips as if I could stop the crying that way and in the gap where he once was is my grandfather. Just as he looks like he's about to say something I scream, 'Don't you dare speak to me,' and so he doesn't. 'I never want to speak to you again. Ever.'

And you're probably wondering why I did it, why all I ever do is make things worse. And the truth is, I don't know, but maybe I just woke up this morning knowing that my whole miserable life and everything in it had never been mine, had always belonged to someone else, and always would, and there was nothing I could do about any of it. Except self-destruct.

Chapter Twenty-Three

Dear Dom,

They won't let you come to me, and so all I do is wait. Any time I'm not with you is just time spent waiting to see you; that's how it's been since the moment we met. But it's harder now I'm in here and I know you can't come to me. Everything is harder now.

I've told you before I'm not strong. This is something that I know about myself, something I have learned to live with and accept. And so I'll admit that I completely flip out when they tell me they are putting me here and keeping me here and that they won't let me see you. You don't even think about how you would feel in this situation until it happens to you, and when it does you know how feeling caged like an animal will make you act like one.

So here I am and I have forgotten how to speak,
and I only need to do this for a little while before
I start to forget who I was before and I start being
something new. So that's how come I end up
as a person I don't know. Someone who doesn't
sleep, who is wound into tight metallic coils by
sleeplessness. This is how little you realise that
sleeping at night is something you need as surely as
oxygen until you don't have it any more. I am so
furious that they are keeping me here, keeping me
from you, and at the same time all I feel is guilt,
because it was me, wasn't it, that caused all this
and so, really, I am the only one to blame for it all,
and so this is what I think about when I should
be sleeping, round and round in a circle with no
respite. Round and round until I am coiled so tight
I can't breathe, and I no longer know if I am hot or
cold, and can't even remember what it feels like to
be tired.

I guess you know that Correctional has two
sections, one for males and one for females. And
each half is divided into crazy and criminal. This
isn't what they call it. They call it Mental Health
and Reformatory, but we all know what they mean.

I am sharing the berths with this woman called
Beth whose life partner somehow ended up dead
before she managed to carry a baby that was born

alive (she carried three that weren't). So, I mean, you know how it works here — the show must go on. They don't let a thing like death get in the way of their precious breeding programme. And the irony is that this last baby actually survived, and now she's so messed up by it all she can't love him, can't even stand to hold him. Everyone wonders why she's depressed but, really, it's not rocket science — she's just got a horrible life.

Along the side of the day room is this two-way mirror and I guess on the other side of it is always a nurse, and it's probably mostly this guy called Ronaldo who has the sides of his head shaved and tattoos on his arms. He is there so he can check that we don't try to bash our brains out on the wall or whatever. And so we don't. Instead we just listen to the hospital noises: the buzzing and the screaming and the way the nurses talk when they are switching shift which feels like something from another world.

Every eight hours this Ronaldo or maybe someone else comes in and takes our vitals, pumping up blood pressure sleeves and taking temperatures, dishing out drugs that put our rational brains in the can and leave us in a dazed stupor. And then on top of all this, come first session he still wants me to put my trainers on and go on the circuit. And look,

I mean, I do it, mostly because it means I get to go out, even though he goes with me, running along next to me with his sweaty elbow against mine all the way and his breath hitching where I can hear it, and all the guys I have seen a million times on circuit leaving this little circle of space around me, as if whatever I have might be catching. But you know, suddenly being out on View and Main feels like a luxury, so I do it, and running has never been so easy. When you are in the position that I am in, running, as if in flight, feels more natural than anything else, and it is the only time my mind stops turning on me, consuming itself.

They tell me from the start that you will not be allowed to visit me, and so I worry and think about you. I wonder how you will feel to be facing these charges when all you ever did was live your life and be who you were, and who you were was someone who was in love with me.

They watch me; they carry on watching me. When I take a shower, Ronaldo stands with his foot in the door. When I wake up at whatever time, pulling the blankets against my chest, convinced they are your arms, deep in a dream, I hear the camera changing angle, and I know they are watching me on the bank of screens in the nurses' station.

Pan comes in one morning just to sit in the day room with me while I hold Deborah on my knee. Pan keeps asking me to talk but she doesn't seem to have any suggestions as to what I should talk about, so I don't. I look at Deborah so deeply, so steadily, that it probably seems weird, but all the time I am wondering about her, about how she will grow, whether she will be crazy too.

My dad comes and just sits, sits next to me and tells me I'm thin, and there is nothing more to it than that, other than the fact that it is the other nurse, Sandra, who is on duty at that time and after he leaves she goes on about what a sweet guy he is, which is probably the kind of thing people will say about my dad in his eulogy, and I find myself thinking that really, when you think about it, it's not much to have to show for your life.

My grandfather doesn't come. He is the kind of man who doesn't come where he knows he will not be wanted.

When Mariana doesn't come I guess she blames me for all this and is as angry with me as I am.

And anyway, look, I begin to be not at all sure if I even want anyone to come and see me the way I am with my big black eye bags and white skin and face that looks, to me, like a death mask, dead and still and stiff and waxy and pale.

I don't eat and, even though it's only been a couple of weeks, I start to fade away, I start to take up less and less space in this world. And I even start to wonder if I will die here, trapped alone deep inside this ship, way out in space, drifting through the stars. Don't they realise that keeping me from you is killing me as surely as turning off the oxygen?

I guess I never told you that your body, your skin, is the first thing I can remember that I have ever felt this way about, the first smell that has soothed me, the beat of your heart the first sound that has ever felt like home. You were not made to be mine, and yet written right through every cell of your being is a message just for me. I guess this only proves something we've known all along: that there are some things you just can't make in a science lab.

And so I spend whatever time I can thinking of ways to escape. But don't worry, because this time things are different. Now, since I've known you, I no longer think about escaping the same way I did before, the way my mother did. Instead I dream of ways to get out of here, to get to you, to find a way to you, my love.

So wait for me.

With all my love,

Seren

Chapter Twenty-Four

It is like a nightmare. Like I didn't wake up this morning and I'm still dreaming those awful, sweaty, early morning dreams that haunt your head like angry ghosts. This is how I feel when Ronaldo comes to tell me it's visiting time but my visitors are coming to my room today, and leaves and takes Beth with him to the day room. It is one of the first times I have actually been alone in this room, which is weird, and I have only just got dressed and realised how skinny my legs and hips have become when they arrive, an invading army, trampling around me with haloes of cold air, towering over me, scaring me to the point that I am basically cowering and covering my head by the time I work out who they are.

Captain Kat, Ezra and Grandpa.

They sit down, Grandpa on the bed next to me and the other two on the steel bench bolted to the wall, but for the first little while they are sitting there not one of them even glances at me. Captain Kat looks around at the walls, Grandpa looks at the floor, and Ezra hangs his head and looks at his hands, twisting together between his spread knees.

'How are you, Seren?' asks Captain Kat, still not looking at me, and of course I don't answer, I just sit there pulling a face and trying not to shiver.

My grandfather sighs. 'Seren, we're here to find a solution. To work out something that'll be in the best interests of everyone.'

'No, you're not,' I say, shaking my head. 'I know you're not.'

Captain Kat sighs musically. 'Seren, really! Why do you always have to be so difficult? You and Ezra belong together. There's no need for your illness to get in the way of that.'

I look at my grandfather. 'Don't any of you listen to a word I say? Ever?'

He turns his hat in his hands and sighs. 'We need to work, within the rules of our society, to find a way through this.'

I get up; I can't help it. 'Stop talking like that. I don't want to talk to you if you're going to trot out that crap.'

Captain Kat stands too, looming above me as she does. 'My suggestion is that you sit down and listen to the people who know a lot more than you do about just about any subject you can name.'

'Except the ones that matter,' I tell her, staring at her so hard my eyes burn.

Ezra leans back against the wall and pinches his nose. 'I told you this was pointless.'

'Ezra, you're not blameless in this,' she says. 'All you two had to do was find a way to get along, to realise what your duty was, where your loyalties lay, and act accordingly.'

'I'm not the one who was sleeping with the fish guy.'

She sits back down, laughing a joyless laugh. 'Oh grow up, this has absolutely nothing to do with him and you know it. He's irrelevant. He isn't going to be an issue for any of us soon.'

'What do you mean?' I ask then. 'What does that mean?'

Captain Kat glares. 'You honestly think someone can endanger the mission by disregarding completely the regulations that have been set in place to ensure our survival and continue to be a part of it? We simply don't have the luxury of tolerating people here who are hell-bent on destroying everything we've created, everything that we are.'

'Dom's never tried to destroy anything. What … what have you done to him?' I spiral into panic then, unstoppable, painful, like something falling from a height. I start to shake, so hard it rattles my teeth. It's only because Grandpa grabs me, takes hold of my

229

wrists, that I don't go for her, that I don't wrap my hands around her throat. 'Tell me where he is.'

'Don't be such a child,' she says. 'I understand that you're ill but you're embarrassing yourself.'

'TELL me!'

'Oh, what does it matter? He's nobody.'

'Captain Lomax, I must insist . . .' says Grandpa.

'You must insist on what?' she hisses.

And by this time I have turned to my grandfather and I am pulling on the front of his black uniform, trying and failing to make him look me in the eye.

'Please, Grandpa, please – tell me he's OK. Don't let anything happen to him. Please, please.'

'Technician Suarez is on bail with a restricted access order.'

'A what?'

'He has been fitted with an ankle tether that will alert us if he tries to leave West before his trial, which will take place once we leave Huxley-3's orbit. This BP Infraction, in addition to his past offences, make a custodial sentence in Correctional look very likely.'

'But what . . . he hasn't done anything wrong! It's my fault – all of it. It's my fault.'

'You're unwell. You're unwell and you're sixteen. You can't be held responsible for it.' My grandfather looks at the floor instead of at me.

Captain Kat sighs. 'Can we move on?'

'Yes, let's. Let's stick to practicalities.' Grandpa rubs his cheek as if he is tired in his bones. 'We came here to form a plan. One that works for everyone. Seren, you must stay here as long as it takes for you to recover, and to come to terms with things.'

'But you can't just keep me here when there's nothing wrong with me.'

They all look anywhere but at me then, mirroring almost exactly the way they were when they arrived.

'The fact is, Seren,' my grandfather begins, reaching to pat my hand a couple of times in a way that makes me flinch. 'The fact is, we can't have you released. Not until we're sure things are ... settled.'

'Settled?'

'You will ... stay here ... where you're safe ... until such time as you are married and you have realised your mistakes and you are ready to take up your position; to fulfil your responsibilities as a member of our community.'

I look at him, feel myself drawing back, feel the snarl that twists on my face as I turn from him to Captain Kat to Ezra. 'I don't have any choices here, do I?' When Ezra won't look back at me I shriek, 'DO I?'

And when he finally does look back he looks pale and hollow-eyed and says, 'And you think I do?'

There isn't a lot to say to that and so we all sit there, breathing in a silence that goes on too long.

'You think it was easy for me, or for any of us?' says Captain Kat, her gaze middle-distance in a way I've never seen it. 'You find out about your Union and you have to make the most of it. I wasn't happy when I was united with Marshall.'

Ezra shifts position then.

'I'm sorry, darling,' she says. 'But it's true.' She shrugs. 'It's true. It was hard, for a long time. But I believe in my people, in my culture, in my place here on Ventura. And by the time I lost Marshall, I ...' She looks down for a moment, then up again, tossing her hair. 'Well, in the end, it turned out that, after eleven years together, I missed him. I missed him a lot more than I ever thought I would, and I still do.'

I don't know what she's doing but for this weird moment she is a person, a real person, and it takes me a moment to realise it's all part of her game, all part of her act, the act she has managed to keep up all her life.

'I can't,' I say, and suddenly they're all looking at me. 'I can't be like you. I'm sorry, I just ... can't.'

She watches me, watches me while I watch her. 'You remind me so much of Gracie.' The way she looks at me then is so intense I nearly turn away, just so I can take a breath, and then she stands so that she is looking at me from her full height, down her nose, and adds, 'But not in a good way.' When she next speaks she is businesslike, as if she is ticking things off a list as she paces the short length of the room. 'There are two options available to you, Seren. Cooperate, and make life better for yourself. Don't, and have every last freedom taken away until you have no choices in any case. You will be the one who decides how it's going to be, but not the one who decides how it will actually turn out. One way or another, in the end, you will be married to Ezra, and you will bear his children. You can do that willingly or otherwise, but that much is already set in stone, and always has been. Come on, darling – we're going.'

Ezra doesn't move at first, just carries on sitting there leaning forward with his fingers in his hair. She glances back at him once before she opens the door and strides out of it, and only then does he look up and when he does it is at me and he is red-eyed and though he doesn't say anything there is such a lot that passes between us and none of it is good, and once he is gone too and I am staring at the empty doorway as the door slides closed behind them, I am feeling something rising inside me irresistibly. Don't ask me how he knows but Grandpa reaches across the room right then for the steel bucket that's used for rubbish and puts it on the floor in front of me just in time for me to fill it with a stream of hot, sour vomit, the last of which I cough up in yellow strings.

I am on my side, shivering, facing the wall with my

knees up at my chest when I hear him sigh, when I feel him switch position as he stands to go.

'Seren, this is the way things are. You know they can't be any different. The only person you hurt by kicking against everything is you.'

'Whoever told you that laying on clichés was going to do the trick was wrong,' I splutter, still coughing, eyes streaming, stomach clenching into knots.

'Seren, will you ... is there any chance you will listen to me and take my advice? As your grandfather who loves you, not as Chief of Security of the Ventura?'

I don't answer but he carries on anyway. 'I know that sometimes life can seem unfair, but things are as they are for a reason. I'm sixty-one years old. I've been around a lot longer than you and for a large part of that time it has been my job to keep us safe, all of us, to guard our way of life and protect the things that we cherish. I'm not always ... comfortable about the decisions I have to make or the things I have to do, but I do them anyway. Living this way, in planned family units, is the very fabric of this mission. Its importance cannot be overstated. Obviously we are all still –' he sighs before he carries on, '– human. And this is why we have ... instincts that we find difficult to ignore. You're not the first and, sadly, you probably won't be the last. But believe me when I tell you I have never seen any good come of allowing yourself to follow those instincts. I mean, Seren, just look at the situation you and Technician Suarez find yourselves in now – was it worth it?'

I want to scream at him then. Scream and scream and never stop screaming. I want to tell him that the only reason we're in this mess is because of him and his rules, is because of this place and its complete disregard for anything that's real and true, is because we have no choice, no freedom, and that what he calls duty I call slavery. I want to tell him that of course it was worth it.

But I don't. I don't even turn to look at him. I know he stands there for a while looking down at me before he leaves, so long in fact that I almost meet his eye, but I don't. I make a point of it.

Chapter Twenty-Five

It's a few days later that Ronaldo brings me into the day room where Dr Mad is forcing Beth to repair Christmas ornaments (apparently it's therapeutic) and talking at her so loud she's practically flinching, so I say, 'She's depressed, Dr Mad, not deaf.'

'Ah, Seren,' he sighs. 'I can see you're feeling back to your old self.'

'Meaning snarky and sarcastic?'

He cocks his head. 'You know I've always loved your sense of humour,' he says, which is a lie, so I just make a face. 'Has Charge Nurse Benitez briefed you on today's activities?'

'Activities?' I glance back at Ronaldo, who looks sheepish.

'Not to worry,' says Dr Mad. 'Nothing to worry about at all. I'm going to help you to manage all your anxieties and navigate your way through the process with the minimum of difficulties. Sit down here, by me, so we

can talk.' He sits on the bench and pats the metal with
a *clang*.

'What process?' I say, not sitting.

Clang clang.

'What process?' Even I can hear I'm getting loud.

Dr Mad sighs and scratches absently at the sharp-
cut outline of his beard. He's one of those people who
looks ridiculous in his uniform. From what I've seen of
Earth and the kinds of clothes psychiatrists wore back
there, he would definitely have made more sense in
that context. He brings his hands together in front of
him and gives me this look. Disappointment. He uses
it a lot.

'I understand that you've had to be sedated recently?'
he says.

He studies me for a response and, when he doesn't
get one, he nods.

'I wouldn't want to think we would have to resort to
that again. I would like to count on your cooperation
today.'

God, it's all I can do not to launch at him. 'So tell me
what you're talking about!'

'You've been summoned to the Security offices. To give
your deposition, your statement, in the BP Infraction
case.'

I do sit down then. Hard. About two metres away
though, rather than next to him.

He watches me for a moment before he adds, 'I'm to act as your advocate.'

'I don't want you to be my advocate, whatever that is.'

He shakes his head slowly. 'Seren, you can fight it if you like, but if they deem you fit to attend without me, that will mean you are eligible for full trial. Then you could be looking at time in Reformatory yourself.' He indicates the other half of Correctional with his head, beyond our wall but not so far that we don't hear noises from there sometimes. Crashes, mostly; sometimes screams. 'I sincerely hope to avoid that outcome for you,' he adds.

'Who's on the case?' I can't seem to take my eyes off my feet.

'Well, Chief Sherbakov will not be overseeing it, if that's what you're wondering. He's removed himself for conflict of interests.'

I nod slow, slower, until I stop, then I look up at him. 'Well, when are we going?'

It's the middle of first session so there aren't many people around and for some reason the emptiness of everything ends up disorientating me, almost as if I've dropped out of the usual timeline and into some alternate reality. I feel like the only people I do see scurry away from me around corners, but Dr Mad tells me I'm being paranoid and the chances are he's right, but still.

'Wait,' I ask him, in the upwards transporter. 'What is this deposition for? Whose case is this? Mine or ...?' I don't even dare to say Dom's name.

'Why?' He arches his eyebrow. 'Would it affect your answers?'

I pause. 'Well, I ...' Then I only shrug.

He's really short, Dr Mad, so when he lays his hand on my shoulder his face is really close. 'Seren, you need to tell the truth. If you are caught in a lie it will cause the kind of trouble you can't afford. You must think of yourself, no matter what it might mean for others. Please tell me you understand that.'

I don't answer, but I feel my pulse beating in my head.

When we get out of the transporter we're directly opposite the door of the Security Station. What I know, because I've been here before with Grandpa, is that the front office has this view right over the plaza from high above, and whoever's on front desk sits there gawping out at it all in case they can catch you doing something you're not meant to be doing, like fighting, drinking too much, falling in love with the wrong person. When I walk through the door in front of Dr Mad with his hand on my elbow, I go straight over to the glass, while he goes to the desk and talks super quiet to the guy there. I know I will know him, I know most of them pretty well because of Grandpa, and I'm desperate to avoid that awkward exchange of glances right now. Down in the plaza, life is going on like it always does. There's no one much down there at this time so the screens are all on and playing to mostly empty tables and chairs but there's a few mothers in smiling groups with pre-Ed toddlers and babies messing around on the floor nearby. It takes me a while to realise that one of the mums is Pan, hair swirled into this loose knot on the top of her head, overalls pulled down so that her shoulder is bare as she feeds Deborah. I watch the side of her face while she talks to someone and then laughs; I can't explain why I feel completely betrayed right then but I do, so much so that I turn away.

We get buzzed through the door that leads into the main part of the station and the Security guy standing just inside takes hold of my hand and shakes it.

'Junior Technician Seren Hemple? I'm Security Officer Elijah Bradman. I'm handling this case.'

I look up at him and, of course, we've met before, at my grandpa's maybe, but he chooses to ignore it and so do I. I'm pretty sure he's also the older brother of Mariana's life partner and was possibly, maybe, at Annelise's party. This is the reason I don't answer him and am full-on panicking as we walk past the vast bank of flickering security screens in the main station area on our way to the interview room, before I manage to convince myself it's actually pretty unlikely as he's got to be late twenties at least and people like that don't generally go to rec room parties.

The interview room turns out to be nothing more than this ridiculous little cubicle with bolted-in seats that face each other over a narrow metal table. There are metal cups of water on it. Dr Mad and I slide in on one side while Elijah slides in on the other.

Before he even says anything he sets his pod on the table and instructs it to record, then he does this whole introduction about what day it is, what time, who's here, all that, and something about it makes my legs really begin to shake under the table. I bounce them up and down in an attempt to hide it.

After he seems to be done he looks at me for a long time, super steady, with his dark eyes. 'You have an advocate present, and you may ask him to speak on your behalf at any time, but really, Seren, all I'm asking you to do is tell me the truth – is that OK?'

I nod.

'OK.' He touches the screen that's recessed into the wall and opens a folder that seems to be full of different documents all labelled 'Hemple–Suarez BPI Case Evidence' followed by a number, and there are a lot of them, and it makes my throat close over. 'It is alleged that you have been inappropriately involved with Technician Domingo Suarez, aged eighteen years five months, of Production – Farm and Fisheries division. This constitutes a Class 3 Breeding Programme Infraction and carries a custodial sentence of up to two years. Understanding that these are the charges, are you happy to answer a few questions?'

I'm not, of course, but since I can't speak, I nod.

'How did you first meet Technician Domingo Suarez?'

'We ...' No voice, so I cough and start again. 'We knew each other a little in Education. He's a generation older than me, so ...' I shrug. 'I don't remember but he does. He says we talked a little at my sister's sixteenth birthday party.'

This settles in the air. Elijah watches me for a moment as it dawns on me: why did I say that? It burns in me, hotter than the surface of a sun. Jesus.

'Everyone knows each other here!' I burst out then. 'I mean, not completely, but somewhat. It's a space traveller – how much anonymity can there be?' I laugh then, look around the table, but nobody else joins in.

Dr Mad pats my hand where it lies on my twitching thigh. 'It's OK, Seren,' he says. 'Keep calm and answer the questions; that's all we're asking of you.'

'Have you had conversations with Technician Domingo Suarez more recently than that?' Elijah raises an eyebrow.

I stall for time. 'Conversations? What, like ... hey, how are you, excuse me do you have the time kind of conversations?'

Elijah stays utterly motionless, just watches me, then says, 'OK, let me ask you a different question: how would you characterise your relationship with Technician Suarez?'

I shrug hard, up then down. 'I mean, I guess we're friends. I see him around.'

'Could you briefly outline the occasions upon which you have been in his company during the last twelve weeks?'

'Look.' I laugh. 'My memory isn't that great. I've seen him places – at parties maybe. I work with his cousin. And ... you know ... that's it really.'

'That's it?' Elijah leans forward over the table, peering at me. In the harsh overhead light, his eyes are completely hidden in shadow. 'Nothing else to tell me at all?'

I pretend to think a little, then shake my head. Elijah sighs then, so hard his breath travels across the table and cools the back of my fingers. He turns to the screen and double touches one of the audio files so that it opens.

' ... that I walked out of the bathroom and they were, uh, let's say, involved in a passionate embrace, up against a wall. They both tried to play it off like it was a one-time thing but it was obvious it wasn't. It's not like—'

He stops it. 'Anything to add now?'

Arnold Witney. Goddamn it.

'I don't know who he's talking about,' I try, shaky-voiced. 'But it's not me.'

'Do you understand that lying in this situation is going to get both you and Suarez into even more trouble than you're already in?' He is leaning all the way forward, low over the table, peering up at me. 'Do you understand that, Seren?'

I nod.

'So do you have anything else about the character of your relationship with Technician Suarez that you want to share with me?'

I shake my head.

'Are you sure?'

I shake my head again.

He turns to the screen again and I swallow a rock as big as a fist. He double touches another audio file. A voice wheedles out of the speaker, a little distorted at first, but after a few seconds I recognise it. One of Dom's room-mates, the one who's also in his band.

'Look, without wanting to be graphic about it … It got so you knew that every time you walked into the room they would be there on his bunk, making out. Ah man, here's the thing – we tried to tell him it wasn't going to end well. You could tell he was in over his head. I can't even count how many times I said to him – that girl has a life partner and so do you and one of these days—'

Elijah stops it, lets a silence settle. 'So?' he says. 'Anything more you want to tell me yet?'

I shake my head, try to shrug but end up messing it up. 'Just sounds like someone with an overactive imagination.'

'OK.' He lays his hands flat on the table in front of him, palm down. 'Let me ask you this: did you ever arrange to meet Technician Suarez specifically? Or speak to him on your pod?'

'I . . .' I pretend to be thinking about it. I feel Dr Mad tense up next to me, sensing something. 'On my pod? I don't think so. Probably not.'

He leaves this gap then, this silence so intense it feels like the world stops. I have this chance right then to realise how dumb it is to lie but it already feels too late, and he gives me this look while he touches a video file and we all know what's coming.

Dom's face, half hidden in shadow, and I swear I shrivel into a husk right then as it starts to play.

'Hey, it's me. I know I shouldn't call you but . . . you know . . . just . . . basically finding it pretty hard, maybe impossible, not to think about you, and last night and everything. Man, what are you doing to me? Come any time once you finish work. I can't wait to see you.'

I doubt anything in the world could be as incriminating as the way I gaze at his face on the screen, soak in his voice, biting hard on my lip and blinking back tears with how deeply I miss him. After it ends we all just sit there, waiting to see what I will say. Not even I know what it will be until I open my mouth.

'Yeah, I guess …' I swallow, swipe at a tear. 'I just … I forgot about that one time.'

'I have more, Seren,' says Elijah. 'Want me to play them?'

With all my heart I do, but I shake my head.

Elijah holds his hand up. 'Before we go on, I want to take this opportunity to remind you that lying to Security officers is a justice infraction and could also have a negative impact on the case for the defence. Now, Seren, is there anything else you would like to tell me in regard to the nature of your relationship to Technician Domingo Suarez?'

And basically at this point, don't ask me why, but I get like this, I just get like … screw you. So I breathe once, in then out, look him straight in the eye, and I say, 'I have absolutely nothing I want to share with you.'

And this is the point at which Elijah and Dr Mad share this look, which pretty much ends in Dr Mad and me standing up and trudging for the door while Elijah watches us and then says, 'Seren.'

So even though I don't want to, I stop and turn.

'Look, if you like you can …' He shakes his head down at his lap as if even he can't believe what he's about to say. 'I won't mind if you come to me within, say, twenty-four hours with a different story. In this kind of case ...' He shrugs. 'Older guy, younger girl, vulnerable kind of girl, you could be stuck in a situation. We're talking about a guy with a history of violence. Nobody would be surprised if you were reluctant to blow the whistle on him. This is the kind of thing we've seen before ...'

And I say, 'Well, it's not what you're seeing this time, OK?'

He looks at me, without moving, so I repeat, pointing at him, 'This is not what you're seeing this time.'

Dr Mad pulls me out of the door then, pulls me out into the main office and straight towards the giant bank of screens only to find me slowing, stopping, when a familiar figure stands, rising slowly from the bench outside the interview room, just to my right.

'Seren,' says Emme, like someone seeing a ghost.

'What are you doing here?' It's all there is to say.

'Well, they ...' She shrugs. 'They called me as a witness.'

I laugh then, step towards her, relieved. 'Oh great.' I take her hands. 'Thank God. So you'll tell them. You're going to tell them – you can tell them we didn't do anything wrong, that there was nothing going on and—'

She looks weird, so weird that I burble to a halt; I stop.

She shifts from foot to foot. 'They want me to talk about the time I saw you together.'

'Well that's stupid ... that's ridiculous! Because you wouldn't; you wouldn't do that.' I am shaking my head. 'Would you?'

She widens her eyes, tries to laugh it off and fails. 'Seren,' she sighs, looks at the floor. 'You know that my training is a big deal for me – an admin job in Science at my age? It's such a great foot in the door. I just can't risk getting caught up in this. And all I have to do is say that I saw you together. I mean, really, it can't make that much difference, can it?'

I can barely look at her as the silence blooms.

'Did our friendship actually mean anything to you?' I ask, watching the way her lip curls up on one side while she stands there taking me in, my skinny, pale face, my unwashed hair, like something she no longer recognises. I guess I look at her tightly pinned-up hair and pursed lips the same way.

I turn then, walk away, knowing it's the last time.

'You never deserved Ezra,' she says to my back, which is what makes me turn just one more time to look at her.

'You're just a ... puppet,' I tell her, loud enough so that everyone in the station stops what they're doing and listens. 'You are no one; you are nothing; you're just a product of this crap. You are the sum total of crap plus crap. Don't speak to me. Don't even look at me again.'

And Dr Mad manhandles me to the door, where I am buzzed out, Emme staring on, hollow-eyed.

Waiting for the transporter I breathe hard, while Dr Mad tries, and fails, to be soothing, flat hands pushing at the air between us while he watches me pace. He doesn't speak, though, won't speak, and this is how I know how angry he is, even before he does.

Once we're in the transporter he says, 'Seren, I wouldn't normally do this,' and laughs. 'But I'm afraid, as your advocate and your psychiatrist, I'm of the opinion that your self-destructive streak has taken over to the extent that you are in serious need of a reality check.'

'A reality check?' I watch the light from the passing floors cross his face.

He looks amazed by my stupidity. 'You just out-and-out lied, during a deposition, to a Security officer.'

'And?'

'And that's a very serious offence – mental health exception or not.'

'And?' I'm seeing red now.

He realises he's not getting anywhere and changes tack, leaning back against the wall, studying me through his glasses. 'OK, just answer me this. What do you know about a man called Charles Darwin? About the theory of evolution?'

The transporter stops and the door opens, but neither of us moves.

'Enough,' I tell him, not breaking eye contact.

As the lift doors close again he keeps talking. 'OK, so, to cut a long story short, in the end it sometimes transpires that certain genetic lines might be better being cut off than continuing. It's something that's been happening for millennia. It's called "survival of the fittest". It's how we got to this point. Look, the fact of the matter is, on Ventura, it's easier for us to lose a man than a woman. This is why they're working so hard to keep you. We need women to incubate and nurture our young. I mean, think about it, really, in purely biological terms, men are almost completely unnecessary. And therefore, that's why, in rare cases, certain men can be deemed to be actually harmful to an effective breeding programme and, consequently, expelled from it.'

He lets that sit in the air between us while I think about it and he watches me.

'Do you understand what I'm trying to tell you, Seren?'

Even though I know he's waiting for me to speak I say nothing.

He shakes his head at the floor. 'Let's just say this: I've been a psychiatrist on Ventura since before you were born, and for much of that time this ship's quote–unquote suicide rate has been completely disproportionate to its population and in many of those quote–unquote suicides neither I nor any of my colleagues in mental health had ever seen the people concerned presenting with the kinds of symptoms you would expect in that scenario.'

The transporter is oddly still with us both standing here, door closed. I feel my own frown forming. 'So ... you ... what are you saying?'

'I'm saying - don't make the mistake of thinking Domingo Suarez is irreplaceable, Seren. Science are prepared for this eventuality. Of course they are. They have other similar donors they can utilise in his place. Knowing what I know of Annelise Gutchenmeyer, I doubt that she is particularly concerned about having a life partner, and, I mean, even if she is there are reallocation options open to her.'

'Meaning?' I shriek at him, knowing but not wanting to believe.

He slams his clenched fist against the transporter wall, hammer-like, where it booms like thunder. 'Meaning that, no matter what you do, no matter how many lies you tell, if they think it better that he doesn't exist, he just ... won't. It's the challenge to the order that you and he represent that's the real threat here. If it's what Command consider to be the tidiest option, they will have him killed, and there is nothing you can do about it.'

I am drawing in hard, shaky breaths when the door slides across and Ronaldo is standing there.

'Everything OK, Dr Maddox?'

Neither of us looks at him; neither of us speaks.

Then, I don't know what it is that makes me do it, but I go for it, I dive past Ronaldo, out into the passage, and I am running and I don't really know where I am going except that I need so hard to be out of here, away from them, that I need to get to Dom somehow.

But I don't think I get more than three metres before Ronaldo has my arms hooked from behind and stops me dead with basically no problem at all even though I am kicking back, my heels connecting with his shins, as he lifts me from the ground.

'She needs to be kept sedated, Charge Nurse Benitez,' exhales Dr Mad, punching a button on the transporter control panel.

Ronaldo and Sandra pin me to the ground in the day room and shoot me in the top of my leg with the little gun they use when they want to sedate you. I hurl a few insults at them then but it's pretty much pointless since there's nothing you can do once this stuff is in your system; you just go down like a sinking ship.

I spend a while looking at Beth's shoe, close to my face, before she squats down and helps me get up and on to one of the benches.

'What happened?' she asks me in slow motion, while I blink at her, and then shake my head.

'Just more crap,' I say, mouth numb.

She watches me. 'Sometimes I wish I was as brave as you, Seren,' she says. 'But most of the time I'm glad I'm not.'

Chapter Twenty-Six

The run circuit takes us round West, where I spend almost the whole time wondering where Dom might be and looking around me just in case I might see him. And this is where we are this one day when we are running and suddenly Ronaldo stops short. The rest of the guys on the circuit are running past us as he turns to whoever has taken his elbow and says, 'Mira hombre...'

And then whoever it is says, 'Hágame un favor, tio.'

And because I would know that voice anywhere, in any language, I turn to him, pull him into my arms, breathe against him; because it is Dom, it's Dom, it's Dom, and he is here.

'It's you, thank God it's you,' I say, pushing my face against his jacket and knowing I'm going to cry.

He is smiling but wet-eyed, palming my cheek and circling me tight with his arm before he turns to Ronaldo and says, 'Cinco minutos, vale?' and even though Ronaldo seems seriously hacked off and looks up and down the passage a little before nodding, he lets us walk away. So this is why I am watching the side of Dom's face as he pulls me in against him.

'How did you . . . ?' I ask.

He shakes his head and says, 'Let's just say that Benitez and I have a history and he owes me a favour and leave it at that.'

So this is how we end up at the seating in View, with Ronaldo at the bottom, pacing back and forth, and us sat way up at the top talking faster, faster, so fast we can barely keep up because he said we only had five minutes and he probably plans to stick with it, and at first all I can say is, 'I'm sorry. I'm sorry. I'm sorry. You were right – I shouldn't have done what I did.' And then, 'How are you? Please tell me you're OK.' At this point I am pulling his leg up, his ankle in my lap, and I am examining the thick black plastic of his tracking tether like it is a cancerous growth. But he pulls it out of my grip and takes my hands, and I look at him and it's only now I notice the matching bruises on his cheekbone and eyebrow, hatched across with broken skin. I reach to touch them but he catches my hand before I get there, presses it between both of his.

'Who did that?' I ask him.

'No, that's not important.' He shakes his head. 'It was just . . . ' He shakes his head again, almost laughs. 'That was Annelise's dad.'

'Oh, right,' I say, not sure if I'm relieved by that or not, but there isn't time to think about it.

'Just listen to me, estrellita,' he says. 'Don't lose hope. Just do whatever you need to do; whatever they want you to do.'

'But are you OK?' I ask him.

'Don't worry about me,' he says. 'Have Security been talking to you?'

I pull his hands in against my chest, close to my heart, and say, 'Yes.'

'And?' he says, swallowing hard.

'They're trying to blame it all on you.'

He almost smiles then, but it's a breathless, panicky kind of smile. 'That's good, Seren, that's the best possible outcome. That's good news.'

'But what ... what will happen to you?'

'Don't worry about that,' he says, his face twisting into pain. 'Don't worry about me. I've been in trouble before, remember, and it worked out OK.' But I don't believe him any more than he does, so to try to convince us both he takes my face between his hands and peers into my eyes as he says, 'I need you to do the right thing for you, estrellita; I don't want you to fight for me.'

'That doesn't mean I'm going to stop,' I tell him. 'I'm never going to stop fighting for you. Never.'

And he leaves his hands on the side of my face but he is shaking his head and saying, 'You know how much I love you, and I always will, but you just have to do as they say. Please listen to me. Please promise me you will listen to me this time. Because otherwise ... '

I look at him, at the face he pulls that I don't recognise, at the way he looks away, down at the floor, struggling, and I say, 'Otherwise what?' and I swallow the big rotten lump of fear that has gathered in my throat and wait for him to meet my eye. 'Otherwise what, Dom? What did they say to you? What did they do?'

But Ronaldo is striding up the stairs and saying, 'Vamos, Seren.'

On instinct I hear myself say, 'No,' and I grab Dom's sleeve, pull him into me, kiss him, hold him, don't let go even though Ronaldo is pulling at my arm and I am saying, 'Five more minutes. Just five more minutes, please.'

I wrap my arms around Dom as tight as I can and I lay my face against his chest, right in the dip of his breastbone in the place I consider to be mine, the only place I have ever really belonged. There is this stillness then, and I can sense their eyes meeting over my head, can feel, even if he himself can't, how torn Ronaldo is to have to take me away.

And right then, right in that one still moment, I open my eyes and see it, out through the quadruple-pane glass, its colour a celestial blue. It is still so beautiful.

Huxley-3.

I hear Ronaldo sigh behind me, saying, 'Venga, guapa,' and he pulls on my arm again.

Dom kisses me as I am eased away from him. 'Please do what's right for you, estrellita. Everything's going to be OK.'

'But you need to keep yourself safe,' I say, shaking off Ronaldo's hand, feeling it rising in me now: the fear. 'I need to know you're safe.' I turn to Ronaldo. 'Please, don't do this.'

He looks surprised. 'I don't make the rules,' he says, and then, 'Vamos, or we'll get back late and they'll know something's weird. Let's move.'

Only because I'm scared of being found out, of what this would mean for Dom, I let him take me, I let him pull me along even though for the longest time I am looking back to where Dom has followed us and is standing on Main, hands on his head, watching us go until we're out of sight.

It's only then that I turn back to Ronaldo and see him studying me. I go to speak but he stops me.

'I don't want to know anything about any of that,' he says, holding up his hands. 'I'll only tell you something I've known for a while – Domingo Suarez has a habit of making things more complicated than they need to be for himself and the people who care about him.'

'Why would you say that?' I frown. He doesn't answer, but I'm not giving up. 'You know each other?'

'From Education.'

'So you know Mariana too?'

He stops, making me stop, and we stand facing each other in the narrow passageway. 'Why are you asking me about Mariana?'

I'm so shocked, seeing the look on his face and the tightness in his mouth, that I stammer a bit before I get my words out. 'Nothing – no reason. She's just … she's a good friend. Well, she was.'

He frowns. 'Why do you say that?'

I shrug. 'I keep thinking she'll come to see me but she hasn't.'

He watches me another few seconds, not speaking, his eyes completely in shadow from the overhead light. 'I think I preferred you before you started talking. Now come on, we're taking too long,' he says, and he runs on.

We're waiting for a downwards transporter when we see this short, red-haired woman from Engineering and she's in maternity uniform and Ronaldo stops to kiss her and they speak to each other too quietly for me to hear and when she leaves I say, 'Your life partner?'

And he nods, and I end up thinking for a moment about how far away it all seems to me now – a normal everyday life like that – but then I'm not sure it ever even did feel that close. Not to me.

Chapter Twenty-Seven

I don't sleep that night. How can I? All I can do is think about Dom; wonder where he is, wonder if he's safe.

So yeah, obviously, after zero sleep, I just don't want to get up, and this is the crime to end all crimes in Correctional. This is the thing that bugs them the most. Seriously, they will do just about anything to get you up and out of bed in this place, like you staying there in your bunk has any effect on anyone whatsoever. So as soon as Ronaldo starts shift they send him in and he sits on the bench opposite my bed, staring at me.

'Mira, get up and get going, huh? Stop making it so hard. Vamos,' he says, no real enthusiasm though and he pouts, stares at the floor, chafes dry palms together.

'What's with you?'

'You're not the only one who got troubles, guapa. Guy ended up getting killed last night. It's all over the screens.'

I turn cold. 'What happened?'

'Accident in a waste chute. Guy called Lucas Brent. Friend of my uncle's.'

'I'm sorry,' I say.

So I get up, for him. Drag my feet along the floor, try to wash with him wedging the door open with his toe and peering through, one-eyed. Just as I'm finishing getting dressed, he says, 'Move it.'

'Why?'

'A visitor.'

'Who?'

But he doesn't answer, just shrugs, and before I can do much more than get into the day room and hyperventilate a little, she steps in, and it is Mariana.

I run to her, pull her into my arms; I know how mad at me she must be but I don't care.

'I'm so sorry,' I say into her hair. 'I know I messed everything up and it was stupid, but I don't want to lose you.' And I step away so I can look at her, the way her pretty eyes are so sad and she is shaking her head just a little.

'If anyone should be sorry around here it's me. I should have come sooner. It's just that I couldn't. Selfish reasons. Took me a while to realise how selfish it was. But then today, what with ... everything ... I had to see you.' This is when I realise her hands are shaking in mine.

I frown, pull her over to the bench, gather her hands into my lap. 'Tell me what's wrong,' I try, but all she does is look around, up at the two fixed cameras in the corners, over at the two-way mirror that gives on to the nurse's station, over at Beth and Jean who are sat in front of the blaring screen but are actually watching us instead of it.

'It's a long story,' she whispers. 'One I can't particularly go into now. But you know I told you before that I ... had experience ... of what you were going through?'

I nod.

'Well, I try to avoid him, as much as anyone can in this place. And coming here meant seeing him.'

And I get it then. Of course. Ronaldo.

She sees it on my face and nods, looks at the floor. 'But I know how lame that sounds, so I'm here now.'

I squeeze her hands. 'Thanks; I'm really glad to see you.'

She shakes her head. 'I guess I should have told you already about what ... happened. It might have made you see things differently.'

I shake my head. 'I doubt it.'

'I owe it to you anyway, seeing as how it involves Domingo too.'

I frown and we both look over to where Beth and Jean have got bored of watching us and turned back to the screen.

She sighs, keeps her voice barely above audible.

'Look, you know how it is, you know that no one tells you anything in this place. We grow up and as far as we know you have this person who is picked for you and that's who you love and they make you a perfect little baby in a bottle and put it inside you when the time is right and that is how life is. They don't tell you how you might feel if you fall in love for real, with someone you're not supposed to. They don't tell you about your instincts, and what might happen if you follow them.'

She doesn't seem to want to go on then, but having looked up at the cameras once, she does. 'They don't tell you what it's like to get pregnant with an unauthorised natural and be told it has to be deleted. They don't tell you how lonely that is. Especially when the guy has a chance to walk away and start his life without it hanging over him and you let him take it.'

She shrugs, makes little noises like it's no big deal, but all the time I am looking at her and I am burning with questions and though I know she won't appreciate hearing all of them I can't help but say, 'Being pregnant, having it deleted – that must have been ...'

She shakes her head, doesn't say anything, just studies our linked hands, then, 'Hemple, it's still the worst thing that's ever happened to me, and I think about it every day. To be honest that part was probably worse than the nine months I spent in Correctional for letting it happen, and for not identifying the guy.'

I feel my mouth drop open. 'Mariana, I … I had no idea.'

'Not here, by the way.' She smiles sadly. 'Next door. Not that there's that much difference really.' She looks around. 'Little cleaner here, less screaming.' She shrugs. 'In my mind it was damage limitation. What was the point in him serving time too? Anyway, that's why Domingo … did what he did. He just couldn't let it go. I have always felt worse about that than I do about the rest of it. That he ended up getting in so much trouble, all because he cares about me. But that's the kind of guy he is. He'll do anything for the people he loves.' This is when her eyes fill with tears so she turns away.

I'm so shocked it throws me for a moment. 'Mariana, I …'

She holds up her hand. 'I'm sorry,' she says. 'It's … There's another thing I need to tell you. I really didn't want to bring this to you but I'm just so worried about him.'

'About Dom?' My heartbeat pushes up into my head, filling my ears and eyes. 'What's happened?'

She swallows, lowers her voice into this breathless whisper. 'You heard about Lucas Brent?'

'The waste chute accident last night?'

She nods, holding my eye. 'That was Dom's shift. His duty. He always does that waste dump. He's done it every shift for the last two years. Lucas only did it last night because Dom had hurt his hand and couldn't operate the lever.'

I lose all contact with my surroundings then. Can't hear, can't see, am only vaguely aware of Mariana as she keeps talking beneath the hammering of my heart.

'That should have been him in there. They're calling it a systems malfunction but we all know what's going on. He's playing it down but I know it was no coincidence. Seren, please, there has to be something you can do to help – someone you can talk to. I can't lose him, and I know you feel the same. What about your grandfather – do you think he would listen to you? Seren?'

And it's only now I realise that I haven't said anything, haven't even moved, that I am sitting here utterly frozen, unable to feel anything but the waves of cold horror which travel through my flesh.

Funny that you never believe what people tell you about fear until you feel it for yourself.

Chapter Twenty-Eight

I don't stop thinking about it. I can't. It just sits there, making laps of my head. They're going to kill him; they're going to kill him; they're going to kill him. This is why I can't eat when they bring in our lunch. There is a physical ache in my throat as I try chewing and swallowing, tasting nothing. This is also why I end up losing it at Sandra when she tells me she is taking me up to Fertility.

'But why am I going there?'

She bites her lips from the inside so that they turn all thin and then sighs. 'Seren, you know what, they don't let me into every little secret here. All I know is I got a docket on my pod that says ship you up to Fertility pronto, and to be honest, that's about all I even want to know.'

'What does that mean?'

'Nothing at all – now let's get moving.'

And she takes hold of my elbow and I yank it away, yelling, 'Don't touch me!'

She shakes her head at the floor with her hands on her hips. 'Now, Seren, come on, we've done all this before. You know that if you fight me I'll just have to dose you. Especially since I've already had to mark you down with a missed meal today.'

She watches me, waiting for me to relent, but I'm not in the mood. 'I'm just not doing it.' I shake my head, which is when she pushes me against the wall and doses me in the leg.

Things unravel slowly once you've been sedated. It's not like you're this drooling wreck or anything, it's more like you just don't mind about anything any more, even the things you normally mind about a lot.

This is the state she delivers me to Fertility in and of course they take one look at me, all skinny and dead-eyed, and basically draw back in horror. They're also doing the kind of loud, freaked-out talking people do when they think they're addressing a crazy person. There's a guy and a girl, both in Med uniform, and they keep making these faces and these little comments to each other that they think I'm not noticing but I am.

'We're going to take you in there now, Seren, check how you're doing for implantation.' This is all enunciated as if maybe I can't understand English.

'I'm not even in my Union though – how can I ...?'

The woman takes over now. 'We won't actually

perform the implantation today. There's just a few things we need to do to make sure you're ready, OK?'

All sing-songy, like this was all something perfectly OK, rather than the most horrible thing in the world. Like they weren't talking about impregnating a sixteen-year-old against her will. Looking at the woman, I find I'm wondering whether it was her who did my egg harvest, the masked woman who almost wore a hole in my leg with her so-called soothing hand.

Cut to me in the lab, treatment room – I don't know. Whatever you call it, this hideous place comes down to the same thing. I lie there while they examine me, while they tell me, by looming into my field of vision, that they're going to put me on a course of drugs to 'ready my womb' in the run-up to the implantation which should take place just after the Union, which they understand will be a private ceremony in the next few days.

In a way, you know, I thank the stars that I am sedated at this point because I just let all this information wash over me.

I'm behind their dirty piece of curtain, struggling back into my overalls, when I hear the door buzz open and a voice I know too well. I tear back the curtain and Ezra looks at me, hands on hips.

'You,' I say.

'Last time I checked,' he says, smug as ever, but

something about his face gives away that he's almost as unnerved as I am.

One of the medics, the guy, says, 'We'd like to give you your pre-implantation briefing, if you'd take a seat over here,' and indicates a bench and table. 'We can talk through any of your questions and concerns and we'd also be really excited to reveal your gender allocation. You can find out whether you're going to be bringing a son or a daughter into the world!' He's gone into some kind of TV-show-host mode now, cheesy white grin and everything. You can tell he's done this a million times. I wonder how many times it's been like this. Like this, meaning that Ezra and I just stand there, looking at him, not cracking a smile between us, leaving a lengthening silence.

'It ... really doesn't ... matter,' I tell the medic guy.

'Uh.' He adjusts his glasses, checks his pod, then looks back at me. 'How so?'

'Seriously?' I ask him. 'You can't even tell that neither of us wants this?'

Which is when the woman says, 'Hey, I know what, how about we give you guys a little alone time?'

'No thanks,' I say, at the exact moment that Ezra is saying something similar.

'All the same,' says the woman, yanking on the guy's arm. 'Five minutes to talk alone is sometimes very beneficial.' They buzz the door and leave.

Ezra scratches his nose and pulls himself up backwards to sit on the examination table, using one of the metal stirrups I just had my leg in as an armrest before staring at me so hard I end up saying, 'What are you looking at?'

He frowns then. 'You ... I just ... You know I don't want it to be this way.'

There doesn't seem to be a lot to say to that so I don't say anything. I just fold my arms across my chest and focus on staying upright.

'Are you OK?' he asks me.

I feel my mouth drop open. 'Of course I'm not OK!' I stare at him. 'How could you ever think that this is OK? None of it's OK. None of anything that's going on is even vaguely OK.' God, I don't know what's wrong with me, but suddenly I'm crying.

'Hemple, Jesus.' He gets off the examination table and takes a few steps towards me. I back away from him so fast I crash into the wall. 'Easy,' he says then, like someone talking to something wild, holding his hands in the air.

'Back up!' I tell him through my teeth. 'I don't want you near me, OK? Not ever.'

And this is when it happens. It happens in such a way that I am thrown forward against him, fetching up on his chest like I was taken there on a tide and then staggering once to the side, the room shifting on its axes so hard that the equipment rattles and rings in its moorings, echoes carrying off into the distant parts of the ship.

Ezra, unsmiling, says, 'They should really warn you when they're going to do that, right?'

I don't answer, don't respond at all; somehow it carries too much import, there is too much story in this single shift of direction and momentum, and the way it pulls at my organs, at the very heart of me, dragging my soul into my feet as if it didn't matter, rendering me into liquid. I guess this is why I sit, way down on the floor, why I slump forward, head down, between my knees, trying to gather myself, while he says, 'I guess that's it for Huxley-3 then,' like it meant nothing; like it meant less than nothing.

I push my fingers into my hair, pressing at my scalp, as I look up at him. I feel so slowed by the dose that I chew my words as they come out. 'Only because of your lies.'

He frowns. 'My lies?'

I stand slowly, with difficulty, and I point right in his face. 'You knew. You went there. You lied. You told us all it was hostile – nothing more than rocks and lava and gases. When all along you knew there were beaches and forests and it was beautiful.'

Now, obviously, look, I wouldn't have said anything about any of this if it wasn't for the sedative but there you go, and luckily he doesn't seem to get too into how

I actually know this because instead he drops his gaze to the side for this long moment and then he says, 'Even if that was true, what difference would it actually make in the final analysis?'

And I say, 'I don't know. Maybe it could have. Maybe I could have ... I don't know ... escaped ... got out of here. Then none of this would ever even have happened.'

'Whatever, Hemple.' He laughs. 'You wouldn't have a clue what to do on an alien planet.'

But I'm not even listening because it is suddenly, all of it, slotting into place in my fuzzy, messed-up head, like perfectly formed puzzle pieces, one by one. It is suddenly so obvious that I say, 'That's it. That's what needs to happen.'

He is smiling then, thinking I'm joking, but once he looks at me his smile fades. 'What are you ...' Quieter now. 'What are you talking about?'

But I'm too busy thinking, my mind cloudy but clearing fast, jumping ahead. 'You. You have access to shuttles.'

Which is when he raises his hands and takes a few backwards steps. 'Oh no, no, no. I am not even going to get into a discussion like this with you. No way. No chance.'

But I'm not really listening and I follow him across the room. 'You could get us in there. You could tell us what to do. It's in your interests to have us gone.'

He looks as stunned as if I just slapped him. His mouth makes shapes and non-sounds for a moment before he says, 'Even if … even if a whole bunch of really unlikely things happen … the fact remains that deserters are shot to kill.'

I turn away, eyes raking the floor in front of me. 'What difference does it make?'

'What?'

I turn to him. 'I said, WHAT DIFFERENCE DOES IT MAKE? The way things are at the moment, it's just a case of die here or die out there.'

'Of course it's not like that. That's just paranoia.'

'Oh really? Are you sure about that? And I know you know what I'm talking about, so don't pretend you don't.' If it were possible to destroy someone with your eyes I would be doing it right now to Ezra.

He shakes his head but goes quiet, walks in a circle and then stops. 'The thing is there's no good solution here,' he says to the floor between us. 'It's just this huge mess. And when you're the one that made it that way I personally think you've got a nerve asking me to get you out of it.' He laughs. 'You know, if you actually do love Suarez, you've got a funny way of showing it.' When I look into his eyes then they are almost entirely black, with just the slimmest rim of blue.

'Meaning?'

'Meaning you must have known the crap-storm it

would cause if the whole thing with you and him was ever found out. I mean, for God's sake, I did everything I could to help you just get over it and sweep it under the carpet. If it were me and a girl I really loved, I would have died with that secret. But you ended up telling forty-five witnesses about it! You've been on self-destruct from the start, Hemple, and now you've taken him down with you. If he does end up dead you can't blame me – it'll be all on you, man.'

So of course I see red and shove him hard in the chest, catching him off-guard so that he staggers back into this trolley of instruments the doctors left and it topples, spilling its contents in this wall of sound. I guess the doctors must have been expecting trouble because it seems they have called Ronaldo to come and get me and within a heartbeat he and the male doctor have burst into the room, taking hold of both of our arms from behind, Ronaldo on me, the doctor on Ezra. This only makes me madder and I kick Ronaldo in the shins, which sends both of us crashing backwards on to the bench. I carry on struggling and shouting until I pull him on to the floor and just as I'm squirming out from underneath him he uses his whole bodyweight to pin me down, his forearm across my throat so hard I yelp.

I look up at Ezra then and he is standing just near my head, towering there, looking down, the male doctor still holding his arms.

Close to my face Ronaldo says, 'You know I don't want to hurt you, guapa. Cálmate. Please.'

I don't have any response at all except to nod my head and wish I wasn't trembling. He gets up and pulls me after him. He's so strong he actually lifts me up a little off the ground as he does so, wrenching my arm in its socket so that I feel something burn in my shoulder.

Ezra barely glances at me as I rub at my arm, but when he does he double-takes, then says, 'You've got a little ... ' and touches his lip on the side, like someone pointing out ketchup after a messy hot dog.

When I touch my mouth my finger comes away streaked in blood, which I stare at for this long moment before looking up at him. I must have bitten down on it as I fell. When I do finally get my voice to escape my throat it is irritatingly small and girlish, wobbling from high to low and back again.

'Can we go now?' I ask Ronaldo, but as I turn to leave, Ezra says, 'Hemple, I ... '

Something in his voice makes me stop, stand there, still for a moment, with my back to him. But there's only silence, so in the end we just leave and I am left wondering about whatever it was that he didn't say, because maybe he is just as much of a loser as I always thought he was.

Or maybe he's not.

Chapter Twenty-Nine

Don't ask me why, when all I've done is cause problems, but Ronaldo still takes me out on the next day's second session circuit. I'm running it hard, so hard he struggles to stay with me, ahead of the others, slippery with sweat, music busting at my ears, and in the plaza, dodging through the people milling, I slip the rest of the pack, almost lose Ronaldo too, but then he has me by the arm.

'What are you doing?'

I pull my earphones out. 'You don't understand. I have to see Dom; it's urgent.'

'Suarez?' he says. 'Impossible.'

'Ronaldo, please,' I pant, spitting it a bit, bending double, too out of breath to speak. 'Just ... please ... I need to see him.'

He takes his bag off, reaches into it, pulls out a flask of water and hands it to me. I take a drink from it without taking my eyes off him.

'Please,' I say afterwards. 'Five minutes is all I ask.'

'Where is he?' he says then.

'I don't know,' I say.

He laughs. 'Then I can't help you, guapa.'

'Lend me your pod.'

He shakes his head.

'Please. Just … please … this one thing.' And he must see it, must see the deep, dizzying horrible fear of it all right there on my face, because he hands me his pod.

'Come to me,' I say when Dom picks up. 'I need you. Five minutes, please.'

He's totally blindsided but catches on quick. 'I'm with my parents. Let me just … I'll meet you, OK? Where are you?'

'Plaza.'

'How about the cinema? That's within the limits of West. Go in, get a seat, over the side near the back. I'll be there, as soon as I can.' He hangs up.

Ronaldo and I walk into the cinema still panting, still sweating. Thankfully the only people here are pretty much all in the middle seats towards the front so this whole back right-hand section is empty. I sit about three rows in and Ronaldo sits at the back, watching the screen. It's some superhero thing that is so noisy it vibrates your skull plates. Dom arrives minutes later and slips from the aisle into the seat next to me, sliding low and wedging his knees up to the seat in front, pulling me down and in against him.

'What's happened?' he says, pushing my hat off and moving sweaty hair off my face. 'Are you OK?'

'I'm fine; I'm OK. Are you?'

And as he nods and smiles, we are nose to nose and it is so weird because how is it possible to be so happy to see someone and so scared and so sad all at the same time, and to know that they feel all those things too. So maybe this is why, when I'm supposed to be talking, supposed to be explaining, supposed to be using the precious time we have to make him understand something that is just so NUTS, so all-out insane he may never actually get his head round it, instead of all this I am kissing him. I am kissing him and he is kissing me back and it is deep and wet and I am pulling at the front of his overalls and he is smoothing the sweat on my face with his fingers and we are both breathing hard, and no amount of close is ever going to be close enough.

In the end it is sheer force of will that lets me pull away, that makes me push on his shoulder until he does too, and when we're apart enough for me to look into his face I see how serious he is, see the frown he wears and press at it with my fingers until it eases a little.

Then I say, 'You have no idea how scared I've been for you. I heard about Lucas Brent.'

'Yeah, it's ... ' He nods, swallows, shakes his head. 'He had two little kids.'

I take his hand, hold it in my lap, run my fingers across the back of it, notice the way it is bruised all along his thumb and forefinger, carrying down his veins, and then look back at his face. 'We have to go. We have to escape. We have to get out of here, back to Huxley-3.'

I watch the light play on his face as he blinks a few times, taking it in, then glances around, pulling his hood up. 'But we … we can't do that. Deserters get shot, you know they do. And even if we didn't, would we even make it there?' And when I look at him, even though I can barely make him out, he is watching me, watching me the way someone does if they think you're going crazy, and I have seen that look a lot in my life, but never from Dom, and this makes me hesitate. But I push on.

'We can work it out. I know we can. I think Ezra could get us access to a shuttle.'

He just watches me, doesn't move, doesn't even seem to breathe, shell-shocked I guess, while some kind of chaotic battle scene plays out on the screen so that the whole room rattles, and then he realises I am waiting for him to say something and says, 'Why would he do that? I'm pretty sure he only acts in his own interests. Only ever has.'

'Exactly why he will do anything to get us out of the picture. I mean, come on, he'd be delighted to help us fly off to meet an almost certain death.'

'Wait, is this why he called me four times this afternoon?'

I hear myself gasp at that. 'He did? Ezra called you? What did he say?'

'Nothing. I didn't answer. Speaking to him is in violation of my parole. I figured he was messing with me.'

'But he's ... Dom, every passing second takes us further away from Huxley. You need to find a way to meet him.'

I look at him, at his sad mouth, which is the only part of him visible since he has his hood up and is partly turned away from me.

'You spoke to him about this already, then?' he says. 'You spoke to him before you spoke to me?'

I push his hood down, lay my palm against his jaw. 'They took me to Fertility. He ... he had to be there too.' I feel him tense up, before I say, 'Dom, we need to get out of here. Soon.'

'But even if we did do this,' he says. 'What about ... your dad, and ... and my parents. And just like ... everyone. Even if we survive we'll never see them again.'

'I can't – we can't – think about that. We just can't think about that. We're not safe here, you know we aren't.'

He looks at me and I see some of the fear that he's been hiding from me, so I take his face against mine.

'Tell me what they've done to you. Tell me what's been happening.'

But he doesn't. Instead he kisses me, breathing me in while I stroke his hair and the back of his neck, his warm skin that carries the promise of sun within it while my own sweat near freezes to my body, bringing on a shiver. And when he stops kissing me he says, 'All I know is when you and I are together it feels like we can do anything, even things that seem impossible,' and his voice cracks a little.

And it is right now that Ronaldo appears, standing in the aisle right next to us, above us, looking around over our heads. I step over Dom's lap and while I do he has his hands on my hips, my face, pulling me into one last kiss, and Ronaldo says, 'Mira, hombre,' exasperated, as Dom speaks against my ear: 'I'll try and work something out, OK?'

Ronaldo traps my arm with his and walks, with me only able to glance back, fingertips slipping out of Dom's, as he stands slowly and watches me, getting smaller, face in darkness, turning away before I do but in a way that suggests that it's hard to do and I am dragged onwards, back to my cell by Ronaldo.

'Your music,' he insists, and I put my earphones in but maybe they are silent and maybe not, I wouldn't know; I am too far inside, or maybe outside, to notice.

Chapter Thirty

Nothing happens, then, until Mariana appears during visiting hours on Christmas Eve, and she's nervous, oddly quiet, so I guess right away that she's trying to give me a message.

'I hear you're going to your dad's tonight,' she says in the end. 'So apparently you should make sure you take what you need.'

'Take what I ...?' Then it dawns on me. 'Tonight? Really? Tonight?'

She sighs. 'I have to go.' And she gets up.

I stand up too, take her arm and lean close, but I'm improvising, and I just hope it doesn't show. 'Come with me for the Christmas thing tonight at my dad's.'

She looks at me, the same what-the-heck look I saw too many times on her cousin's face the other day. 'Your dad won't mind?'

I shake my head. 'Of course not. Come. I want him to meet you anyway.'

She makes a face. 'You want him to meet me?'

I shrug. 'Sure. Believe it or not, you're my friend and I care about you.'

She raises an eyebrow. 'Cool it, Hemple. Don't get all warm and fuzzy on me.'

So yeah, because it's Christmas Eve, I am, for one night only, allowed out of Correctional to have dinner in the cantina in East with my dad and Olivia and then go back to their quarters to watch the Christmas movie and play games. God only knows what she and her kids are making of having his crazy daughter over for the evening but that's not my concern. My concern is that Ronaldo is taking me over there and coming to bring me back before midnight Mass begins on the screens, and obviously somehow, on the way back, I need to work out how to give him the slip. So here I am, getting ready, getting dressed with shaking hands, wishing I could talk to Dom, knowing that I can't.

All the way there Ronaldo walks next to me like he senses something (which he probably does) but anyway once we get to the cantina there is hideous Christmas music playing, same as every year, and all this forced jollity and people wearing paper crowns, and a smell of food that is almost like the bathroom drains, and in among it all is Olivia waving at us from where they are sitting.

'Well, you sure are a pretty little thing still, Seren,

even though you let yourself get thin. Now come and eat something,' she says, while my dad stands slowly and kisses me, and Olivia carries on. 'Will you stay, Ronaldo – will you join us?'

'No,' I answer for him, while everyone looks embarrassed. 'He has to work,' I say, to cover it up. 'Don't you?'

And he watches me while he says, 'I do.'

'Not exactly the Christmas spirit, Seren,' sighs my dad as we watch him leave and then sit.

'I know, it's just I invited someone, a friend, and they don't get on.' As I look around for Mariana I see her and wave. 'There she is.'

And even though she's a little jumpy and quiet, especially when we finish the food and have to do the carol singalong, it seems they like her plenty, and back at the quarters the kids show her their little standard-issue Christmas tree and pull her on to the bench to play some weird game on their pods. I guess this is about when Pan and Cain arrive, having had dinner over in South with Cain's parents, both pretty drunk and talking over each other about how Cain made a little mobile for Deborah for Christmas in the metal shop and then someone thought it was offcuts and crushed it and don't we think she's grown already and look how she's got Cain's nose. And all this time Mariana is shooting this wide-eyed look over at me which makes me wonder if she's about to bolt for the door, but before I can go to her my dad takes my arm and steers me through to the bedroom to give me my present. It's a printed picture on a magnet and once I look at it for a moment I realise it is my mum.

'I thought you should have it,' he says.

I look at it, look at her, and she is in maternity uniform, a two-year-old Pan on her hip and pregnant with me, twenty-one and beautiful, and I say, 'She's so much prettier than I will ever be.'

And my dad says, 'Oh I don't know about that,' and even though I know he agrees with me, it's sweet that he says it. 'I think it's one of the last pictures we took,' he adds. 'Before . . .'

This is about as vocal as my dad ever is on this. Knowing of old that he won't be drawn out, I say, 'Why are you giving me this now?'

And he says, 'Because it kind of feels like we're at a crossroads right now,' and while I frown he sits back on his desk. 'And I don't want you to go forward thinking the way you do about Mum.'

'So . . . how should I think about her?'

He sighs. 'There are things your grandfather advised me to keep from you and your sister, but over the years, I've wondered if it was the right thing to do.'

I watch him. The others are calling us to come and watch the movie but he tells them to wait, closes the door, answers my frown with one of his own.

'Like what?' I ask him.

He sighs. 'Look, all I ever knew, all they ever told me, was that she went into the airlock and released it. But ... I don't know. It has never quite fit. Just before it all happened she had been making quite a few enemies at work. You know she worked in Command, in communications. I guess she and I always had a lot of ideas about how life could be made better for us all. There were a lot of people who thought our ideas were just jeopardising the mission and so ...' He holds his hands out, palms up. 'Look, I don't know. I was never able to prove anything either way. But after that, I kept my mouth shut, just in case. I had you girls to think of.'

I frown. 'What are you saying, Dad?'

He shifts his position, pulls his hat off and rubs at his hair in the way he does when he's thinking. 'I don't know. Nothing, I guess. Gracie did have times when she was incredibly low, so maybe it's just wishful thinking on my part. Maybe I'd just like to think she didn't choose to leave us. But you are like Mum in so many ways, and so I spend a lot of time thinking about you, and how we can make sure things turn out better for you than they did for her.' He sighs. 'I'm not trying to scare you, Seren. I guess all I want is for you to find a way through this.'

I look at him and suddenly I wonder if this is some

kind of warning. My throat constricts but I manage to say, 'Are you trying to tell me something?'

He shifts position, shrugs a little. 'Only that I love you and I don't want you to take any risks. Play their game. Do what they want you to do. I tried fighting it once and realised there's just no point. You will find a way to be happy in the end.'

I look at him, and we are listening to the sounds of *It's a Wonderful Life* as they leak in round the door, the same film they show this time every year. And all the time Dom is the name I dare not speak, but maybe I am thinking that one day, when my dad looks back on this, I want him to understand.

'You know, it probably would have been OK if I hadn't met Dom.'

Dad just shakes his head and says, 'Not something you should waste time thinking about,' and then adds, 'For his sake, as well as yours.'

I sigh, look back at the picture.

'I just want you to be happy, Seren, you know that.'

I don't know if I have ever had him pull me into his arms the way he does then, and all the time I am wondering whether he knows about their plans for me, and I am about to ask him when suddenly I realise there's no point. There's just no point. Nothing would make me turn back now anyway. So instead I take this long deep breath of the skin on his neck, the rough rash on it he gets from the intense cold of the loading bays, and I am already missing him SO BADLY that it burns in my eyes, but right then Olivia's oldest boy comes bounding in and says, 'Uncle Jamie, Mum says it's your favourite part coming up.'

My dad pats me on the back a little before he goes back in and sits on the bench and so, after a second of frowning at the photo, I follow him.

Later I am outside the door with Pan because Deborah is screaming her head off and the others are watching the film which I can't bear to watch anyway, and we are passing Deborah back and forth but basically realising from the way she is bobbing her head up and down that she just wants to be asleep and I am trying not to think about never seeing my sister again, about not seeing Deborah grow up, and feeling surprised that this is what bothers me the most, while at the same time I am also so scared that I can't stand still, can't even think straight.

'What's the matter with you?' Pan says, watching me take deep breaths in an effort to slow my heart.

'Nothing. I'm fine,' I say. 'I just ... I'm glad you're happy, Pan, OK? And I am glad Dad is happy. And I hope you would be glad for me, you know, if I was happy too.'

And she is just watching me out of the side of her eyes and saying, 'Seren, please don't get weird tonight. You only need to hold it together for a few hours. If you can't manage that they are never going to let you out of Correctional, you know that, right?'

'I know.' I am taking deep breaths. 'OK.'

'Even if you don't care if you're in there for ever,' she says, face all pinched, 'it bothers Dad. And it bothers me. It really bothers me.'

I lunge for her then, pull her in so tight that Deborah yelps between us, so that Pan pries herself away and shoots me a look before trying to take the baby back, but I keep hold of her and say, 'I want you to know that whatever happens I ... Just don't worry about me, OK? Don't feel sad for me.'

And I am just looking down at Deborah when she all of a sudden stops crying and looks at me and I kiss her tiny cool cheek but Pan is taking hold of her, pulling her away, frowning at me and she is saying, 'I really should get her home now, and I think you should be getting back soon too.' When she opens the door to call to Cain he is asleep with his head on my dad's shoulder. I watch them while they mess around and kiss people until Cain hugs me and Pan is looking at me over his shoulder and then she says, 'I'll try to come and see you tomorrow, OK?' and then they are gone.

It is only now I think about the time. I look at Mariana and she is wedged in among everyone, looking completely haunted by all the festive cheer with the light from the movie playing on her face, and I pull her out by her hands and take her to the bathroom with me where I lock us in and she backs into the corner looking freaked out.

And I say, 'Look, we haven't got much time until he gets here, and I need your help.'

And she swallows, wide-eyed. 'It's OK – Dom told me yesterday.'

'He did?'

'Yeah, why do you think I've been jumping out of my skin all damn night?'

I can't help hugging her then but she shoves me away and says, 'For the record it is the dumbest plan in the world with a basically zero per cent chance of success but since I know neither of you will listen to me no matter what I say, I don't have any choice but to help you.'

Just then we hear the door buzz and within a couple of seconds my dad yells, 'Seren, Ronaldo's here.'

And we look at each other and by this point I am trembling, not sure whether to laugh or cry, and Mariana says, 'Is there any point in me asking you not to do this?' and after watching me shake my head, she adds, 'Well, then I'll tell you the same thing I told Domingo ... I'll help you on one condition.'

'Anything.'

She swallows. 'That you take me with you.'

I'm so shocked there is just this silence where all I

hear is us breathing, me and her, almost panting in the fear and exhilaration of it all and then I pull her into my arms and scream into her shoulder because it is perfect. Of course. It was always meant to be this way.

And she is saying, 'This is probably the stupidest decision I have ever made, but I hate my life here, and you two just happen to be the only people I don't want to live without.'

But my dad is at the door then, pressing the intercom. 'What's going on, girls? We're a little worried here.'

So there's no time to say anything else, because he is overriding the door lock and it is sliding back and they are standing there frowning, and it is happening.

My dad must wonder why I hug him goodbye because I don't usually do it, but I guess he puts it down to my delicate mental state, especially when I hug Olivia too, and then we are gone, and I don't look back, not even once.

I have no idea how it's going to play out as I walk between Ronaldo and Mariana in a horrible atmosphere and total silence. I never even got to ask her where we are meeting Dom so all I do is look for him, look at everybody who passes us in their stupid Christmas hats and wonder when and how.

Then, just as we get to the pool and I watch the way the light that comes up through the water dances on the ceiling, Mariana says, 'Ronny, I need to talk to you.'

And it feels like all of us hold our breath until he says, 'Sure, what's up?'

I stand looking around, wondering, every one of my senses turned up so high that I struggle not to cower beneath it all, amazed that she can actually get it together to speak, but she does.

'You need to do something for me, OK? I did something for you once and now I'm calling in the favour.'

He leaves this long silence, during which he is absolutely still, a statue of himself, and then, when he finally accepts that this is really happening, he says, 'Mari, I don't want to talk about the past; there's no point.'

And she says, 'I agree. I'm talking about the future.'

He checks his pod. 'I need to get this patient back. Let's go.'

But neither of us moves so he stops, turns, touches his hand to his eyebrow, so that Mariana says, 'I know it'll get you into trouble but you have to let us go.'

He frowns. 'Go? Where to?' He gestures around, laughs a little, then sees our faces and lets the laugh die on his lips.

'It doesn't matter,' says Mariana. 'All I'm saying is: I let you move on and live your life. Can you do the same for me?'

He steps closer, lowers his voice. 'I don't understand what you're asking me to do.'

'Nothing,' she says and she reaches back and takes my hand. 'Nothing at all. We all know this is a blackspot for the security cameras. Just wait a while before you tell anyone we're gone. That's all. Is that so much to ask, Ron, after everything?'

He looks weird then, studying his feet. 'Where are you taking her, though? I'm the one who's responsible for keeping her safe.'

With her free hand she bats his question away. 'She'll be fine with me.'

And then we are backing away, slow at first but getting faster, and I only notice one last thing before we turn to run for the service stairs, and it is the way he looks at her and she looks at him and suddenly I realise why he has never really looked at her until now, because it is all there on his face, all the love that was never allowed to be, all the hurt he wishes he'd never caused, all the goodbyes and sorries he couldn't really say.

And then we are gone.

Chapter Thirty-One

Dom is waiting on the service stairs one flight down, backpack on, jacket done up, cap jammed down, and he pulls me against him, touches his lips to mine, takes my cold hand in his and we are running so hard, so fast, that I can barely speak, that I can barely hold on to Mariana as she follows me.

'Mariana's coming too,' I manage to say, and he says, 'I know, isn't it perfect?' And I want to kiss him then but I can't because all we do is run, run, run until we get to one of the West service transporters and we call it. And while we are standing there listening to the grinding sound of it arriving and praying it will be empty, he pulls me into the crook of his arm against the warmth of him and I am looking up into his eyes and I am saying, 'How did this all happen so fast?'

And he says, 'I spent all last night in the explorer with Ezra.'

'You did?' And I think about Ezra then, about how

he didn't need to help us at all and he did anyway and for a moment I think it's sad that I will never get to say thanks. And goodbye.

But now the transporter is arriving and, rather than look at it myself, I watch the light of it cross Dom's face and when he hits the door release with his free arm I know that it is empty.

'He got me a study pass for West Dock, no idea how but I guess he can pull strings the rest of us can only dream about.' As he talks we are sinking, deeper, passing floor after floor, and as the light stripes over us we stay back, all three half-turned to the wall and hoping that no one gets in. 'We were there all night, most of the day today too, programming the nav computer, figuring out the life systems. Flying it seems simple enough. I got a B in Basic Flight at school, so it's no big deal.'

Mariana laughs but just then we realise we are slowing, stopping, and a woman, middle-aged, engineer uniform, gets in and barely nods as she goes to lean on the side at the front and makes a call on her pod to her kids, and doesn't seem to notice that we are all three holding our breath until she steps out three floors later.

In Dock there are two guys in the gate office, visible through the window as they drink coffee and watch midnight Mass just starting on the screen, but they don't even seem to register our presence as we head for the service entrance and swipe through.

'I just knew that being stuck in Maintenance would have its perks one day.' Mariana smiles, kissing her all-access key fob, and we are in the Dock break room where the coverage of the procession is playing to an empty L-shaped bench and some crumpled paper crowns.

Out of the other door we are in the vast lower hangar and there are disembodied voices bouncing off the distant ceiling and someone singing 'Silent Night' over their own echoes. Disorientated, Dom looks back and forth before he spots the access gate to the rafts and pulls us over to it, where he swipes in and the door opens and at the same time the lights ping on in a wave all down the long, long corridor of hatches. And as we run we are passing hatch after hatch and the light down here is so blue and the walls are so white and there is this eerie intermittent buzzing sound and I am suddenly so scared that it feels like my stomach might actually just drop out and I nearly, nearly, say I don't want to go and then we are there, and Dom is releasing the hatch. I stand there watching him, I stand there shaking, while next to me Mariana looks up and then down the passage, her head flipping one way then the other then the other and her fingers twining between mine absently and then Dom is down on his knees, peering into the hatch and reaching back to take my hand and when I don't take it Mariana goes first, crawling in ahead of him while he studies me and says, 'You coming?' Watching me while I shake my head and say, 'I didn't think we'd get this far.'

And he stands and pushes my hair back off my face and says, 'But we did.'

'This is a story that ends up with us dead.'

He smiles and shakes his head. 'One day it will of course, but not today.'

'How do you know that?'

He smiles into my smile, shrugs. 'I just do. Come on, let's just see what happens. I think it'll all work out.' And I realise this, right here, is why I love him, why I can't imagine spending my life with anybody else. I am always expecting the worst and he is always expecting the best, and he makes me believe him so easily, without even trying, and the whole world looks different, and this is how I find myself in Explorer 37, looking out of the front window at the stars, lost in thought completely until Dom says, 'Amor, I need your help, OK? Get the life systems booted up,' and he is pointing at a set of screens to my left and just as I turn to them there is the sound of the hatch door releasing and opening and we all freeze and I think ... man, we almost made it.

And it is Ezra.

'What are you doing here?'

He doesn't answer, though, just takes hold of the top of the little round doorway and slides in feet first in one movement, pushing the button so that it closes after him. Then he heads to the pilot's seat and edges Dom out of it, pulls on the headset, brings the computer online and starts the checks. Dom shoots me a look but follows orders when Ezra starts pointing out switches and swiping at the nav screen.

'What's he doing here?' asks Mariana then, pulling my fingers into her palm and squeezing them too hard. 'This is a trap, Hemple. I warned Dom about this.'

I look at her, her pupils immense, a sheen over her skin, all the fear I feel right there on her face.

'It's not a trap,' I say, but my voice dies, fails me, and I don't even believe myself.

She shakes her head. 'Then why is he here? Tell me that. Domingo said he had learned how to set the computer, how to command the system. What is he doing here? He's screwing us, Hemple. This is a set-up.'

I watch Ezra's face in the wide convex mirror above the front windscreen, giving the system his voice commands through the headset, the way he keeps licking his lips, the sweat along his hairline, and then I see it: blood, just a little of it, a smear in the corner of his mouth, a pink trace along his left-side front teeth. Something is off.

'Ezra.' His name is out of my mouth before I have time to stop it and so now he has turned to me, is watching me, his eyes huge and black too, his chest rising and falling too rapidly and our eyes are locked for this long moment in which I am trying, and failing, to work it out.

Dom says, 'Ezra, I can take it from here, man – we need to go.'

'Yeah,' sighs Ezra, and it's as if for a moment he is actually sad that he is never ever going to see us again; that's what it looks like when he just sits there, but he still doesn't actually move, he still doesn't get up. And this is when the communicator goes.

Bing bong.

Pause, in which we are all looking at each other.

Bing bong.

No one moves.

Then Dom says, 'Tell them it's you. Tell them you're training.'

Ezra laughs, but Dom just watches him until he flips the switch and speaks.

'Control, it's Junior Airman Lomax. I'm just taking the chance to get some practice in ahead of my assessment, over.'

The voice comes back: 'That's affirmative, Lomax. Your dedication to gaining cockpit experience is an inspiration, over.'

'Thank you, Tower, over.' He pulls the headset off and tosses it into Dom's lap, blowing all his breath out in a rush.

'How can we launch now?' says Mariana, shaking her head. 'They're watching us.'

'They're not,' says Ezra, glancing back at her. 'They'll be watching the Mass, waiting for my brother to fluff it. You know they will. By the time they notice something's weird . . . ' He shrugs one shoulder.

'Thanks, man,' says Dom, offering his hand, but then: *Bing bong.*

It's the com again. We all look at each other.

'Answer it,' says Dom, but Ezra shakes his head.

'Jeez, don't screw us now, man!' yells Mariana from behind me, and I can hear her panting with fear. 'Just help us – get them off our backs!'

But Ezra doesn't speak again. Instead he just sweats, heavy breathes, swallows, looks an awful lot like someone who's about to vomit. There's this long few beats where all I can do is hope he's coming up with a plan, and then he swipes at the control screen some more and . . . *What the . . .* This is when we hear the release brackets grinding open and the airlock hissing and the boosters fire and this is when we realise that – *oh man* – we have just launched. And for this long, silent moment, it is just us and a hundred thousand distant, drifting stars.

'My God, Lomax, what have you done?' Dom is torn at this point between screaming at Ezra and screaming at me to get my belt on.

The com isn't politely *bing bong*ing any more; instead it has set up a steady *bing bing bing bing* while we pick up pace and I am pushed back deep into my seat and can only vaguely hear Dom and Ezra yelling at each other. Across from me Mariana has her eyes closed, head back, tears at the corner of her dark eyelashes that form into tiny globes of glass and break free to drift in the air, our first sign of zero gravity.

'Mariana,' I call, and she rolls her eyes in my direction and watches me point at the floating beads of her tears.

'Oh God, I think I'm going to puke,' she says.

The com is now on override and there are hails coming through.

'Explorer 37, you are on an unauthorised flight path in a misappropriated vessel. Please correct your trajectory and return to dock.'

'Oh man, they're on to us.' Dom glares across at Ezra, and then reports it in exactly the same voice but looking back at me. 'They're on to us.'

Ezra isn't responding to the hails; he is just swiping at screens and flicking at switches. On the big screen next to him he pulls up our rear view image.

'Suarez, stop talking crap and watch this for me, will you?'

Dom peers at it, then at Ezra. 'Why? What am I looking for?'

'You're checking if they're coming after us.'

'Coming after us?'

'A combat vessel. We're deserting. Perhaps you aren't aware, but we're not allowed to do that.'

'Of course I'm aware.'

'Then I guess you'll know what the penalty is for it.'

He doesn't answer that. No one does. And just then Dom says, 'There's something launching.'

I look across at Mariana and she is talking quietly, shaking her head, maybe praying, more little crystalline tears breaking free of her closed eyes, her hand, hard-knuckled, gripping the belt.

'Can you outrun them?' I ask Ezra, while he flicks a few more switches, sets a few things beeping, ignores two more nearly identical hails, shakes his head.

'In this? No chance.'

'Not even at full pelt?' asks Dom.

'Suarez, this is full pelt.'

Dom and I watch each other in the mirror and then both look away. Another hail comes through:

'Explorer 37, you are being ordered to return to Ventura immediately or you will be subject to the Clarke Protocol and will be dealt with as deserters.'

And while I am blowing into my pinched nose and trying to equalise the dagger-like pain in my ears, wondering for a moment if I will be sick, it comes to me.

'Your mother,' I ask Ezra. 'Does your mother know you're here?'

He sighs. 'I think so.'

I shake my head. 'I don't.'

He doesn't look at me, just watches the rear view screen as the combat launch gains on us, gleaming silver against the blackness.

'I'm pretty sure it wouldn't take her long to work it out. I was just with her. I had to fight with one of her goons to get away while we were heading to Mass. And I spoke to Tower a second before we launched. I haven't exactly been trying to hide it.'

'But why would she think you would be here? It's the last thing she would think. It hasn't got through to her yet.'

'It has, Hemple!' he yells, instantly flushed. 'She knows. She just doesn't care. I'm not worth anywhere near as much to her as her career is, as her reputation, as the mission. That's who she is, that's what makes her her. I took a gamble. I gambled that me being here might save us. I was wrong. I was wrong, OK? And I'm sorry.' He grimaces into his palms before reaching for the control screen and swiping at something that makes this weird robot voice say:

'Manual control activated.'

Ezra releases the steering column from the dashboard.

Dom looks at him. 'What are you doing?'

'What do you think I'm doing?'

'Well, to be honest, I have no idea.'

'How do you expect to get away from a combat shuttle on an automatic launch and cruise sequence? Now do something useful and increase the engine power output.' And when Dom looks blank he points and yells, 'THAT SCREEN THERE!'

In the silence that follows there is just the climbing whine of the small-scale fusion engine and the beeping of the com, and over all of this, almost audible, is me making up my mind. I shake my head.

'Ezra, I'm telling you – she doesn't know. It's just taking a while to get through, to work its way up. Then they'll be called off. They will.'

He shakes his head again, while Dom checks the rear view screen and says, 'They're closing in.'

This is when Mariana spasms forward in her chair, hurling what looks like a huge ball of pale vomit into the ziplock sick bag she just managed to find in the storage panel. Flecks of it escape and wobble through the cabin, the smell of it hitting us all while she wipes the sleeve of her uniform over her mouth and apologises. She is white, white-green, sheened in sweat as she struggles to slide the zip with trembling hands. And then we get another hail.

'Junior Airman Lomax, report immediately, over.'

It's Captain Kat, no doubt about it. There is this long moment of silence before we all watch Ezra flick the switch.

'Junior Airman Lomax reporting, Captain, over.'

'Airman Lomax, you must return this vessel and the personnel within it to the Ventura or you will be subject to the Clarke Protocol and dealt with accordingly, have I made myself clear? Over.'

Ezra doesn't meet anyone's eye, but I can see his face in the cabin view mirror and I notice he is almost smiling. 'You have made yourself clear, Captain Lomax, but unfortunately I am not in a position to return the craft nor the personnel at this moment in time, over.'

There is what may be a minute then, a whole long, seemingly endless minute in which Dom and Ezra start yelling at each other about the engine power output and the wing flaps, and I watch Mariana for a bit while she just lies there totally white and shivering.

'Ezra.' That is the only word Captain Kat says at first, low and harsh and definitely coming out of a million childhood moments when he overstepped the line. A warning. 'Ezra, I don't think you want to call my bluff. As you know, I don't bluff.' Then, as an afterthought, 'Over.'

That right there is the moment I realise we are really in trouble, and there's a silence that makes me sure the others do too. But there is one thing we, all of us, to a man, know for sure, even Mariana who can't seem to open her eyes. There is no going back. There can't be. There is nowhere and nothing to go back to. This has always been a one-way ticket.

And so Ezra says, 'I guess there's no point asking you to turn a blind eye? Show some leniency due to the fact that I'm, oh I don't know, your son? Over.'

There's this pause that we all listen to, listen to even though the sound of the engine screaming is so loud and Ezra keeps saying, 'Come on, come on, come on,' as he jams the steering column forward as far as it will go and it is hard to tell if it is the shuttle he is willing on or his mother, and then she says, 'Ezra, don't do this – please don't make me do this.'

I watch him squeeze his eyes tight once before he opens them and looks round at us all, each of us in turn, and though no one actually reacts at all he sighs and says, 'We're not coming back, Mum, the rest is up to you, over.'

And there is another super-long pause before she speaks again. 'You know that my priority has to be with the Ventura, no matter what my heart might tell me. I love you, I hope you know that, but where would we be right now if it wasn't for people like me – people who are prepared to do what's best for the mission at the cost of all else? Even when it hurts like hell.' Her voice breaks before she says, 'Over.'

This is when we are shunted forward hard, before hurtling into a sickening spin, tail over nose over tail over nose, and all the time I am screaming, and Dom and Ezra are yelling, and I have no idea what just happened or how this is going to end, if it ever is.

'We're hit,' Dom shouts, checking the external view screens. 'We're breached, back starboard.'

There are so many alarms going off it is a wall of unintelligible sounds and automated voices. Several of the stow holds fly open and tip stuff out on us that then flies around the cabin. All this time I am biting down so hard I start to taste blood. When I look at Mariana she is white and unresponsive, more like a toy than a person as her limbs flop sickeningly.

'Mariana!' I scream, making Dom twist in his seat for a second.

Ezra yells, 'Suarez, do a status check!' while our spin seems to slow a little. 'Status check!'

Dom squints at the screens and switches in front of him. 'I can't ... I don't ...'

'Operations, life systems – run status checks on them now, before they get a fix on us again.'

This is when I hear my grandfather's voice coming over the com: 'This is Chief Sherbakov, Chief of Security on the Ventura.'

They both turn to me then and I feel my eyes close tight, almost to block it out, but then he says, 'I am here to ensure that you are all safely returned to the Ventura. Who am I talking to? Over.'

There's dead air while Ezra slides his eyes to me. 'Junior Airman Ezra Lomax, sir, over.'

'And are you piloting the vessel at present? Over.'

'Affirmative, sir, over.'

'Identify your co-pilot, over.'

'Technician Domingo Suarez, sir, over.'

'Identify other crew members, over.'

'Petty Officer Mariana Moreno and Junior Technician Seren Hemple, over.'

He barely misses a beat then, which must mean that the news has already reached him.

'I want you to listen very carefully to me, Junior Airman Lomax. My priority is ensuring the safe return of this vessel and its crew to the Ventura. I'm going to talk you through every step of what you need to do to make that happen. What is the status of the vessel, over?'

At which point Ezra seems to run out of patience. 'The status is not very good to be honest with you, sir. The status is we've been hit on our starboard side and from the looks of it we are breached. Over.'

'A swift return to the Ventura is essential for your own safety and that of your passengers, Junior Airman Lomax. I will talk you through the procedures – stand by.'

Pulling us into the closest thing to a steady position we have held since we were hit, Ezra pulls the headset off and throws it at Dom. 'Someone else deal with him,' he says.

Dom turns to me but I shake my head. 'Come on,

Seren.' He looks away from me then, out of the front window at the stars. 'You know you're the only person here who has a hope of changing his mind.'

'I have pretty much no hope at all of changing his mind on anything, believe me.'

Dom watches me while Ezra leans across his lap to press some of the switches on his side.

'At this point, "pretty much no hope" is all we got,' Ezra says, and Dom hands me the headset, holds my eye as he does.

I slide the headset on with closed eyes. 'We're hanging up now,' I tell it. 'Just so you know. I don't think there's anything else useful we can achieve, over.'

'Seren, this is your grandfather.' And because it's suddenly so undeniable, so inevitable almost, I open my eyes.

This is when we are hit again, sent pelting out into the universe on a sickening, looping diagonal that swirls our guts, our insides, the very fluid in our cells, sets another three or four alarms flashing and beeping on the screens and starts Ezra and Dom yelling again.

'Stop doing that!' I yell at him. 'Grandpa, stop them. Stop them! Just let us go – let us go. What difference does it make to you whether you kill us or you let us go?'

'Seren, your craft is so badly damaged at this point that the only way I can keep you alive is by bringing you back, do you understand that? I have to bring you back. If I let you go now, I may as well kill you. Please, Seren, I don't want to lose you. Come back and we can work this out. We can find a way. Over.'

I am shaking my head even though he can't see me. 'You don't understand; there is no going back, there never was.'

'There can be. Come back safe, and let me work it out from there. Over.'

But I carry on shaking my head. 'I'm sorry, I just ... can't. I'm sorry, Grandpa. It's too late.'

'It's not too late. There's no such thing as too late.'

But even I know that's not true. I look around at the others then and I can see how it would turn out for us if we went back now. 'There is, Grandpa, there definitely is.'

And I pull the headset off and even though we still hear him come through on the system I don't respond, even when he spends a while saying, 'Seren, Seren, talk to me; please talk to me,' because instead I am listening to Dom and Ezra figure out where we have been hit and how screwed we really are, and it is only after we've done this that we notice that the combat vessel is dropping back. And then something makes the whole shuttle start to shudder, rattling around us like something that's just about to break apart.

'Explorer 37, come in,' says Grandpa, but I don't

bother answering. 'Come in, Explorer 37. Combat 55 has been ordered to withdraw.' And this is the point at which he starts to break up, churning into off-minor chords of sound that chop in and out. 'This is to facilitate your return to the Ventura, Explorer 37. REPEAT: Explorer 37, you must return to the Ventura immediately. YOU HAVE BEEN FATALLY BREACHED and are in distress. Come in, Explorer 37. Are you reading me? Are you …?'

And right there is where we lose them.

Chapter Thirty-Two

We spiral out into space, still full speed, running like we're being chased even though it seems like maybe we no longer are. While Dom and Ezra check read-outs, I undo my belt and go to Mariana, my legs drifting to the ceiling against my will so that I have to pull myself to her by gripping her harness and I am now completely upside down, basically doing a handstand, and for a moment it is all so weird, so nauseating, that I lay my head against her chest, squeeze my eyes as far closed as they will go. That's when I feel her breathing, feel the rise and fall of her chest, her light outbreaths in my hair.

'Mariana,' I say, but she doesn't respond, and when I look at her she is slack-mouthed, the skin around her closed eyes dark and still.

'Hemple, you need to get back there,' calls Ezra.

'Back where?'

'You need to patch the hole. It's small but you need to do it fast. Locker one five five one.'

'Locker – what?'

I realise he is glaring at me in the convex mirror. 'That's where the emergency patch kit is.'

'Ezra, I ...'

But just then Dom says, 'I'll talk you through it – just find the locker.'

I squint at the cream-coloured wall just to my side and notice the little recessed handles, the embossed numbers printed under each. Even though the shuttle is small, from this angle the selection of them looks infinite and I feel it crushing me. Then I take hold of the first with my fingers and pull myself close, read it: 738. Diagonally to the right: 752. Way off. Must be on the other side. I haul myself over there, swallowing mouthfuls of the hot metallic liquid that is filling my mouth, signalling the vomit I am only just managing to fend off. 1169. Closer. I pull myself up and down and up with my fingertips.

'Hemple, what the heck?' says Ezra.

'Leave her. She's doing it,' says Dom. 'Just get us back on trajectory.'

'What do you think I'm doing? Man, Suarez, what you don't know could fill a book.'

And while all this is going on I have found it, popped it open, and am now holding bags of tape rolls and this weird metal mesh in my hands.

'OK, I have it. Where's the hole?'

Dom checks a screen. 'Back part, sector five – it's in behind the insulation panels so you'll have to pull them off first but we are losing pressure at quite a rate so we need to get this done.'

'We're talking minutes!' yells Ezra, like this is helpful.

'OK!' I tell him, hauling myself to the back portion near the access hatch and trying to fit my fingers into the tight edges of the insulation panels.

'Be careful,' says Dom. 'When you pull that panel off you're going to feel the suck, big time.'

'Suarez, will you please watch your screen. If you let that power output slide, in manual, the rear thrusters will die and we'll go into a flat spin again,' says Ezra, through his teeth.

'I'm just trying to help her.'

'We all need help. Just do your job, man.'

But I notice that Dom still flicks his eyes to me in the convex mirror. 'That's it,' he says. 'That's the one. Just get ready for the suck. Don't let it pull you in, OK? Just get the stuff ready and bang it straight on.'

'This mesh thing?' I ask him, feeling myself begin to shake hard with the fear, feeling it spread down to my hands.

'That "mesh thing" is high tensile titanium,' smirks Ezra. 'The tape is a reinforced liquid fibreglass. Get them on and get them right and they will stand between us and the vacuum of space. You could just get on with it or we could talk about it for the next several minutes and all lose consciousness. You decide.'

I pull them out of the bag while I am shaking so hard that my teeth start banging together. I pull deep breaths in and force them out, as slow as I can. *I can do this.* I unfold the sheet of meshed metal and manipulate it between my fingers for a moment. Then I trap it under my knee, clamp the end of the tape in my teeth and start edging the insulation panel out again.

'It isn't coming,' I tell them, after a few seconds. I can feel that it is being kept in place by suction and when I think about it I realise I have absolutely no faith that I can do any of this. It's space versus me – how could I ever win?

'It will come,' says Dom, 'The insulation panel is a honeycomb texture. The suction is only acting on a small surface area. Keep pulling.'

So I do, until finally it gives, downwards, all of a sudden, firing itself into me and cutting my leg, a fact I don't notice until later since right now I am pulled immediately towards the shining surface it has revealed, irresistibly, only stopping my face from mashing into the metal wall by planting my hands and pushing with all my strength.

'I don't see anything!' I scream, the alarms drowning out everything, including my own voice. 'I don't see the hole!'

Something makes the shuttle start to shudder again

then, rattling everything, including my brain inside my skull, so that my eyes stop focusing. Ezra yells something but I can't hear it.

'What?' I scream, but it is stolen right from my mouth like it was nothing. 'What?' I try again and when I look towards them I see that he is pointing at the screen that is up on his right, moving his fingers on it until it displays this green line drawing of the panel I am looking at, a red X-shape flashing in the top-left corner. A map. X marks the spot. Everything is juddering so hard I can barely make it out but I manage to long enough to figure it out, and when I turn back to the panel I see it – not even a hole as such but a line, hissing and drawing me to it in a way that is almost overwhelming – and all I can do is picture it taking me all the way, sucking me out through there like milkshake up a straw, in a million little pieces.

'I see it!' I yell, just as Dom hurls something back at me and it spins once in the air before hitting me in the shoulder. It's a depressurisation mask. I've had one on a thousand times during depressurisation drills, back on Ventura. I pull on the mask and tighten the strap, switch on the com.

'Mariana!' I say first, but Dom has already undone his straps and is bracing himself against the ceiling while he pulls her mask on. In the process he kicks Ezra in the side of the head.

'Jesus, Suarez, really?' his voice booms in the com.

Dom's back in his seat by now, pulling his own mask on and strapping in.

'What do you expect me to do – let her die?'

'We'll all die unless you maintain the goddamn thrusters.'

I have laid the mesh into the corner of the panel and once I do it basically stays there, the intense suction creating its own seal, and so now I am yanking at the tape roll so that it gives a length which I push straight across the sheen of the metal patch in a diagonal and then can't cut.

'How do I cut it?'

'Suarez, check the inventory. Search for wire cutters.'

'Why would they not include those?' I yell, feeling the panic spiral out of me for a horrible second.

Dom presses at a screen and then says, 'Six forty,' and points just behind Ezra's chair. 'In there.'

I dive forward and crash into the back of Ezra's chair, jarring my elbow and getting caught in Mariana's drifting legs.

'What number again?'

'Six forty,' he says, peering down at me over his shoulder and though I can only see his eyes because of the mask he still manages to make me feel better. 'OK?' he says and I nod, swallow, move Mariana's leg and pull open the locker. The wire cutters are clipped to the back of the door.

I tape the patch all the way round, even though cutting the tape takes every bit of strength I have and seems just about impossible with how much I am trembling and can't see all that well because of the mask. It also leaves me covered in this black, peanut-butter-textured gunk which seems to be its adhesive and sticks two of my fingers together so firmly I can't get them apart.

'I'm done,' I tell them, just as a couple of the blaring alarms stop, only leaving about another two or three still going and this red strobe light up above the front windscreen that pops once every few seconds.

'Good work,' says Dom. 'Just put the insulation panel back on and then get back in your seat.'

It's only once I'm hefting the insulation panel back in that I notice my leg, a growing dark patch in the mid-shin area of my overalls shedding blobs of blood, one of which breaks free as I watch and hits the nearest locker door, spreading into a jelly-like puddle.

'Listen,' I say, 'it's no big deal, but search the inventory for a first aid kit.'

They both look at me wide-eyed in the convex mirror and Dom says, 'Why? What happened? What's wrong?'

'Nothing, I'm absolutely fine, I just cut my leg – but it's not bad. I guess it's just a little messy and I should bandage it, that's all.'

'Under your seat,' says Ezra.

I'm crushed into the footwell between his seat and mine, pulling out the first aid bag, when Dom takes hold of my upper arm and pulls me up between him and Ezra, so that my backside hits the windscreen before he scoops me out of the air and into his lap, trapping me between his arms.

'Show me where you're hurt,' he says, not looking at me because he's watching the screens, his mask knocking into mine. 'Show me.'

It isn't easy because I'm kind of squashed between him and the control panel and all the time he's trying to maintain the power output on this one screen on his left and the direction of the thrusters with this sliding control on his right but I haul up the leg of my overalls and he glances at it and says, 'It's pretty deep,' and then, nodding at the screen on the left, 'Take over here. Move this up or down so that it stays in the green.' He leaves me panicking over it a little while he leans back to where the first aid bag is half pulled out and grabs an elasticated bandage that he pulls on to my shin and shifts into position.

'You're OK,' he says, more to himself than to me, eyes meeting mine for a split second, before he takes over from me on the screen and says, 'I've got this. Just rest a minute. You did good.'

And it's just so like him, so Dom, to want to rescue me like that, that I actually smile, that I fall back into him and lie there for this long moment, feeling his body flex and move beneath me, feeling the adrenaline as it surges under his skin and mine, feeling his elbow knocking into my hipbone in a way that should hurt but doesn't.

After a while there's this moment that almost seems calm and I say, 'How are we doing?'

In the com, Ezra laughs. 'You really want to know?'

'We haven't finished running the status check yet,' says Dom, and I feel the way he glares at Ezra over my head.

'Not altogether necessary when you have that pretty picture to look at.' His hand comes into my view, pointing to the screen high up on Dom's side, the rear view monitor, where a spiral of white spews out behind us into the black, painting our trajectory.

'What is that?' I swallow.

'That, my friend, is the powdered remains of our tail section, as well as most of the coolant out of our heat shield. If I'm not mistaken it may also be the fluid from our heating system.' He sounds almost gleeful, and it occurs to me that this is his version of sheer panic, of horror.

'We haven't finished running the status check yet,' repeats Dom, same even tone, same glance in Ezra's direction, before he clips a few switches. 'Isn't there any way to override these alarms?'

Ezra laughs. 'No, that's kind of the thing about being utterly screwed – it's inconveniently noisy.'

Dom peers down at me then. 'You OK?'

I can just see his eyes, the way he smiles with them as I nod, through the screens of his mask and mine.

'Status is in,' says Ezra. 'And yep, I was right, we are SCREWED.'

'Is that a technical term?' asks Dom.

'You want the good news or the bad?'

Dom says the good and I say the bad, both at the same time.

'Well the good is –' Ezra pulls his mask off and his voice gets distant and faint, '– that, yep, cabin pressure is normalised. For now.'

'And the bad?' I ask, pulling my own mask off, watching Dom do the same, noticing the red marks it has left along his cheeks.

'Where do you even want me to start?' says Ezra, studying lines and lines of code and text as he leans way over and swipes down the systems screen on Dom's side.

'Just give us the highlights,' says Dom, as I twist and lean all the way back to ease Mariana's mask off and stroke her hair back from her face.

'Well, to summarise, the back landing flaps and starboard tail section are gone, the cabin heating system is so badly damaged I am surprised it's still functioning, and one of our oxygen filtration systems is also lost. The hits we took, it's pretty much a million to one that we're still on the map.'

Mariana groans, bends double and twists in her seat, all without opening her eyes. 'I don't like those odds, Lomax,' she says on an outbreath.

Ezra laughs. 'No, me neither.'

Dom asks Mariana if she's OK and she nods, tries to smile, fails.

There's a silence before Ezra adds, 'Still, it's not all doom and gloom. Entering a flat spin was pretty good for our progress. Nothing motors like an explorer that's completely out of control. And without all the extra weight of the stuff we've lost we should be able to double our speed. It's just a shame that by the time we get there we'll be dead. It's bound to put a crimp in it, you know?'

'Make one more dumb joke like that and it'll be your last, Lomax,' says Dom, shaking his head.

'It's probably my last anyway, man. You need to get yourself some new threats.'

'It's not a threat, it's a promise.'

'Well, good luck lasting five minutes without the only person who knows how this thing works.'

'OK,' I interrupt, taking Dom's hand to calm him. 'What's the upshot?'

'The upshot is ...' While Ezra says this I am peering over my shoulder at him, watching his frown forming.

'The upshot is I think it somewhat unlikely that we will make it to Huxley-3, which, according to the nav, is twenty-three hours at full speed from where we are now, and in the unlikely event that we do make it, I have never entered an orbit or a gravity field in a real-life situation and I would self-assess my ability to do that as having a twenty per cent success rate.'

Dom swallows. 'Twenty per cent?'

'That's with a fully functional vessel. In a vessel with this amount of damage . . . '

We wait for what seems like for ever.

'Maybe three to five?' he says finally.

'Per cent?' I ask.

Ezra nods. 'Give or take.'

Dom looks at me, touches my lower lip, shifts his eyes to the side for a moment, to the side and down. For a moment I see the fear in him, the doubt, and it feels like a precipice I'm about to fall into, or something draining out of me, dizzying. There is a drop of sweat creeping out of his hair, near his ear, a shake in the hand that cups my jaw, but then he swallows, nods at me, and says, 'We'll make it.'

And Ezra laughs. 'If you say so, but if we do it'll be no thanks to Hemple. I could be wrong but I'm pretty sure sitting on the hydraulic actuator was not in the flight manual last time I checked.'

I'm about to climb away when I take hold of Dom's

hand where it rests on my cheek and turn my face to it, kissing his palm, lips parted. He pulls me back then, presses his mouth against mine so that we fall into the deepest part of a kiss, the kind that shuts out everything and is full and sweet. I lay my hand on his neck, move my fingers into his damp hair, feel him pull me in as if he had his own gravity. He does, of course, for me. Always has had. I manage to pull away eventually, though it feels like one of the hardest things I've ever had to do.

And it's only once I'm strapped into my own seat again that I notice Ezra watching me in the convex mirror, but when I look back at him he looks away.

Chapter Thirty-Three

This is how you go to the toilet on an explorer. You shut yourself in this tiny little compartment, basically like the storage lockers, only just about big enough for a person to stand in. The rest of it involves rubber funnels and tubes and none of it is particularly pleasant or easy and actually borders on almost impossible when it's the first time you've ever done it.

And if you're me you then spend this extra few minutes in there, bracing off the ceiling and peering into the little square of mirror that's on the back of the door, looking into your own eyes and wondering what you're thinking, trying not to ask yourself out loud. Then you look down at your body, laid out in this tight little space and suddenly it is so like a coffin that you nearly scream, and you can't stop wondering if you're dead already, or whether you're just way too close.

Back out in the cabin every axis has shifted. With no

gravity it's just a case of aligning yourself, so the toilet unit is actually a door in the floor. When you're in there you feel like you're standing but you're actually lying along the bottom of the shuttle and when you come out you have to convince yourself of where up and down is all over again.

I am clinging to the back of my chair when Mariana turns to me.

'You OK?' she says, almost all out of voice and watching me nod.

'Yeah,' I say, with not much voice of my own.

'I have to go too,' she says, unclipping her seatbelt, and I help her clamber around the wall in a spiral on her way there.

I take hold of the back of Dom's seat in time to watch him yawn so hard it makes him shudder. When he opens his eyes and sees me he curls his arm around my shoulders while I watch the light from the screens play on his face.

'Let me do this for a bit – go get some sleep,' I tell him.

He shakes his head. 'Nah, I'm OK; I'm fine. Not sure I could, anyway, in this.' He waves his hand up at the strobing red light which has never yet given up, even though most of the other alarms have.

'I think Dom should go get some sleep,' I tell Ezra, who takes a moment to turn his head.

'Oh sure, let's just bed down, let's just chill out, everything's under control.' His voice is thick with sarcasm.

'I can take over,' I tell him.

After a beat he says, 'Go get some sleep, Suarez,' without looking up from the monitor he is checking.

Dom looks at him, then at me, then yawns again even though you can tell he's trying not to.

'OK, so ...' He blinks a little while he looks around the multicoloured consoles, dials and swipe screens around him. 'This one is the—'

'I'll tell her,' says Ezra. 'You just go.'

Dom looks at me again, makes a face while he's unclipping his belt and shifting on to the ceiling, kissing me upside down before he leaves.

Clipped into Dom's seat I sit and look around and realise I don't remember anything, not even the first thing from Basic Flight. But since the systems screen is in front of me I peer at it, swiping between the oxygen monitor, fuel tank, life support systems and speed. Then I gaze out of the front windscreen. Huxley-3 is football size at the moment, mostly blue; a blue you only dream of. Looking at her fills me with something I have to swallow down, something that threatens to break out of me.

I turn to Ezra then and he is eating a protein bar, studying the nav screen while he holds the steering control with one hand.

'Are you OK?' I ask him.

'Well.' He shrugs. 'I've been better, but in the circumstances . . . '

I smile. 'What happened?'

'When?'

'Back there, on Ventura.'

'Nothing much,' he sighs, shrugs. 'I was on my way to midnight Mass, with her, and this call came through and, you know, maybe it was about you, maybe it was something totally unconnected, either way she said she had to go and I tried to stop her, and she went anyway and maybe she knew what I was thinking because she told her Security guy to keep me there, but I . . . got out anyway . . . and here I am.'

I shudder then, suddenly freezing against the chill plastic coating of the seat beneath me. Ezra reaches behind his back for his jacket, and tosses it so that it drifts at me, silently unfolding itself while we watch. Once I grab it, I tuck it round my legs.

'God, what are we doing?' I say then, shaking my head.

He laughs. 'Well, Hemple, if you don't know then I don't know who does. You're the one who was desperate enough to get away from me that you were prepared to stake your life on it. Which, you know, ironically, utterly backfired on you, since I'm now one of the only three people in your life that you are ever going to see again.'

We both let that sit there for a moment before I say, 'It wasn't you I was trying to get away from, Ezra. You know that, don't you?'

But he is holding his hands up in the air between us and only says, 'Are you actually going to do any work or are you just going to talk?'

He talks at me then, pointing to all the screens and going on about maximum efficiency velocity, damage bias and other things I don't understand, until in the end I say, 'Why don't you just let me drive?'

And he looks at me for this long moment before he says, 'You? Drive?'

'Why not?'

He looks at me a little longer, and then says, 'OK then, you said it, let's go.'

And I get up, climb on to his lap, take hold of the steering column while he slides out from under me.

Immediately I start to lose Huxley-3 out of the windscreen and feel us veer.

'Ah man,' I say. 'Help me!'

He just smiles. 'You said you wanted to drive. Just bring it back. You're the one in charge. Pull it back. Think differential.'

Even though that means absolutely nothing to me I pull hard on it, swing it one way then the other, and nothing seems to help until he reaches over and grips it, his hand on mine. 'Like this, OK? Just like this.'

And he pulls it back into my knees, between them, tilting to the right. 'Just like that,' he says, his voice close to my ear. 'And then just hold it steady. You'll feel her pulling, always pulling over to the right; with half the tail gone that's what's going to happen, inevitably, so you've got to steer into it, just like this. Nice and easy.'

Huxley-3 comes in sight, swinging into view, swaying a little, circling, then holding, dead centre. Almost like he put her there.

'I think I've got it,' I say then, hunching up my shoulder a little on his side, which makes him shift back over on to his seat, mess with his hair, glance round at a few screens.

I feel bad then. 'Ezra, I—'

But this is when another alarm goes off, so loud it nearly makes me shriek.

'What have I done?' I ask him, but he shakes his head as he checks the flashing messages on the systems screen.

'It's not you.' He pushes his hair back as he talks. 'It's the heating system.'

'What about it?'

He smiles. 'It just failed. So we're about to get really, really cold.' And then, 'I may need my jacket back.'

I look at Dom in the convex mirror, asleep in my seat. Mariana must still be figuring out the bathroom.

'Do we have anything we can use? To keep warm?'

Ezra taps a few keys on the information screen. 'Looks like there are some survival blankets,' he says, shaking his head and shrugging. 'Spare uniforms, I don't know, but you know what, at some point ...' He looks at me and he is still shaking his head. The light from the console shines on him from below, making him look different.

'At some point, what?'

He does that weird smile of his, no joy. 'At some point, we're just going to have to start accepting it.'

'Start accepting what?'

He widens his eyes at me. 'That we're not going to make it. We're just not. Everything's against us, Seren. There are just too many things against us.'

'I ...' I start to reply without planning my answer, then stop because I'm wondering what I'm going to say. 'I ... I'm not going to do that. I can't. And even if I did, what would that look like? What would accepting it even mean? Opening the airlock to have done with it?'

'All I'm saying is ... we can fight it. We can keep fighting it every inch of the way, but the time is going to come when we've done all we can. This is NOT going to end with us on Huxley-3, it's just not. We're still seventeen hours out, minimum. So if you have unfinished business I suggest you finish it.'

'NO!' I yell at him, making him jump. 'I will not! I won't do that.'

'OK,' he says. 'Don't do it. But don't stop me from doing what I need to do.'

'I won't!' I say, and then, quieter, 'I won't.'

'OK then.' He nods, going back to looking at the systems screen.

The alarm fills the silence – a pulsing sound like a submarine's radar on an old movie, and meanwhile I am trying to think about steering but actually just wondering.

'OK then,' I say. 'Here's some unfinished business for you: I have a question.'

And he sighs, yawns, says, 'Fire away.'

'Why did you do this? Why did you care enough to give up everything, to risk your life for us?'

He shrugs, scratches his head like even he isn't sure. 'There was no way you were going to make it without my help. You just weren't. Suarez means well but he's no pilot. And I guess I just didn't want to live in a world where you were dead and it was my fault. It's like, I don't know, somehow ... we were meant to be together and I have always known you and now, whether I like it or not, you're a part of me.'

He looks over at me then but I look away, out of the front window at the drifting stars but without seeing them, nodding a little, blinking, recalibrating to this world where Ezra talks to me this way.

'Well ... thanks,' I say, realising right away how lame it sounds.

We sit in silence then while he messes with the systems screen and my chair shifts under me as Mariana uses it to lever herself back into her seat.

'What's that noise?' she says, leaning between us.

'Heating's packed up,' says Ezra.

She sighs through her nose. 'Anything we can do?'

'Like what?' I ask her.

'I know a little about those systems, from work. I could take a look if I could access it.'

'Access is external,' says Ezra.

'Then we're screwed.'

Mariana locates the right locker for the blankets. They are the same silver sleeping bags we have on Ventura; they roll up into these little tube-shapes but when you pull them out they puff up. I watch her tuck one in around Dom and then she hurls two more forward at us. We can already feel it, seeping in: a cold even worse than the one we've spent our lives dealing with.

With the sleeping bag pulled up to my waist I'm actually able to feel fairly warm though I am aware of the air temperature plummeting against my exposed cheek and locking my hands into position on the steering column, frosting up the corners of the windscreen. Looking at the orange light of Huxley as it pours through the window on to us it's hard to believe it won't be enough.

I don't realise I'm drifting off at the wheel until a new alarm sound jolts me out of it. I look at Ezra and he is totally out, on his side, curled away from me. I call him but I've got no voice so nothing comes. I see Dom moving behind me, shedding the blanket which drifts into the back of the cabin while he pulls himself forward between the seats to the systems screen to check the alert, breathing out a cloud of frozen breath.

'Madre de Dios,' he says, wrapping his arms around his body and shuddering hard.

'The heating system failed,' I tell him, as he blinks round at the screens, while I add, 'It happened while you were asleep.'

He leans over Ezra's lap to squint at the line of flashing red text on the systems screen.

'And that's a warning on the air filter,' he says through chattering teeth.

'What?' I ask him.

'We're depressurising, a little, and it's making the air filter malfunction.'

I swallow. 'Is that a big problem?' I ask him, before watching him shake his head, force a smile. He's no more convinced by it than I am. He lays his hand on my forehead and kisses my eyebrow.

'I didn't know you could drive,' he smiles.

Dom figures out how to put music on and we listen to something we used to listen to a lot on Ventura. I battle with an urge to tell him to turn it off just because I almost can't bear it. I spend a while trying to work out how something that was basically just a few hours ago can feel like a million years in the past.

'I didn't bring my guitar,' says Dom, hanging on the back of my seat and meeting my eye in the mirror even though his chin is on my hair.

'Oh man.' I can't even explain how sad that feels.

He makes this pout but then says, 'I've got everything I ever wanted right here, estrellita, so don't worry about it,' and he kisses my ear, breathes there.

When he wakes Ezra to try to get him to swap seats, he won't.

'I wasn't asleep,' he keeps saying.

'You were,' laughs Dom.

'Suarez, if I leave this to you and Hemple we'll be dead within seconds.'

'We managed fine while you were asleep.'

'I wasn't asleep!'

In the end he agrees to move but rather than getting some sleep he picks a fight with Mariana over the fact that he thinks it's ridiculous that, having worked in Maintenance for two years, she can't fix any of the failing systems.

'You're the one who said the access panels are outside.

To get to it from here I would have to start taking the place apart!' she yells at him.

'Do it then,' he yells back.

This is how they end up yanking off most of the side panels without any real plan. Having hung off the bottom of the Ventura for eighty-something years the whole thing is pretty thick in space dust which soon covers their hands and faces and fills the air in clouds and is weirdly black and pervasive. They continue to argue basically the entire time while they pull out sections of trunking, set off more alarms, have moments of success and then ultimately decide it's pointless. By this time the shuttle is largely dismembered and the life systems computer isn't even working any more and when Dom decides they should maybe quit before they kill the nav or autopilot they both get so mad that he ends up having to put it all back together. Ezra and Mariana take over the driving and I wedge myself in under our seats next to Dom while he sniffs and sneezes in the dust, handing him tools and sliding them back into their pouches while the others figure out how to drive with half the systems gone, and after a while he says, 'Well if nothing else, keeping busy warms you up.'

Just then the systems computer comes back online and starts beeping.

Because the air filter has failed.

Chapter Thirty-Four

'Yeah,' says Ezra, yawning. 'That's the air filter giving up. I thought that might happen.'

'So what now?' I say.

'Well,' sighs Ezra. 'If memory serves me from emergency drill procedures, this is about the point at which we put our masks on.'

'How much air do they have in them?'

He shrugs. 'Eight hours maybe.'

Dom tries to wipe some of the black space dust off his face with his forearm and just smears it around. 'So really we should see how long we can last without them first.'

'Without passing out,' says Mariana.

Ezra laughs. 'Yeah – it's about to get pretty ugly, basically.'

We all sit with that for a moment, trying to process something that is basically impossible to process.

I sit in one of the back seats and run a finger back and

forth along my lip for a minute before I say, 'Look, the way I see it it's a simple case of conserving our energy. All we need to do is chill, keep taking one calm breath after another and we'll be fine.' When I look at Dom, he is watching me, this smile on his lips, and when I say, 'What?' he says, 'Nothing.' But he keeps on watching me, same smile.

'How many hours are we from Huxley-3 now?' I ask Ezra, and he looks at the nav screen and says, 'Eleven.'

Which is more than I expected since it seems like we have been here for ever, but I don't say that. Instead I say, 'Well, look, you know, it's like getting through a long night. A night you're not sure how you're going to get through. In the end all you can do is take each minute. Just get to the end of each minute and say to yourself that you're still here, and just … keep doing it.'

Dom pulls my hand down on to his shoulder and then kisses it.

I don't know when or how I fall asleep. I only know I wake up with numb tingling legs and my mouth so dry I can't even swallow, and there is this new noise. Three low honks, then a gap, then the honks again. I lift my pulsing head and see Dom peering round the front seat at me.

'Masks on,' he says, eyes wide while he waves his at me. 'Oxygen level's too low.'

I pull mine on and tighten the straps at the back. Ezra pumps up the volume on music that is already loud, no lyrics, surging noises that make me gaze out at the dark side of Huxley-3 through the ice that is lacing up the windows and think about how close we were.

Finally, over the com, Mariana says, 'What happens now?'

And no one answers, no one moves; we all just sit in our seats, hoods up, quilts pulled up to our chins, until finally Ezra says, 'I used to love that swimming pool, the one on main deck. Back when I was a kid. Got so close to being able to do a whole length underwater. Jonah hated me for it,' and he laughs a little.

'What's that got to do with anything?' asks Mariana.

'Nothing really, just ... came into my mind.'

'So, I take it you're cracking up?'

'What would you rather I said at this point in time, Moreno? Would you rather I just came out and said that we probably have five hours of oxygen left for a seven-hour journey? Is that the kind of thing you want to hear right now?'

'If it's the truth then yes!' she yells, before Dom says, 'Please, guys, let's just conserve, OK? No shouting right now, please – it's not helping. Let's just ... think happy thoughts.'

I notice Mariana blinking her eyes and if she was anyone but her I would think she was crying but she's her, so she can't be. But all the same I reach my hand to her and when she sees it she takes it.

'For the record,' I say, 'I still think we can make it.'

'Give it up, Pollyanna, you're driving me nuts.' Mariana takes my hand, and we stay that way for a while, hands clasped across the gap between us.

Sunset. Huxley-3 fills our view, and the sun slides down her flank, the last rays dark pink and gleaming off her sea just before they disappear. We are in the planet's shadow. Ezra drives; Dom sits in co-pilot. He pushes his mask up to eat a protein bar and drink some water and asks me to do the same. I shake my head.

'Please,' he says, eyes sad. So I do.

It happens fast; or maybe it's in my mind. Either way I soon begin to feel it. It's dizzying and it starts making my thoughts come strange, untidying them, so that at times it seems almost like I might be dreaming. Instead I concentrate on being awake or looking out of the front window at our beautiful view, filled by the blue-jade planet and the islands round its middle. How cruel to be so close.

'I loved this view,' I say, even though when I look at Mariana her eyes are closed. 'When we were in orbit, there was just something special about this place. She was talking to me, she was … calling to me. I knew I would be back here. I just knew this place would be … important in my life. Do you know what I mean?'

At this point her hand slips out of mine and I realise she's asleep, or maybe unconscious. I watch her pale face and try to decide for a while, before I realise it doesn't matter as long as she is breathing. When Dom unclips his belt and holds my knee as he glides between the seats it seems almost as if he wakes me from sleep.

'Suarez, what the hell, man?' Ezra sighs hard.

'It's on cruise, Lomax – give me a couple of minutes,' he says as I unclip and he takes my place in the chair and then pulls me into his lap. He doesn't say anything at first and so we just lie there, icy fingers locked, masks knocked together so we can see each other's eyes, both of us trying not to breathe but breathing more if anything.

'Hey,' he says after a while, quietly, though I guess both of us know that we can be heard by everyone over the com.

'Hey,' I answer, realising I don't care who's listening.

'How are you?'

'Better now.'

He tightens his arms around me and says, 'I've been thinking about what we'll do once we get to Huxley-3.'

And I don't even care whether it's delusion or whether he's just doing it for my sake, because right now it is exactly what I need.

'What?' I ask, playing the game. He takes my hand

and flattens it against his chest, pressing my fingers with his and speaking slowly.

'Well, we will stick our little flag into the sand and say, "I name this place Seren Land," and we'll find a nice spot to lie down and start making up for all the years of sun we missed out on.'

'Seren Land?'

He smiles. 'Sure, why not? I just know it's going to be amazing and beautiful, so what name could be more appropriate?'

'Nice,' I laugh. 'Perfect answer. Very smooth.'

'You like that?'

I nod. 'I love you,' I tell him.

And Ezra says, 'Oh man, seriously?' and disconnects his com with a beep.

Dom laughs a little at that, before he says, 'I love you too. So much.' And I watch as his smile fades, watch as his gaze drops from mine to where he still strokes the back of my hand with his fingers, watch the happiness drain out of his face like something tangible, and I feel the fear welling in me, because I know what's coming. And sure enough he says, 'Just in case something should happen ... '

And I shake my head. 'Don't do that.'

He takes my head between his palms and makes me look at him. And that's when I see it, only slight but I see it, the paleness in his face, the slow movements of his eyes, and I want to scream. He pulls at his mask then, pushes it up on to his head and I do the same, and when I look at him he is trying to smile, frowning as well, an expression I've never seen before, and when he kisses me, I hear this noise escape me, this ugly sob of panic, but he shushes me, freezing thumbs on my jaw as we press our cold faces together, talking against each other's skin. He kisses my neck and I kiss his ear and breathe in the sweet smell of his hair as he pulls at the snaps of my overalls until he has his arm inside, curved behind my back, icy fingers on my spine and shoulder blades, pulling my chest against his. I slide my hand down his sides as he shifts beneath me, and he is cold, so cold, so I move my hand down to his hips to where he is still warm. I lay my face against his neck and feel the way his blood moves beneath his skin. I press my thumb against the corner of his mouth as I kiss him and then peer right into his eyes from zero distance, my eyes into his eyes. And all the time I am trying not to cry.

This is when we completely lose our breath and have to pull our masks back on. Once we have, I clunk my mask against his, as close as we can get, and I say, 'I bet you wish you'd never met me.'

'You couldn't be more wrong,' he says and, because over the com his voice sounds like it does on a pod call, I am taken so vividly back there, to Ventura, to the start of us, and suddenly it's all so clear.

I actually flinch under the weight of it as I say, 'Everything was fine for you until I came along. All I brought you was trouble. And now you're ... dying out here ... and it's my fault.'

He just shakes his head, smiles, but he is wet-eyed and it pulls at me. 'You are so wrong, estrellita. You have to know that being with you has been like a dream, like something I never thought I would have. Something so perfect and precious that it meant more to me than anything, that it meant I could give up everything without even stopping to think about it. Didn't even have to think about it. You're worth it. You are so worth it. You're worth it times a million. I love every damn thing there is to love about you. And would I do it again? Of course. Every time. I would do it a thousand times with no hesitation.'

And I shake my head and shake my head and shake my head as if somehow I could stop it happening, and I say, 'I refuse to say goodbye to you,' and just then I am so dizzy, my lips buzzing with numbness, and it is pulling me under and I know how much easier it would be to pass out, and my eyes drop closed without me meaning them to and I hear Dom saying my name and he is begging me to stay with him, to keep talking, and so because I want him to know that I am still OK I manage to produce this voice that sounds so faint and tiny to my ears: 'I just wish I'd had more chances to dance with you. I just wish I'd ever had the chance to lie close to you and have you be near to me in all the ways you could be . . . ' I want to carry on talking but I can't. The words have thickened inside me like a gel and are stuck and now I know they will never come out I am twisted into rings of grief, a pain I now know I will die with, but then I manage to add, 'You have made me feel so strong. No one ever made me feel strong the way you have. You have been like a gift to me. The gift. The gift I was waiting for all my life and never thought I'd get.'

And then we hold each other, and I try to think myself inside him, be inside him, be right inside the person that I have known most, loved more than any other. And suddenly I realise how lucky I have been. And it all just . . . melts away. And I can let go of so much, maybe all of it, because I have known him, because I have loved him, because someone has known me as well as he did, because someone has loved me as much as he did. What else matters? What does it matter if we never got to spend our lives the way we wanted? We lived that way for a while anyway, and that's more than some people get in a lifetime.

And this is how I embrace the moments where the oxygen monitor is beeping and I feel this life escaping us, ebbing away, the reality of Huxley-3 getting too far away to imagine, so far away it seems as if she was never even real. And I feel it come to claim me; I feel my body telling me it's time to sleep.

But just when I'm about to, Dom says, 'Estrellita,' and he is easing my mask off, cold air rushing in against my damp skin. 'Your mask, something's wrong with it; switch with me.'

And though I am shaking my head and telling him no, he is tightening the straps of his at the back of my head, accidentally pulling my hair so hard that it wrenches at my neck and brings me round a little.

'No!' I tell him, because I know him too well. 'No, don't do that. Don't do that.' And I lock eyes with him as he pulls mine on.

'I know what's wrong with it, Seren – I can fix it.' He takes my hands, nearly crushes them.

'Promise me you're telling the truth?' I ask him, almost shrieking it.

'I can fix it,' he says, not answering my question, slow blinking, eyes almost rolling back.

'No, Dom!' I scream. 'No! I am not going to let you do this!'

He coughs, squeezes his eyes shut and then opens them again. 'You need to go help Ezra, estrellita, OK? Can you do that for me? I'll stay here and look after Mari but you need to go get in that seat and help while I fix this mask.' He pulls at my hands even though I keep shaking my head. 'That's what I need you to do, OK?

345

Please?' And when I look at him he knocks his mask against mine and says, 'Please. Do that for me?' And then, 'Right, Ezra?' But because he switched his com off he doesn't hear until Dom pulls on his shoulder and he startles, flicks the switch, turns a little as Dom says, 'You need Seren to come help you, right?'

Despite sounding frighteningly vague and breathless Ezra manages to say, 'Well, yeah, I'll take whatever help I can get at this point.'

And so I realise I have to go, go to leave but don't, try not to cry but do it anyway, hearing my own ugly yelps of horror in my ears as I try to pull myself away from Dom but can't, just can't.

'You'll be OK,' I say, not sure if I'm asking or telling.

'Of course I will,' he says, trying to smile. 'Now go fly us home.'

And so, somehow, I go, because he makes me believe it's the right thing to do, even though I leave my heart with him, as I have done every time we've parted since the moment I first knew him.

Chapter Thirty-Five

I wake up suddenly, who knows how much later.

I suppose I must be dead. Except I'm not.

I didn't even realise I had passed out until now, and obviously Ezra hadn't noticed either, as he is talking at me so fast and so hard it takes me a minute to tune him in.

'... in orbit, so all we need to do at this point is slow down, and if we can slow down enough we will just fall, basically fall through the atmosphere. This thing is built for that kind of passive entry in an emergency so, you know, as long as the heat shield holds without any coolant, in theory, it could work.'

'What could ...?' I shake my dizzy head. 'What are we talking about?'

He blinks. 'You weren't listening? We're in orbit. If we slow this thing down enough we could get into the atmosphere.'

'Tell me what to do,' I say then, pushing the words out

of my mouth like glue, stuck as I am at the bottom of a hole. 'Tell me what to do to help.'

He turns and looks at me, blinks once, eyes rolling back and not returning right away. 'Reverse thrusters,' he says, as if through water. 'We just need to get our speed down enough for the planet's gravity to take over.' And he starts pulling switches and swiping at the screens. Something rumbles under the seats then, a deep rumble that pulses into us in waves and roars in our ears. He shouts but at first I don't hear it, and then suddenly his voice stabs me in the eardrum.

'The sluice!' he yells. 'It's behind you, Hemple.'

'The what?' I twist in my seat.

'We need to dump our weight.'

'Dump our weight? What weight? Our water?'

His eyes find mine, sad, and his voice comes over the com. 'You can still actually think that far ahead? Jeez, Hemple, dump it! Pull the lever round there, the sluice lever – it should be black.'

Straining against my harness I see it, centimetres from a red lever that releases the inner door. I wrench at it, expecting it to be stiff, but actually it ends up being ridiculously easy to slide across, and I watch it then, watch it spray out behind us like our lost innards.

'It's done,' I say, and I lean my head back to where it vibrates with the guttural throb of the thrusters, rattling my teeth, loosening them in their sockets, whipping the blood in my head into foam, scrambling my thoughts.

'Dom,' I say then, flinching with a penetrating fear that he won't answer me. And he doesn't. 'Dom,' I say again, feeling it take hold of me. I try to turn to look at him but can't; the pressure forcing me into my seat is too immense. 'Dom,' I sob. 'Please talk to me. Please.'

'He can't hear you,' says Ezra. 'No mask.'

And when I look at Dom in the mirror I see him – face slack, eyes closed, no mask.

'It's OK,' says Ezra then. 'He's OK.'

'How is he OK?' I scream, but there is nothing I can do to move, to get to him; I am just being beaten back by the kind of forces I have never even imagined, pummelled into the seat until I am almost a part of it, so all I can do is fight the tears and talk to myself and say, *No no no no no.*

I don't know how long it goes on like this. So long that I think I lose consciousness again, or nearly anyway, rescuing myself just in time before sliding into it, knowing that if I did it would definitely be a one-way trip. I think it's the heat that brings me back, building as it does, as rapid and solid as physical weight. Something I've never felt before, not like this. When I open my eyes I see it, the front window filling with flame, and I find myself trying to speak through my vibrating jaw. 'We're on fire.'

'It's the heat shield burning off,' says Ezra, his voice a blur.

I don't know what happens then; I don't know. All I do know is that Ezra keeps talking, and I hang on to it like a rope in the darkness under my eyelids. I just wish he wouldn't keep making me talk too, because it's so hard, and just gets harder and harder, and I really can't even think of anything to say, and in the end I can only think of a song, and so I sing it, and it's the one that goes *twinkle, twinkle* and it makes Ezra laugh, but it is so soft, so weak now, that I wonder whether I am losing him too and, if I am, whether there is even the smallest hope of us making it and I guess the answer must be no but then I realise that there never was anyway so we didn't lose anything, not really, we only gained.

And I bury myself then, bury myself in the darkness, the roar, the vomit that issues down my chin with only the slightest sensation of lifting in my stomach, the sudden calm, the quiet, a high whistling sound I can't place but that seems to start in the very centre of my skull and radiate outwards, one of those noises you can hear any number of infinite layers in, including some that sound like music.

And then, there is nothing.

Chapter Thirty-Six

The impact is what brings me round. A noise louder than any I've ever heard and a bone-shattering crash that thunders through me in echoes for minutes and leaves me so heavy I can't move except to roll my head to Ezra who is coughing and blinking in the seat next to me.

'Dom!' I shriek, struggling with my belt and falling on to the floor, dragging myself to his feet and pulling myself up his legs, into his lap, on to his chest where I can look at his face, speckled in dark ash, leaking dark blood from his nose, blue around his lips. 'Dom!' I hear myself shriek in a voice that isn't my own.

Ezra has pulled Mariana's mask off and has his hands on her neck. 'She's breathing,' he says, and comes to me, forcing me aside, pressing his fingers into Dom's neck, frowning.

'Suarez?' He tilts his face up and leans close; listening, feeling, shaking his head.

'What?' I scream.

Ezra keeps listening, looks at me. 'Help me.' He unclips Dom's belt, takes hold of his arms. 'Help me, Hemple,' he says, snapping me out of it so that I go and take Dom's legs and we get him to the floor between the seats.

'Suarez!' he yells at him, tilting Dom's head back, pinching his nose and pressing his mouth to his, breathing into him twice before starting chest compressions while all I can do is watch, fist pressed against my mouth, blinded with tears. And there are no words for how long and how lonely these minutes are; I can only say that I know they will always be a part of me. I will always hear the way my voice sounded as I said his name, squeezing my eyes shut, hard, against something that couldn't, mustn't, be true.

'Hemple, get ready to take over from me.' When I open my eyes Ezra is watching me, flushed, face covered in Dom's blood, sweating as he pushes and pushes and pushes at his chest so hard that some instinct almost makes me tell him to stop.

I get on my knees, next to Dom's hips. 'I don't … I can't … ' I swipe at my tears and shake my head.

'You can,' pants Ezra. 'We know this. We did this every year with Dr Pen. I'm going to find the defib, but you have to do this, OK?'

'The defib?'

'Next set of breaths are you, Hemple.' He looks at me hard. 'OK? For Christ's sake, don't give up now.'

But there is just too much, too much of everything, and I can barely see. 'It's my fault,' is all I can say. 'This is all my fault. He can't die. He can't be dead. I can't do this without him.' And then, 'No, no, no, no, no,' stuck on a loop but getting louder.

'Hemple, don't you dare do this now!' he screams, utterly out of breath. 'Take over!'

And he hauls me in next to him, his hands on my hands, showing me. 'Just keep doing this. It has to be this hard. Thirty times. Then do two breaths, right?'

I do it. I push just the way he showed me, and all I can do is think about how many times I have heard Dom's heartbeat before, his precious heart. His face is still deeply beautiful even now that it is so pale, so slack, pretty lips blue. Tears burn down my face and I sob and my heavy breath is nothing but this ugly rattle. Then I take that face in my hands that I have kissed so many times and feel it lifeless beneath my lips and though it is a bottomless horror, I give breath to the man I love, to the person I have loved most, and in between the breaths I say, 'Please come back to me.' And he is so very still and the new gravity is pulling on me so much that it is melting my bones.

All this time Ezra is hauling things out of the storage lockers around me so that the world seems to be collapsing in on itself in a way that doesn't surprise me at all. Then suddenly he is kneeling next to me, clipping the switches on the small yellow defib, which begins a high-pitched whine as it charges.

'I don't even know how this works,' says Ezra, pushing sweat out of his eyes with his forearm.

There's such a chasm of fear in me then that I shut my eyes and almost let it take me right over the edge. There just doesn't seem like there's anywhere else to go but there. My mind fails me, just like it always does. It's only my body that doesn't, that keeps up the compressions, knowing about the strength I have that's kept a secret even from me. It's one of those slow moments; my perception of time is so utterly shifted that I take in all of it, every dreadful detail, and in amongst it I notice the tiny rhombus of sunlight that touches Dom's head, his face, his ear, his hair. And this is when I know that this is not the way the story ends for him. It can't be.

I am just pinching his nose and giving him the next breath when it happens. It's a choking sound at first, a gasp, and I swear I see the way life floods back into him, moving under his skin. He convulses then, jerks up into a cough, our faces crashing together so that I haul him against me as he pulls in a huge noisy breath. He comes back to life, there on the surface of Huxley-3, soaked in my tears and covered in our ashes, retching out blood in strings like something being born, or reborn, before falling back against the floor. And I cover him, crying harder than I ever thought I could, pulling his head up and in against my chest, kissing him all over his hair and his face and his arms and his neck as he stirs, shifts, and finally, with no voice left to speak of, says:

'Estrellita.'

Chapter Thirty-Seven

At the moment we open the door hatch here's what we don't know: whether we will die the second it is open. But we don't. Instead we breathe in an air that is rich in oxygen, and we live; we finally really live.

I guess anyone who hasn't spent their life the way we did would never be able to imagine the moment we breathed air for the first time, smelt it and tasted salt and felt the wind move across our skin. You can't know, you never will, how it was to see an ocean, to float on it, this endless mass of water, moving beneath us, urging us onwards like something alive, a living entity.

You will never know the feeling of looking up at the sky for the first time when you have only ever lived on the outside of it. Here was the secret that I had never known, and it was so beautiful that it terrified me and all I could do was cower beneath it, beneath all that beauty. And I knew suddenly why people who live on planets believe in God and all that stuff but I couldn't speak to tell anyone and so I never did, but right then, looking at that endless eternal work of art, blue and white, like a dream somebody once had, I could feel something inside me that I couldn't name.

It's not like we'd been in zero gravity for that long but all the same we flopped out of the hatch like boneless fish and found ourselves clinging to the side of the shuttle, limbs too numb to swim, the warm saltwater embracing us, drawing us in and under.

The island is two hundred, maybe three hundred metres away, low and pale and still. We plan to tow Mariana but once we get her in the water she comes alive, suddenly gasping and screaming and looking around at us wide-eyed, and when she clings to me, nearly pulls me under, I hold her face between my palms and she says, 'Are we dead?'

And I say, 'No. We did it.'

We pull our uniforms off; kick them off to the seabed like we're shedding a skin. We're still about fifty metres out when I feel the sand beneath my feet, when I feel Dom behind me, sliding his arm around my waist and giving me the strength to stand in the moving water.

It's only as we are wading to the shore that I get scared, that I turn to him and hook my arms around his back and I want to hide, want him to hide me from the dark-leafed trees that I have never seen before, the things that may be moving in the treeline, the way the sun is slipping lower, reddening, bleeding its light from the sky. He pulls me against him, kisses me, smiles against my lips.

'We're OK,' is all he says, but there are dark shadows of bruising on his mouth and under his eyes that I can barely stand to see.

'You nearly died,' I say, choking it out, immediate tears mixing with the seawater on my cheeks.

'But I didn't,' he says, cupping my face in his hands.

Above us the stars are appearing in the fading light, the two moons are waxing, and suddenly I am so gripped by the fear that space is coming to claim me back.

'I've told you before I'm not brave like other people,' I tell him, trying to justify my trembling.

And Dom just laughs and says, 'No, estrellita, you're not like other people at all.' And he kisses me once more, watches my face, shakes his head. 'You're like no one I've ever known.'

And he takes my hand.

And so I keep on walking.

Acknowledgements

Thanks to Madeleine Milburn for the late night email that told me she believed in *Loneliness*, and would do a great job persuading others to do the same (along with Cara Lee Simpson and Therese Coen). Thanks to Karen Ball and all at Little, Brown Books for Young Readers for being persuaded. Thank you to Sophie Burdess for the beautiful and haunting cover. Thanks to Becca Allen, and also to Catherine Coe, but most of all to editor Kate Agar for being the best pair of fresh eyes anyone could hope for, and helping me make this story into what I always wanted it to be.

Thanks to my parents for believing in the dreams of an odd little girl enough to give her a sky-blue typewriter for Christmas. Thanks to my husband for getting things off high shelves for me, literally and metaphorically, across three continents and seventeen years so far (and being ignored almost every evening the whole time for his trouble). Above all, thanks to my girls, for putting up with the fact that I'm not as good at being a mum as I am at writing, and for being the best possible reason to never stop trying to be better at both.